INTEGRATED ENGLISH
LANGUAGE ARTS

Currents in Literature

American Volume

Harold Levine • Norman Levine
Robert T. Levine

AMSCO

Amsco School Publications, Inc.
315 Hudson Street/New York, N.Y. 10013

Contributing Writer: Mary L. Dennis

Reviewers
Krista Chianchiano, English Teacher, Indian Hills High School, Oakland, NJ
Rachel Matthews, Social Studies Teacher, Passages Academy, New York, NY
Erin M. Stowell, English Teacher, Huntington Beach High School, Huntington Beach, CA
Howard Withrow, Reading Teacher, Ida S. Baker High School, Cape Coral, FL
Melissa White, Instructional Specialist Secondary Reading and English Language Arts,
   Montgomery County Public Schools, MD

Cover Design: Wanda Kossak
Text Design: A Good Thing, Inc.
Composition: Publishing Synthesis, Ltd.
Illustrations: Anthony D'Adamo
Cover Art: Trophy © istockphoto.com/Jonas Staub

Please visit our Web site at: *www.amscopub.com*

When ordering this book, please specify:
either **R 059 W** *or* CURRENTS IN LITERATURE, AMERICAN VOLUME.

ISBN: 978-1-56765-144-7
NYC Item 56765-144-6

To the Student

Most famous writers say that while they were growing up they read the work of many different authors, and that they continue to be insatiable readers. Reading good literature as young people provided them with examples they could follow as authors, and gave them inspiration and motivation to write their own stories, poems, articles, and plays.

With this book, you can do the same. In each unit, you'll find four carefully chosen selections by American authors. Each one is linked to its own unit theme: "Freedom and Opportunity," "Identity," "Love and Friendship," or "Defining Moments."

Along with each selection, you'll find a strategy to help you become a better reader. Using these methods will lead you to deeper understandings of literature and of life as you think about the unit themes and your own experiences.

With a bit of effort, you will soon find yourself becoming a better writer. You'll build a more powerful vocabulary and learn to correct common mistakes. You'll feel the pride and satisfaction of writing an essay, story, or poem that represents you at your best.

In addition, you will enjoy the work of sixteen different authors who all have something interesting for you to think about, write about, and discuss. They are the inspiration for everything this book has to teach you.

Enjoy your journey into the fascinating world of language!

The Authors

Contents

Introduction

What Is American Literature?

American Literature courses and textbooks used to have a fairly limited focus. They often concentrated on nineteenth-century white male authors such as Nathaniel Hawthorne, Herman Melville, and Walt Whitman. While these authors' works are extremely valuable, and deserve a place in the canon, or accepted body of works, focusing only on them was problematic because it left out a lot of other important American writers. Fortunately, however, scholars and educators have come to realize this, and expanded the study of American Literature to include a wider range of authors. After all, since one of the things we celebrate most about our nation is its great diversity, a study of our literature should reflect that. In this volume of *Currents in Literature* we include an assortment of authors of different ages, regions, races, and ethnicities. You'll read about people's individual struggles in school, in relationships, and in forming their identities, and you'll also read about some of the larger issues we all face as citizens of this country. And that is a great virtue of our nation—that we can retain our individuality, while still coming together.

Our Journey Across America

The readings in this volume are organized thematically, not chronologically. In other words, they're grouped according to essential concepts or ideas, not by time periods. We did this to help you make connections between the selections. Comparing and contrasting is an important skill that will help you become a sharper reader and critical thinker. In addition, looking at these big ideas will help you find more personal meaning in the readings and relate them to your own life.

Unit One, "Freedom and Opportunity," highlights the people who have fought for our nation's independence and the freedoms we still hold valuable today. In the first selection, "Crispus Attucks, Martyr for American Independence" (1958), Langston Hughes describes a former slave who sacrificed his life for our country. The second reading, the poem "Concord Hymn" by Ralph Waldo Emerson (1837), looks back from his time to the American Revolution, and celebrates ordinary people who fought for America's freedom. Next, is a selection from E.B. White's *Salt Water Farm*, written in 1939. White discusses issues of freedom of the press during time of war, but the questions he raises are still relevant today. Should a writer or citizen be able to criticize the government, or is that unpatriotic? What does freedom of press really entail? Finally, we end with an excerpt from President Franklin Delano Roosevelt's speech "Annual Message to the Congress" (1941); Roosevelt discusses which rights of U.S. citizens he feels must always be protected.

Unit Two, "Identity," explores how we form our identity, or sense of self. Is it shaped by our backgrounds? By our assimilation to American culture? By our social class or by the way others view us? We begin with an excerpt from *The Woman Warrior,* a memoir by contemporary Chinese-American writer Maxine Hong Kingston. Kingston describes how her cultural traditions made it difficult for her to feel as if she belonged in the U.S. Then you'll read an excerpt from the nonfiction book *Where We Stand: Class Matters* by African-American writer and professor bell hooks, who explores how our social and economic classes continue to divide us. The next selection is from *Hunger of Memory* by Mexican-American writer Richard Rodriguez, who tells of his own struggles accepting his parents' culture and fitting into his new U.S. environment. Finally, we end the unit with an excerpt from Dorothy West's novel *The Wedding* (1995), which describes how a wealthy black family deals with an interracial relationship.

Unit Three's theme is "Love and Friendship." The first reading is a humorous selection from Mark Twain's novel *The Adventures of Tom Sawyer* (1876), where Tom tries to get closer to a girl he has a crush on. Next is an excerpt from Willa Cather's *My Ántonia* (1918), which also tells of a boy trying to win someone's affections—in this case, the protagonist Jim acts boldly with the hope of getting closer to his friend Ántonia. This is followed by an excerpt from Edith Wharton's *Ethan Frome* (1911) about a difficult love triangle between a married couple and the wife's cousin. We wrap up the unit with a short story from a contemporary writer, Judith Ortiz Cofer. "American History," published in 1993, explores the feelings of a girl whose infatuation with a boy in her school is doomed due to circumstances beyond her control.

In Unit Four, we look at "Defining Moments." Barbara Kingsolver's essay "Setting Free the Crabs" (2002) explores the tough decision her daughter faces while on a family beach vacation. Kate Chopin's short story "A Pair of Silk Stockings" (1897) tells of a woman who learns to think about her own needs for once. Next, you'll read an excerpt from *The Way to Rainy Mountain* (1969) by Native American writer N. Scott Momaday. What does he learn about his tribe and why is that important to him? And finally, you'll read "Sparrow's Sleep" (2005), by M. L. Smoker, a Native American writer from Montana. The poem's narrator struggles with a big life change when she has to leave her reservation.

The authors in this volume are from different time periods and backgrounds, but the feelings they experience and the issues they give voice to are ones we all may face as Americans. We hope this volume celebrates the value of a shared experience while recognizing our differences.

Freedom and Opportunity

Chapter One

Prereading Guide

Words to know and ideas to consider before you jump into the reading.

A. Essential Vocabulary

Word	Meaning	Typical Use
conceal (*v*) cun-SEEL	to put out of sight or cover up; hide	Britney *concealed* her journal in a secret place so her sister would not find it.
conspicuous (*adj*) cun-SPIK-yu-us	easily seen or attracting attention	My cousin Andrew's bright red hair makes him *conspicuous* in any crowd.
embattled (*adj*) em-BAT-uld	prepared for war; fortified	The *embattled* troops boarded the plane that would take them to the war zone.
gravely (*adv*) GRAVE-lee	in a serious manner; seriously	"I have something important to tell you," she said *gravely*.
indignation (*n*) in-dig-NAY-shun	anger aroused by something unjust, unworthy, or mean; righteous anger	Many students, parents, and teachers expressed their *indignation* at the very idea of doing away with football.
recover (*v*) re-KUV-ur	to get back; regain	It will take Manuel at least a month to fully *recover* from the accident.
redeem (*v*) re-DEEM	to balance, to make up for, to compensate for	Your good behavior today will *redeem* your rudeness yesterday.
sentinel (*n*) SEN-ti-nul	person or soldier who guards or watches; sentry	A *sentinel* was posted day and night outside the command post.
taunt (*v*) TAWNT	to provoke someone with insulting language; jeer	Even though his friends were *taunting* him and calling him "chicken," Jake could not bring himself to parasail.
votive (*adj*) VO-tiv	expressing gratitude or devotion; commemorative	A *votive* plaque was placed on the courthouse wall to honor the departed judge.

B. Vocabulary Practice

Exercise 1.1   Sentence Completion

Using your new vocabulary knowledge, choose the best way to complete the following sentences. Circle the letter of your answer.

1. Disproving the taunts of her friends, Sarah _____ snowboarding.
   A. never tried
   B. eventually excelled at

2. Pilar tried to _____ the remote, but her brother found it and changed the channel.
   A. conceal
   B. recover

3. Filled with indignation, the _____ marched down the street.
   A. band
   B. protesters

4. Jamal was afraid he would _____ while standing sentinel.
   A. fall asleep
   B. ruin his uniform

5. After the New Orleans _____, it took the city years to recover.
   A. flood
   B. Mardi Gras party

6. The speaker at the meeting spoke gravely of the _____.
   A. upcoming bake sale
   B. challenges faced by the club

7. Votive candles are often lit for the purpose of _____.
   A. showing devotion
   B. lighting up the room

8. If they had been better embattled, the soldiers would have _____ the fight.
   A. won
   B. lost

9. We told her not to be conspicuous, but she was very _____ when she walked into the room.
   A. sneaky
   B. loud

10. "I have lost your _____. How can I redeem myself?"
    A. pencil
    B. trust

Exercise 1.2   Using Fewer Words

Replace the italicized words with a single word from the following list. The first one has been done for you.

conceal   conspicuous   embattled   gravely   indignation

recover   redeemed   sentinel   taunted   votive

1. Winning our country's independence from England somewhat *made up for* the loss of lives during the Revolutionary War.

1. __redeemed__

2. Though the British were better equipped and *prepared for war*, the colonists had more reason to fight on.

2._____

3. For years, many colonists had expressed *anger aroused by unjustness* over unfair taxation.

3._____

4. They spoke *in a serious manner* about "taxation without representation."

4._____

5. Colonists often *provoked and insulted* the soldiers sent by England to keep order.

5._____

6. A(an) *soldier standing guard* was often a target for their resentment.

6._____

7. The colonists made little effort to *cover up* the way they felt about their new country being occupied by British soldiers.

7._____

8. The soldiers were *easily seen and attracted attention* because of their red coats.

8._____

9. England was determined to *get back* complete control over the colonies, but the minutemen were just as determined to win the colonies' freedom.

9._____

10. If you visit Boston today, you will find a number of *gratitude-expressing* markers commemorating these early American freedom fighters.

10._____

Exercise 1.3 Synonyms and Antonyms

Fill in the blanks in column A with the required synonyms or antonyms, selecting them from column B. (Remember: A *synonym* is a word similar in meaning to another word. *Autumn* and *fall* are synonyms. An *antonym* is a word opposite in meaning to another word. *Beginning* and *ending* are antonyms.)

	A	B
_____	1. synonym for *jeer*	votive
_____	2. synonym for *anger*	conceal
_____	3. antonym for *lose*	embattled
_____	4. synonym for *striking*	redeem
_____	5. antonym for *jokingly*	recover
_____	6. synonym for *fortified*	sentinel
_____	7. synonym for *compensate for*	taunt
_____	8. antonym for *display*	indignation
_____	9. synonym for *guard*	conspicuous
_____	10. synonym for *commemorative*	gravely

C. Journal Freewrite

Before you begin the reading on the next page, take out a journal or sheet of paper and spend some time responding to the following prompt.

TIP: Don't worry about grammar and spelling; just write what comes to mind. The purpose of freewriting is to explore ideas, not to produce a polished work.

> What is your definition of a hero? Give an example of a person you know who you think is heroic and explain what he or she has done that shows this trait.

Crispus Attucks, Martyr for American Independence

by Langston Hughes

About the Author
Langston Hughes (1902–1967) was one of the most dominant figures of the Harlem Renaissance, an artistic movement in which African-American writers, artists, and musicians celebrated their heritage and culture. Hughes wrote more than 60 books, including poetry collections, fiction, biography, and children's books. His writing spoke out for racial and social equality and portrayed African-American characters in a realistic light. He lived to see the effects of his lifelong struggle when the Civil Rights Act of 1964 was signed. Hughes died just three years later in Harlem, New York City, where he lived most of his life.

Reader's Tip: The following is Hughes's account of the Boston Massacre, a historical event that occurred five years before the outbreak of the Revolutionary War. It was caused by the tension between the people of Boston and the British troops that had been sent to their city.

Near the waterfront, in the crowd milling about between Dock Square and Long Wharf, a gigantic man of color stood out above almost everyone's head. A mulatto[1] of light complexion then in his forties, his name was Crispus Attucks. He was a seaman but lately discharged from a whaling vessel, and little is known about his life except that in his youth Attucks had been a runaway slave. Twenty years before that fateful night of moonlight and blood this advertisement had thrice appeared in the *Boston Gazette*:

Ran away from his Master, *William Brown* of Framingham, on the 30th of Sept. last, a Mulatto Fellow, about 27 Years of Age, named Crispus, 6 Feet two inches high, short curl'd hair, his Knees nearer together than common; had on a light colour'd Bearskin Coat, plain brown fustian[2] Jacket, or brown all-Wool one, new Buckskin Breeches, blue yarn Stocking, and a check'd woolen Shirt. Whoever shall take up said run-away, and convey him to his abovesaid Master, shall have ten pounds, old Tenor Reward, and all necessary Charges paid. And all Masters of Vessels and others are hereby caution'd against <u>concealing</u> or carrying off said Servant on Penalty of the Law.

Boston, October 2, 1750

But, so far as is known, in spite of the repetitions of this ad, William Brown of Framingham never <u>recovered</u> his runaway slave. Crispus Attucks had taken to the high seas as a sailor. So on that night of March 5, 1770, with snow on the ground and a bright moon in the sky, he felt himself a free man allied with[3] the citizens of Boston in their <u>indignation</u>

---

[1] a person of mixed black and white ancestry
[2] heavy cotton and linen fabric
[3] on the side of

that freedom to run their own affairs should be denied them by the English.

About nine o'clock that night, <u>taunted</u> by youngsters, a <u>sentinel</u> had knocked a boy down in front of the Custom House. Whereupon, other boys began to throw snowballs at the Red Coat as a crowd of men came running to the scene. Crying for help, the sentinel ran up the steps of the Custom House while someone else of his company rushed to call out the guard. A group of British privates officered by Captain Preston trotted doublequick up King Street and were met by a crowd of citizens that included the towering Crispus Attucks, and these were armed with sticks and stones. As the soldiers ran with drawn bayonets[4] through the street, they were pelted[5] by chunks of ice and handfuls of snow. Then the Red Coats encountered this group of men with stones and sticks in their hands. Crispus Attucks cried, "The way to get rid of these soldiers is to attack the main guard! Strike at the root! This is the nest!" And the men began to use their crude weapons against the well armed British.

Then the guns went off. An order to fire had been given. The very first shot killed Crispus Attucks. Maybe, being tall and Negro, he was the most <u>conspicuous</u> person in the crowd. At any rate, Attucks was the first man to lose his life in the cause of American freedom, pierced by a British bullet in the streets of Boston.

To his aid came Samuel Gray, a white man. And Gray, too, on the instant was shot dead. The next to fall was a sailor, James Caldwell. Then Patrick Carr and a boy of only seventeen, Samuel Maverick, <u>gravely</u> wounded, tumbled to the cobblestones. The boy died the next morning and Carr nine days later. A half dozen others were shot, but not fatally.

---

[4]steel blades, usually attached at the muzzle of a firearm and used in combat
[5]struck

Understanding the Reading

Complete the next three exercises and see how well you understood "Crispus Attucks."

Exercise 1.4 Multiple-Choice Questions

Answer the following questions about the reading. Circle the letter of your answer.

TIP: Don't try to answer the questions from memory; go back to the text as often as necessary.

1. Altogether, _____ persons were killed by the soldiers.
   A. eleven
   B. six
   C. five
   D. nine

2. When he lost his life, Crispus Attucks was about
_____ years old.
   A. 47
   B. 20
   C. 27
   D. 50

3. Of those who were shot by the Red Coats,
   A. one was a sailor.
   B. two died at the scene.
   C. six recovered.
   D. all eventually died.

4. Which statement about Crispus Attucks is not supported by the reading?
   A. He was the tallest person in the crowd.
   B. He had a passion for freedom.
   C. He felt the citizens of Boston should manage their own affairs.
   D. He learned military skills when he was a sailor.

Exercise 1.5   Short-Answer Questions

Respond to the following questions in one to two complete sentences. Go back to the text, as you did on the multiple choice.

5. What are some possible reasons that the captain of Attucks's first ship allowed him to join the crew?

   _____

   _____

   _____

6. Framingham is in Massachusetts. Does knowing this affect your previously held ideas about slavery in the U.S.? Explain why or why not.

   _____

   _____

   _____

7. A 1925 poem written by Hughes ends with the line, "I, too, am America." Keeping this in mind, why do you think he wrote this selection about Crispus Attucks?

   _____

   _____

   _____

Exercise 1.6   Extending Your Thinking

Respond to the following question in three to four complete sentences. Use details from the text in your answer.

8. The theme of this unit is "Freedom and Opportunity." How does Crispus Attucks exemplify this theme?

_____

_____

_____

_____

_____

_____

Concord Hymn

by Ralph Waldo Emerson

About the Author

Ralph Waldo Emerson (1803–1882) is one of America's best-known writers and philosophers. He was at the center of the circle of writers, artists, and musicians who were part of the American Renaissance, a period from about 1835 to 1880 when art in all forms began to blossom. Emerson was part of the transcendental movement. Transcendentalists stressed the spiritual connection between human beings and nature, the value of self-reliance, and the importance of social justice. Emerson opposed slavery and spoke out against the displacement of Native Americans. He lived in Concord, Massachusetts, not far from Boston, but traveled and lectured widely.

Reader's Tip: Before you read the poem, here is some historical context. In the years leading up to 1775, American colonists had begun stockpiling weapons and supplies at Concord. On April 19, British General Gage sent 700 soldiers to Concord to destroy the arms depot. The British were successful there, but they were ambushed all along the way by the Minutemen, everyday American residents who had trained to be ready "in a minute" to answer a British attack. The British Red Coats retreated to Boston with 270 casualties, while patriot casualties were fewer than 100. No one knows who fired the first shot, but it began the American Revolutionary War. Sixty-two years later, Emerson was asked to write the words to a hymn to be sung on completion of the Concord Monument, which honored the Minutemen. The words he wrote have lived on as this poem.

By the rude bridge that arched the flood,
    Their flag to April's breeze unfurled,
Here once the <u>embattled</u> farmers stood
    And fired the shot heard round the world.

The foe long since in silence slept;
    Alike the conqueror silent sleeps;
And Time the ruined bridge has swept
    Down the dark stream which seaward creeps.

On this green bank, by this soft stream,
    We set to-day a <u>votive</u> stone;
That memory may their deed <u>redeem</u>,
    When, like our sires, our sons are gone.

Spirit, that made those heroes dare
    To die, and leave their children free,
Bid Time and Nature gently spare
    The shaft we raise to them and thee.

Understanding the Reading

Complete the next three exercises and see how well you understood "Concord Hymn."

Exercise 1.7 Multiple-Choice Questions

Answer the following questions about the reading. Circle the letter of your answer.

TIP: Don't try to answer the questions from memory; go back to the text as often as necessary.

1. The word *rude* in the first line most likely means
   A. impolite.
   B. impassable.
   C. small.
   D. roughly made.

2. What do the "foe" and the "conqueror" in stanza 2 have in common?
   A. Neither of them won the battle of Lexington-Concord.
   B. They were both fighting for independence.
   C. Everyone who fought is now deceased.
   D. Time spared them both.

3. According to stanza 3, what will redeem the heroes who died?
   A. the actions of their children and grandchildren
   B. the memory of what they did, represented by the monument
   C. the tendency to keep fighting wars
   D. the power of nature

4. In stanza 4, Emerson asks that
   A. the heroes' reputations be treated gently.
   B. the heroes' children remain free.
   C. neither natural forces nor time will harm the monument.
   D. time will be kind to the heroes.

Exercise 1.8 Short-Answer Questions

Respond to the following questions in one to two complete sentences. Go back to the text, as you did on the multiple choice.

5. Why did Emerson call the first shot fired "the shot heard round the world"?

   _____

   _____

   _____

6. Emerson valued self-reliance (relying on your own talents and efforts). How does this poem celebrate that quality?

_____

_____

_____

7. Patrick Henry, an American patriot who lived at the time of the Lexington-Concord battle, said, "Give me liberty or give me death." For what would you be willing to fight—and possibly die?

_____

_____

_____

Exercise 1.9 Extending Your Thinking

Respond to the following question in three to four complete sentences. Use details from the texts in your answer.

8. Compare what Hughes, through his story of Attucks, and Emerson, through his poem on the Minutemen, might be telling us about the kind of people who fought for America's freedom. (*Who* fought for it and *why*?)

_____

_____

_____

_____

_____

_____

Reading Strategy Lesson
Using Context Clues

What Is Context?

Context literally means "with text." When you come across a word you don't know, looking at its context—the text that surrounds it, whether it be a phrase, sentence, or paragraph—can help you determine its meaning. Even if you can't come up with a precise definition of the word, you may be able to come close enough to understand what it generally means in the selection you are reading. In this lesson, you'll learn several ways to look at context.

1. Sometimes the context restates the meaning of the word.
Example:

> Some *veterinarians*, doctors who care for animals, volunteer their services at animal shelters.

The phrase "doctors who care for animals" tells you what the word *veterinarians* means.

2. Word meanings are not always stated so simply, but sometimes writers give examples that you can use as clues to the meaning.
Example:

> Although modern medicine has made great strides in preventing or curing serious illnesses such as heart disease and cancer, doctors still haven't found a cure for *maladies* that nearly everyone experiences: the common cold and the "24-hour bug."

What does *malady* mean? The colon after "experiences" tells us that the common cold and the "24-hour bug" are examples of maladies. Since these are illnesses, and the beginning of the sentence is about illnesses, *malady* must be a synonym for *illness*.

3. Another kind of context clue tells you what a word means by telling you about its opposite.
Example:

> Unlike Danielle, who is usually *decorous*, Stephanie is noisy and unruly.

The word *unlike* tells you that Danielle and Stephanie are different. Stephanie is noisy and unruly, and Danielle is the opposite. So Danielle must be quiet and well behaved, or *decorous*.

4. You can determine what a word means by reading the words or sentences around it and making your best guess, or inference.
Example:

> During the American Revolutionary War, not all of the soldiers in the British army called England home. England hired *mercenaries* who were willing to fight for any country that would pay them to do so.

In this example, there are two clues to the meaning of *mercenaries*. They were not British citizens, and they would fight for any country that paid them. So you can infer that a *mercenary* is a soldier who is hired by a country to join its army.

Exercise 1.10 Practice the Reading Strategy

On the line below each sentence or passage, write a brief definition of the italicized word.

1. In many cases, the penalty for drunken driving is the *revocation*, or suspension, of the driver's license.

---

2. We went to the home improvement store to gather the *implements* we needed to paint the room, such as a roller and pan, a scraper, and brushes.

   _____

3. On the *façade*, or front, of the building, the sculptor had carved scenes from Greek myths.

   _____

4. Slinky, our cat, always maintains his *dignity* when we have company, but our dogs act like silly fools.

   _____

5. Luke may seem uncaring, but he's not really as *callous* as he appears.

   _____

6. In spite of the *impairments* of deafness and blindness, Helen Keller lived an extraordinary life.

   _____

7. Mosquitoes are particularly *prolific* during wet, rainy summers because they lay their eggs in standing water.

   _____

8. After a week's vacation, Mrs. Martinez seemed *revitalized*, full of new life that bubbled out in happy giggles.

   _____

9. Scientists have determined that animals, including people, release *pheromones* that make them attractive to possible partners. When lots of these natural chemical substances are produced, romance is more likely for the producer.

   _____

10. While lions, tigers, and other big cats eat primarily meat, the giant grizzly bear is *omnivorous*. It will make a meal of vegetation, insects, fish, or meat.

    _____

Exercise 1.11 Apply the Reading Strategy

Choose four of the vocabulary words listed. On the next page, write a sentence or short passage for each word that contains context clues to the word's meaning. Use a different kind of context clue for each word. Write one sentence with a **restatement** clue, one with an **example** clue, one with an **opposite** clue, and one with an **inference** clue. You may use any form of the words you choose.

conceal	conspicuous	embattled	gravely	indignation
recover	redeemed	sentinel	taunted	votive

1. Restatement:

_____

_____

_____

2. Example:

_____

_____

_____

3. Opposite:

_____

_____

_____

4. Inference:

_____

_____

_____

Writing Workshop
Thinking About Audience, Purpose, and Task

When you have an assignment to write an essay, you are either given a prompt or choice of prompts, or you choose your own topic. Professional writers are in the same situation. They are either assigned topics by their editors, or they write something because they want to. Langston Hughes wrote the article about Crispus Attucks because he made the choice to do so. Ralph Waldo Emerson, on the other hand, was asked to write the words to a hymn that would be sung at the dedication of the Concord Monument.

Both Hughes and Emerson had to do three things before they started to write. Each writer had to think about his **audience**, his **purpose**, and his **task**.

Audience

The essay about Crispus Attucks was included in a book called *Famous Negro Heroes of America*. Hughes wrote the book in 1958—when civil rights issues were at the forefront of American minds. Hughes's audience varied widely, but the book was of special interest to African-Americans who wanted to know more about the history of their people and to others who felt the time for equality had come.

Emerson's audience was a very specific one—the people attending the dedication of the monument. His audience probably included politicians and officials from Massachusetts and the nation's capital as well as local townspeople. While this was the audience he undoubtedly had in mind as he wrote, his hymn survived as a poem with a much wider audience.

Hughes and Emerson had to consider their audiences before they wrote. You need to do the same thing. Why? Because you have to tailor your language and tone to your audience.

When you write an e-mail or text message to a friend, you are probably unconcerned with punctuation and spelling. You simply want to communicate your message.

- But suppose you want to apply for a job as a counselor at a summer camp. You decide to write a letter to the camp director to inquire about possible jobs. In this case, the camp director is your audience, and your goal is to make a good impression.

- Maybe you want to complain about a DVD recorder that quit working two days after the 90-day warranty expired. You might try sending an e-mail to the company first, but it should *not* be informal, like those you write to friends. Your audience will be the person who answers customer service e-mails, and your e-mail should have a formal, serious tone.

- If a teacher assigns an essay, a research paper, or another written project, the teacher is likely your main audience. Your work may be read to your classmates, but you should write it with your teacher in mind. Essays for standardized tests are read by a panel of teachers or others with educational backgrounds. The members of the panel do not know you. You should usually use a more formal tone and style for standardized test essays.

Purpose

Hughes's purpose was to celebrate African-American heroes. He probably wanted to point out to the public that not all heroes in American history were white men. His purpose was to inform his readers and expand their thinking.

Emerson's purpose was to honor those who died at Concord and to celebrate the courageous fight for American freedom.

- Think about your letter to the camp director. Your purpose is to get a job. Your letter is your first contact with the director, and it can open the door if it is well written. Your purpose is to inquire about job openings and to inform the director about your experience and interest.

- Your purpose for your e-mail about the broken DVD recorder is most likely to get a refund or a replacement. You want to convince the company that you will never buy any of their products again unless something is done.

- Most school and test essays ask you to either inform or persuade your readers of something. Personal narratives are another type of essay that you may be asked to write. In a personal narrative, you respond to a prompt with reference to your own experiences. You can use the pronoun *I*, but your style should remain fairly formal. The purpose of this kind of writing is usually to entertain.

Task

A task is the work that you actually do for an essay prompt. Your task might be to write a paragraph, an essay, a letter, an article, a story, a poem, or something else. Hughes's task was to write a collection of short biographies about African-American heroes. Emerson's task was to write the words to a hymn.

- Your tasks in the previous examples are to write a letter to a camp director and to write an e-mail to a customer service department.

Before you write, you can identify your audience, purpose, and task by asking yourself these questions:

1. For WHOM am I going to write? (**audience**)
2. WHY am I writing this? (**purpose**)
3. WHAT am I going to write? (**task**)

Exercise 1.12 Practice the Writing Lesson

Read the following writing prompts. Identify the audience, purpose, and task for each.

1. Your favorite park is going to be sold to developers, who plan to build a large condominium community around the small lake where you've enjoyed walking and watching wildlife. Write a letter to the editor of your local newspaper protesting the sale of the park.

Audience: _____

Purpose: _____

Task: _____

2. What does "courage" mean to you? Write a five-paragraph essay defining the term in your own words and giving examples of courageous people and acts.

Audience: _____

Purpose: _____

Task: _____

3. Some parents at your school feel that teachers should assign less homework. The teachers say homework is essential for learning.

Write an informational flyer you can hand out to fellow students stating reasons for your position on the issue.

Audience: _____

Purpose: _____

Task: _____

4. Your school board has removed a number of books from the library because they are on a "banned books" list. Among the books removed are *The Adventures of Huckleberry Finn*, *Of Mice and Men*, and *How to Eat Fried Worms*. Write an article for your school newspaper stating your position.

Audience: _____

Purpose: _____

Task: _____

5. Emerson said, "The only reward of virtue is virtue; the only way to have a friend is to be one." Write a paragraph explaining what you think Emerson meant.

Audience: _____

Purpose: _____

Task: _____

Exercise 1.13 Apply the Writing Lesson

Fill in a possible audience and task for each purpose listed in the middle column. An example of each has been done for you.

Audience	Purpose	Task
computer users	inform	*Write the directions for defragmenting a disk.*
my parents	persuade	*Write a letter persuading them to extend my curfew.*
a first-grade class	entertain	*Write a story about a family of otters.*
	inform	
	persuade	
	entertain	

Grammar Mini-Lesson
Writing Complete Sentences

A **sentence fragment** may look like a sentence. It can start with a capital letter and end with a period, question mark, or exclamation point. However, it is not a complete sentence unless it has two parts: a *subject* (the person or thing doing the action in the sentence) and a *predicate* (the verb, or the action in the sentence). If it's missing one of those two parts, it is not expressing a complete thought and it is not considered a sentence.

Look at the following fragment in italics:
I spend a lot of time inside having fun. *Play video games.*

The fragment is missing a subject. It doesn't say *who* plays video games. Let's add a subject:
I play video games.

Now we have both a subject (*I*) and a predicate (*play video games*), so we have a complete sentence.

Here is another example. Can you tell what is missing?
I am in a grouchy mood. *Losing at tennis.*

We don't know *what* losing at tennis does. Does it make her frustrated? Does it make her motivated to try harder next time? We have the subject, what the sentence is about ("losing at tennis"), but we don't have a predicate. Let's add a verb (*frustrated*).
Losing at tennis frustrated me.

Now we have expressed a complete thought.

Sometimes, you will encounter a fragment that *does* have a subject and verb, but still does not qualify as a complete sentence. Here are some examples. Can you tell what is missing from these?

Because eggs have a lot of nutrition.

Which makes me very proud.

Although I am considering.

All of these fragments are *subordinate clauses*. This means that they are less-important parts of a sentence. They do have a subject and a predicate, but they don't make sense on their own.

You can correct a sentence fragment by adding words before or after it:
Because eggs have a lot of nutrition, I eat them frequently.

I made the honor roll, which makes me very proud.

What can you add to the third fragment?

You can often recognize fragments by spotting subordinating words: *although*, *because*, *except*, *including*, *instead of*, *that*, *which*, *who*, and *when*. You can look for them when you check your writing for fragments. Make sure the whole sentence is there!

Exercise 1.14 Practice Identifying Sentence Fragments

The following is from Emerson's essay "Self-Reliance." In the space before each item, write an **F** if it is a fragment and an **S** if it is a complete sentence.

_____ 1. There is a time in every man's education when he arrives at the conviction that envy is ignorance.

_____ 2. That he must take himself for better, for worse.

_____ 3. Though the wide universe is full of good.

_____ 4. No kernel of nourishing corn can come to him but through his toil.

_____ 5. Nor does he know until he has tried.

_____ 6. But what he has said or done otherwise, shall give him no peace.

_____ 7. We but half express ourselves.

_____ 8. Do not think the youth has no force because he cannot speak to you and me.

_____ 9. Bashful or bold, then.

_____ 10. He will know how to make us seniors very unnecessary.

Exercise 1.15 Apply the Grammar Lesson to Revise Sentences

Turn each fragment into a complete sentence. Write your new sentence on the line provided.

1. Just the other day

   _____

2. Which were original

   _____

3. Because I believed him

   _____

4. A person should

   _____

5. Although I lost the book

   _____

6. Familiar as the voice was

_____

7. Learning to be a better writer

_____

8. My uncle being nervous

_____

9. Speaking her mind

_____

10. Which makes me happy

_____

Polish Your Spelling
Base Words

Being able to spot the base of a word is an important skill because it can help you determine what that word means. For example, if you did not know what *embattled* means in Emerson's "Concord Hymn," you could look and see that the base is *battle*. Therefore, you can safely guess that *embattled* has to do with being *in battle*.

Learning to switch between base words and derivatives (words formed from base words) can also help your writing, because you'll be able to play with different ways of saying things. Let's say you were writing about a time you asked a friend a question, and he gave you an unclear answer. You could write, "His response lacked coherency," or you could say, "His answer was incoherent," or you could say, "His answer was not coherent at all." When you know how to spell and use different forms of a word, you can vary the ways you express yourself.

Look at the following diagram. It shows all of the words that you can make from one base word, *cover*.

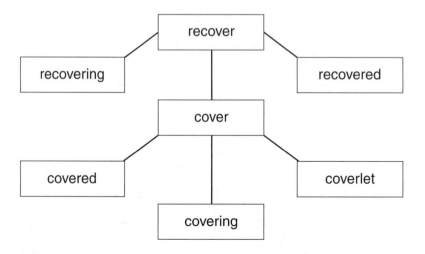

In this lesson, we'll focus on how to find and spell the base of a derivative. Later in this volume, we'll look at how to form a derivative *from* a base.

Derivatives to Base Words

- It is often possible to change a derivative back into the base word by simply dropping prefixes and suffixes.

    Examples: discontent – *dis* = content

    developed – *ed* = develop

    unbuttoned – *un . . . ed* = button

- Sometimes you need to restore a letter to the base, such as an *e* that was dropped when the suffix was added.

    Examples: blazing – *ing* = blaz + *e* = blaze

    unimaginable – *un . . . able* = imagin + *e* = imagine

- If a final consonant was doubled when the prefix was added, you will need to "undouble" it, that is, drop one of the consonants.

    Examples: committed – *ed* = committ – *t* = commit

    baggy – *y* = bagg – *g* = bag

- If a final *y* was changed to *i* when the suffix was added, change it back to *y*.

    Examples: hurried – *ed* = hurri – *i* + *y* = hurry

    happiness – *ness* = happi – *i* + *y* = happy

Exercise 1.16 Practice the Spelling Strategy

On the blank lines, write the base of each word.

1. unforgettable   _____
2. dislocation   _____
3. rereading   _____
4. unrecoverable   _____
5. inconspicuously   _____
6. irredeemable   _____
7. consciousness   _____
8. unaffected   _____
9. nonconformist   _____
10. unnecessarily   _____

Chapter Two

Prereading Guide
Words to know and ideas to consider before you jump into the reading.

A. Essential Vocabulary

Word	Meaning	Typical Use
amalgamate (*v*) ah-MAL-ga-mate	to combine into a single unit; merge	The school *amalgamated* its two lunchrooms.
appall (*v*) uh-PAWL	to horrify or dismay; shock	Teenagers often like to listen to music that *appalls* their parents.
deleterious (*adj*) dell-uh-TIR-ee-us	harmful or hurtful; injurious	The medicine helped indigestion but was *deleterious* to overall health.
despot (*n*) DESS-pit	a ruler with complete power; tyrant	The Russian czars were *despots*.
flimsy (*adj*) FLIM-zee	insubstantial or unbelievable; inadequate	Tired of Josh's *flimsy* excuses for not practicing, Mr. Tolliver canceled his violin lessons for good.
flourish (*v*) FLUR-ish	to grow strongly and vigorously; succeed	Art, writing, and music *flourished* during the Harlem Renaissance.
forswear (*v*) for-SWARE	to pledge to give up; renounce	She decided to *forswear* gossiping when she realized how seriously she was hurting people's feelings.
gainful (*adj*) GANE-ful	producing profit; lucrative	He has found *gainful* employment and is now looking for an apartment.
revoke (*v*) re-VOKE	to reverse or recall; void	After his third ticket, his license was *revoked*.
unimpeded (*adj*) un-im-PEED-ed	without interference; unhindered	Fortunately the fog had cleared, so the rescuers were *unimpeded* by poor vision.

B. Vocabulary Practice

Exercise 2.1   Sentence Completion

Using your new vocabulary knowledge, choose the best way to complete the following sentences. Circle the letter of your answer.

1. Melissa has forsworn _____ in an effort to be healthier.
   A. celery
   B. candy

2. He loved to paint but had to _____ because painting was not gainful for him.
   A. buy new supplies
   B. get a paying job

3. There was _____ discussion since everyone had amalgamated on the decision.
   A. lots of room for
   B. little point in

4. Justin's parents were _____ when he brought home straight A's.
   A. appalled
   B. pleased

5. The house was built with flimsy materials, so it _____ in the tornado.
   A. blew apart
   B. held up

6. Keisha was _____ that the updates to her computer were actually deleterious.
   A. relieved
   B. annoyed

7. Wildlife flourishes in areas with a _____ of pollution and human activity.
   A. minimum
   B. large amount

8. _____ was a despot.
   A. Ivan the Terrible
   B. George Washington

9. We _____. We were unimpeded.
   A. could not move
   B. moved ahead steadily

10. The legislature is voting on whether to revoke the _____.
    A. school year
    B. bicycle helmet law

Exercise 2.2   Using Fewer Words

Replace the italicized words with a single word from the following list. The first one has been done for you.

amalgamated	appalling	deleterious	despots	flimsy
flourish	forswear	gainful	unimpeded	revoke

1. "The dog ate my homework" is the classic *insubstantial and unbelievable* reason for not turning it in.

   1. _flimsy_____

2. After his career as a singer became *profit-producing*, he was unsure how to handle the prospect of becoming a star.

   2._____

3. The two small classes *combined into a single unit*.

   3._____

4. Some people view video games as *horrifying and dismaying*.

   4._____

5. People in drug rehab have to *pledge to give up* their habit.

   5._____

6. In the spring, wildflowers *grow strongly and vigorously*.

   6._____

7. My grandma took that medicine for years, but now studies are showing that it can actually be *harmful and hurtful*.

   7._____

8. It's not too late to *reverse or recall* your privileges.

   8._____

9. Saddam Hussein was one of the worst *rulers with complete power* in history.

   9._____

10. Their movements toward the fort were *without interference*.

   10._____

Exercise 2.3   Synonyms and Antonyms

Fill in the blanks in column A with the required synonyms or
antonyms, selecting them from column B. (Remember: A *synonym*
is a word similar in meaning to another word. *Autumn* and *fall* are
synonyms. An *antonym* is a word opposite in meaning to another
word. *Beginning* and *ending* are antonyms.)

	A	B
_____	1. synonym for *merge*	appalled
_____	2. synonym for *void*	gainful
_____	3. antonym for *delighted*	despot
_____	4. synonym for *unhindered*	flimsy
_____	5. antonym for *helpful*	amalgamate
_____	6. synonym for *lucrative*	unimpeded
_____	7. synonym for *tyrant*	forswear
_____	8. antonym for *strong*	flourish
_____	9. synonym for *renounce*	revoke
_____	10. antonym for *decline*	deleterious

C. Journal Freewrite

Before you begin the reading on the next page, take out a journal or
sheet of paper and spend some time responding to the following
prompt.

*TIP: Don't worry about grammar and spelling; just write what
comes to mind. The purpose of freewriting is to explore ideas, not
to produce a polished work.*

> Think about what life in the United States would be like if
> everyone agreed on politics and social issues (such as health
> care, education, and law enforcement). Explain whether you
> think such a situation would strengthen or weaken the
> country.

Reading 3

from Salt Water Farm

by E. B. White

About the Author
**E. B. White
(1899–1985)** was born in Mount Vernon, New York, and said he began writing "as soon as I could spell." He lived in New York City from 1924 to 1939, writing articles and essays for *The New Yorker* and *Harper's* magazines. He then moved to a farm in Maine. He continued to write essays, including the one excerpted here. While living on his farm he also began to develop ideas for children's books. *Charlotte's Web, Stuart Little,* and *The Trumpet of the Swan* were the well-loved results. In addition, he revised a classic writer's handbook, *The Elements of Style,* still in use in many classrooms. White advocated for human rights, simple living, and respect for nature. He was awarded a Pulitzer Prize special citation in 1978.

Reader's Tip: This essay was written in January 1939, eight months before the start of World War II. People all over the world were growing anxious about events in Europe: The dictators Adolf Hitler, Benito Mussolini, and Francisco Franco were in power in Germany, Italy, and Spain.

I was sorry to hear the other day that a certain writer, <u>appalled</u> by the cruel events of the world, had pledged himself never to write anything that wasn't constructive and significant and liberty-loving. I have an idea that this, in its own way, is bad news.

All word-mongers,[1] at one time or another, have felt the divine necessity of using their talents, if any, on the side of right—but I didn't realize that they were making any resolutions to that effect, and I don't think they should. When liberty's position is challenged, artists and writers are the ones who first take up the sword. They do so without persuasion, for the battle is peculiarly their own. In the nature of things, a person engaged in the <u>flimsy</u> business of expressing himself on paper is dependent on the large general privilege of being heard. Any intimation[2] that this privilege may be <u>revoked</u> throws a writer into a panic. His is a double allegiance to freedom—an intellectual one springing from the conviction that pure thought has a right to function <u>unimpeded</u>, and a selfish one springing from his need, as a breadwinner, to be allowed to speak his piece. America is now liberty-conscious. In a single generation it has progressed from being toothbrush-conscious, to being air-minded, to being liberty-conscious. The transition has been disturbing, but it has been effected, and the last part has been accomplished largely by the good work of writers and artists, to whom liberty is a blessed condition which must be preserved on earth at all costs.

But to return to my man who has <u>foresworn</u> everything but what is good and significant. He worries me. I hope he isn't serious, but I'm afraid he is. Having resolved to be noth-

[1]writers
[2]hint

ing but significant, he is in a fair way to lose his effectiveness. A writer must believe in something, obviously, but he shouldn't join a club. Letters <u>flourish</u> not when writers <u>amalgamate</u>, but when they are contemptuous of one another. (Poets are the most contemptuous of all the writing breeds, and in the long run the most exalted[3] and influential.) Even in evil times, a writer should cultivate only what naturally absorbs his fancy, whether it be freedom or chinch bugs, and should write in the way that comes easy.

The movement is spreading. I know of one gifted crackpot,[4] who used to be employed <u>gainfully</u> in the fields of humor and satire, who has taken a solemn pledge not to write anything funny or light-hearted or "insignificant" again till things get straightened around in the world. This seems to me distinctly <u>deleterious</u> and a little silly. A literature composed of nothing but liberty-loving thoughts is little better than the propaganda it seeks to defeat.

In a free country it is the duty of writers to pay no attention to duty. Only under a dictatorship is literature expected to exhibit an harmonious design or an inspirational tone. A <u>despot</u> doesn't fear eloquent writers preaching freedom—he fears a drunken poet who may crack a joke that will take hold. His gravest concern is lest gaiety, or truth in sheep's clothing, somewhere gain a foothold, lest joy in some unguarded moment be unconfined. I honestly don't believe that a humorist should take the veil today; he should wear his bells night and day, and squeeze the uttermost jape,[5] even though he may feel that he should be writing a strong letter to the *Herald Tribune*.

---

[3]admired; glorified
[4]someone with odd or whimsical ideas
[5]joke

Understanding the Reading

Complete the following three exercises and see how well you understood the excerpt from "Salt Water Farm."

Exercise 2.4   Multiple-Choice Questions

Answer the following questions about the reading. Circle the letter of your answer.

TIP: Don't try to answer the questions from memory; go back to the text as often as necessary.

1. When the author says, "artists and writers are the ones who first take up the sword," he likely means that writers and artists are
   A. the first to cause trouble.
   B. the first to point out challenges to freedom.
   C. always fighting among themselves.
   D. the first to join the military when there is a war.

2. According to the author, writers have a double allegiance to freedom
   A. because they are twice as patriotic as most people.
   B. because they have a strong belief in freedom of expression.
   C. because they need to express themselves freely to make a living.
   D. for both reasons described in B and C.

3. The author is worried about the man who "has foresworn everything but what is good and significant" because he
   A. feels writers should write about what naturally attracts them.
   B. thinks the man is overly optimistic.
   C. thinks writers should write mostly about trivial things.
   D. feels writers should face up to evil and write about it.

4. Which statement about E. B. White is *not* supported by the selection?
   A. He was not afraid to speak his mind.
   B. He felt liberty should be preserved at all costs.
   C. He was concerned about the trend to write only liberty-loving articles.
   D. He thought people were making too big a deal of liberty.

5. When White says, "I honestly don't believe that a humorist should take the veil today," he probably means that humorists should
   A. not join convents.
   B. continue to write humor.
   C. not get married.
   D. stop writing humor.

Exercise 2.5   Short-Answer Questions

Respond to the following questions in one to two complete sentences. Go back to the text, as you did on the multiple choice.

6. E. B. White says, "In a free country it is the duty of writers to pay no attention to duty." Explain what you think he means and why you do or do not agree with him.

   _____

   _____

   _____

7. What influence do you think the conditions in Europe had on the writing of this essay? (Look back at the Reader's Tip.)

   _____

   _____

   _____

8. Why do you think White included the sentence, "Only under a dictatorship is literature expected to exhibit an harmonious design or an inspirational tone"?

_____

_____

_____

9. Which of the statements in this essay do you find most powerful or surprising? Why?

_____

_____

_____

Exercise 2.6   Extending Your Thinking

Respond to the following question in three to four complete sentences. Use details from the text in your answer.

10. How does E. B. White's essay relate to the unit's theme, "Freedom and Opportunity"?

_____

_____

_____

_____

_____

_____

Reading Strategy Lesson
Thinking Aloud to Find Meaning in a Text

In the last chapter, you learned about audience, purpose, and task. Think about the essay excerpt you have just read. What do you think E. B. White's audience, purpose, and task were?

From the author information, you can infer that White wrote for a sophisticated audience of educated, well-read people. He set himself the task of writing about writing at the time, which he felt was becoming too serious and nationalistic. In other words, he felt writers were possibly becoming afraid to write anything critical of the government or anything lighthearted and humorous. His purpose was to defend writers' freedom to write what they wanted to.

Determining a writer's audience, purpose, and task can help you accomplish your goals as a reader: to find meaning in the text and possibly to connect what the author is saying to your own life.

A helpful tool for reaching your reading goals is called "thinking aloud." This means that you talk to yourself or to a classmate or teacher about what you are thinking as you read the selection. You can even carry on a conversation with the author.

For example:

E. B. White Writes:	You Think Aloud:
I was sorry to hear the other day that a certain writer, appalled by the cruel events of the world, had pledged himself never to write anything that wasn't constructive and significant and liberty-loving. I have an idea that this, in its own way, is bad news.	*Hmm . . . "cruel events"—he must be referring to the events in Europe. This writer thinks the world situation is too serious to be writing anything that isn't about freedom. But Mr. White, are you saying it is bad to love liberty?*

You are now becoming involved with the essay. You want to find out what White is talking about. Why does he think it's bad that people wanted to write constructive articles? Didn't he realize how serious things were?

Keep in mind that writers often like to keep their readers awake and interested by posing ideas that may at first seem a bit shocking. In fact, in the next four paragraphs, White explains exactly what he means by "bad news." By carrying on a conversation with him as you read, you can determine the essay's overall message. In addition to asking questions, write down in your own words the ideas you understand. Here is part of the second paragraph, along with some thoughts you might have as you read:

E. B. White Writes:	You Think Aloud:
All word-mongers, at one time or another, have felt the divine necessity of using their talents, if any, on the side of right—but I didn't realize that they were making any resolutions to that effect, and I don't think they should. When liberty's position is challenged, artists and writers are the ones who first take up the sword. They do so without persuasion, for the battle is peculiarly their own. In the nature of things, a person engaged in the flimsy business of expressing himself on paper is dependent on the large general privilege of being heard.	*Ok, so you're saying all writers have thought it was their duty to promote good things, but you think they shouldn't do only that. Are you saying they should be on the side of the wrong? Or maybe just what people sometimes think is the wrong side? You say that artists and writers are the first ones to point it out if liberty is being challenged. Why is liberty especially important to them? Are you talking about freedom of speech?*

Exercise 2.7 Practice the Reading Strategy

Part I. Here is the remainder of paragraph two of "Salt Water Farm." With a partner, take turns reading it aloud and talking through what you think it might mean. In the space to the right, jot down your questions and comments, using the previous examples as a model.

Any intimation that this privilege may be revoked throws a writer into a panic. His is a double allegiance to freedom—an intellectual one springing from the conviction that pure thought has a right to function unimpeded, and a selfish one springing from his need, as a breadwinner, to be allowed to speak his piece. America is now liberty-conscious. In a single generation it has progressed from being toothbrush-conscious, to being air-minded, to being liberty-conscious. The transition has been disturbing, but it has been effected, and the last part has been accomplished largely by the good work of writers and artists, to whom liberty is a blessed condition which must be preserved on earth at all costs.

Part II. You and your partner should now join with another pair and discuss your questions and comments. Did you have the same questions or come to the same conclusions? Can you get closer to the paragraph's meaning by thinking about what someone else has written?

Exercise 2.8 Apply the Reading Strategy

Part I. For the remaining three paragraphs of the essay, work with a partner and jot down your notes from thinking aloud on a separate sheet of paper. When you are done, share your questions and thoughts with another pair, as you did for the previous exercise.

Part II. In a whole-class or group discussion or on your own, answer the following questions:

- Does E. B. White say anything with which you can identify?

- Is his treatment of this subject biased or balanced?

- Is he qualified to write about this topic? Why or why not?

- What are some qualities you picture this author having?

Writing Workshop

Gathering Ideas

Overcoming Writer's Block

Have you ever looked at an essay prompt and thought, "I have no idea what to write about"? Don't worry. Everyone has had that feeling. Even professional writers experience writer's block, where they stare at a blank computer screen or pad of paper, and nothing comes to mind.

In the previous chapter, you learned that when you read an essay prompt, the first thing you should do is identify your audience, purpose, and task. Jotting down those three things is a first step in overcoming your own writer's block. The next thing you need to do is gather some ideas for your writing task.

The Writing Prompt

Let's suppose you need to gather ideas for this writing prompt from Chapter One:

> What does "courage" mean to you? Write a five-paragraph essay defining the term in your own words and giving examples of courageous people and acts.

You've defined your audience as your teacher, your purpose as "define and give examples of courage," and your task as a five-paragraph essay.

The first thing you need to do is *think* about courage. One productive way to do this is by *brainstorming*, which is similar to what you did when you used thinking aloud to better understand the E. B. White essay. You can brainstorm with another person or a group, or you can have your own individual brainstorming session. To brainstorm, you concentrate on your topic—in this case, courage—and write down everything that comes to mind that is related in any way to the topic. It's important to write down even things that seem silly or irrelevant. You might find out later that they will be of use.

A cluster map is a good way to gather your thoughts as you brainstorm a topic. Let one thought lead to another, and write everything down. Neatness doesn't count, and don't worry about spelling. Use abbreviations. You want to get each thought down quickly and be ready for the next one!

Look at the sample cluster map on the next page, which is from a brainstorming session for "courage."

This student started at the top with a definition of courage: when something is hard to do but you do it anyway. That takes care of the first part of the task: to define courage in your own words. Next, the student began quickly writing down everything else that came to mind about the idea of courage.

Exercise 2.9   Practice the Writing Lesson

Choose one of the writing prompts from Exercise 1.12 on page 18. Brainstorm and create a cluster map for it on a separate sheet of paper.

Exercise 2.10 Apply the Lesson to Your Own Writing

This time, invent your own topic. On a separate sheet of paper, brainstorm and create a cluster map for your topic.

Grammar Mini-Lesson
Subject-Verb Agreement

One of the most common mistakes people make in writing and in conversation is incorrect subject-verb agreement. In this lesson, we'll review how to make sure your subjects and verbs agree, to ensure that you're communicating as effectively as possible.

> GRAMMAR REFRESHER:
>
> The **subject** of a sentence is the noun or pronoun, the person or thing doing the action in the sentence.
>
> The **verb** is the action or state of being.

1. A **singular subject** requires a **singular verb**. A **plural subject** requires a **plural verb**.

Examples:

> The *movement is* spreading.
> Singular subject (*movement*) + singular verb (*is*)
>
> A *writer believes* in something.
> Singular subject (*writer*) + singular verb (*believes*)

> Notice what happens if we change the subjects:
> The *movements are* spreading.
> Plural subject (*movements*) + plural verb (*are*)
>
> *Writers believe* in something.
> Plural subject (*Writers*) + plural verb (*believe*)

TIP: Verbs ending in s *are usually singular:* is, was, knows, has, does, eats, sleeps, *and so forth. This is easy to remember:* s *at the end is a* s*ingular verb.*

Mistakes often occur because of uncertainty as to which word in the sentence is the subject. Normally, the subject comes before the verb. In the following cases, however, you will find the subject after the verb:

- In a question:
  > Are the children here yet? (The subject is *children*. The *children are* here.)

- In a sentence beginning with *There is, There are, Here is, Here are*, etc.:
  > Here are your books. (The subject is *books*, not *here*. The *books are* here.)

Be careful: An "of" phrase between a subject and its verb has no effect on agreement.

> A can *of peaches* is in the refrigerator. (It doesn't matter how many peaches are inside. We're talking about the one can. A "*can . . . is,*" not "*peaches is.*")

If you aren't sure which verb to use, try reading the sentence without the "of" phrase.

> A can is in the refrigerator. (The singular subject *can* requires the singular verb *is*.)

Exercise 2.11 Practice the Agreement Rules

Choose the correct verb and write it in the space provided.

1. Here (is, are) _____ a bushel of potatoes.

2. There (was, were) _____ three dogs in the street.

3. (Where's, Where are) _____ their owners?

4. Many word-mongers (feel, feels) _____ the necessity to use their talents on the side of right.

5. A bag of apples (sells, sell) _____ for $3.29.

6. (There's, There are) _____ several reasons for writing the truth.

7. How much (have, has) _____ prices gone up?

8. A flock of pigeons (was, were) _____ on the sidewalk.

9. (Doesn't, Don't) _____ they know how to speak correctly?

10. One of the girls (seems, seem) _____ to be missing.

Exercise 2.12 Apply the Grammar Lesson to Revise Sentences

Read each sentence. If the subject and verb do not agree, rewrite the sentence correctly. If they do agree, write OK, and write the verb and subject.

1. The teacher give the students time to do their homework in class.

_____

2. The bag of vegetables need to be put in the refrigerator.

_____

3. We all sleeps late on the weekend.

_____

4. Don't this bus ever come on time?

_____

5. Many products in American stores are made in other countries.

_____

6. The results on the test is good.

_____

7. Hasn't the boys come back yet?

_____

8. All of the tickets have been sold.

_____

9. Has you seen my cell phone anywhere?

_____

10. Prescription drugs has become unaffordable for some people.

_____

Polish Your Spelling
Adding Suffixes to Form Adverbs

In Chapter One, you removed prefixes and suffixes to find base words. Now you will practice *joining* suffixes to base words. In this lesson, we'll focus on a common suffix, *-ly*, which is used to turn adjectives (words that describe nouns) into adverbs (words that describe verbs). Adding *-ly* to the end of the word can seem simple, but there are certain spelling changes you should know.

Rule: To change an adjective to an adverb, we usually just add *-ly*.

ADJECTIVE	+	SUFFIX	=	ADVERB
gainful		ly		gainfully
effective		ly		effectively
deleterious		ly		deleteriously
eloquent		ly		eloquently

Exceptions:

1. If the adjective ends in a consonant plus *-le*, change the *-le* to *-ly*.

ADJECTIVE	ADVERB
impeccable	impeccably
idle	idly
single	singly

2. If the adjective ends in *-y* preceded by a consonant, change *y* to *i* before adding *-ly*.

ADJECTIVE	+	SUFFIX	=	ADVERB
hasty		ly		hastily
angry		ly		angrily

3. If the adjective ends in *-ic*, add *al* before attaching *-ly*.

ADJECTIVE	+	SUFFIXES	=	ADVERB
drastic		al + ly		drastically
scientific		al + ly		scientifically

4. Note that the *e* is dropped in these three special exceptions:

ADJECTIVE	ADVERB
due	duly
true	truly
whole	wholly

Exercise 2.13 Practice the Spelling Pattern

Change each adjective into an adverb and write it on the line provided.

ADJECTIVE   ADVERB

1. constructive + ly   _____
2. terrific + ly   _____
3. hearty + ly   _____
4. disturbing + ly   _____
5. large + ly   _____
6. flimsy + ly   _____
7. whole + ly   _____
8. remarkable + ly   _____
9. intellectual + ly   _____
10. natural + ly   _____

Chapter Three

Prereading Guide
Words to know and ideas to consider before you jump into the reading.

A. Essential Vocabulary

Word	Meaning	Typical Use
accountable (*adj*) uh-KOWNT-uh-bul	responsible for one's actions; answerable	They held the vandals *accountable* for the damage.
antithesis (*n*) an-TIH-thu-sis	the exact reverse of something; opposite	My dignified cat is the *antithesis* of my friendly, silly puppy.
appease (*v*) uh-PEEZ	to make concessions to others in order to keep the peace; placate; pacify	If you always try to *appease* other people, you may never get your own way.
assail (*v*) uh-SALE	to attack violently or vigorously; assault	The icy wind *assailed* me as I waited for the bus.
attainable (*adj*) uh-TANE-uh-bul	able to be achieved, such as a goal; reachable	Her mother was happy when Alexis told her she'd decided a college degree was *attainable*.
discord (*n*) DIS-kord	incompatibility or conflict; disagreement	The newspaper article described the *discord* between the two nations.
peril (*n*) PEHR-ul	a danger or hazard; jeopardy	He realized that the *peril* of not wearing a motorcycle helmet isn't worth it just to look cool.
tyranny (*n*) TEER-uh-nee	cruel oppression; domination	American colonists rebelled against the *tyranny* of Great Britain.
unalterably (*adv*) un-ALL-tur-ub-lee	in a way that is not subject to change; stubbornly	Her interest in becoming a concert violinist changed her *unalterably*; she began to devote her life to that aim.
vindicate (*v*) VIN-duh-kate	to validate, defend, or prove; justify	Being editor of the school paper does not *vindicate* your right to publish anything you want; always check the facts first.

B. Vocabulary Practice

Exercise 3.1   Sentence Completion

Using your new vocabulary knowledge, choose the best way to complete the following sentences. Circle the letter of your answer.

1. We all should be accountable for _____.
   A. our actions
   B. tomorrow's assembly

2. The discord between the neighbors made Island Road an _____ place to live.
   A. unpleasant
   B. inviting

3. "Good" is the antithesis of _____.
   A. excellent
   B. bad

4. The _____ has a sign that says "Enter at your peril."
   A. doctor's office
   B. haunted house

5. He _____; his decision is unalterable.
   A. has made up his mind
   B. is still thinking about it

6. The team vindicated itself by _____ the Cougars.
   A. losing to
   B. beating

7. The mother tried to appease the crying child by _____.
   A. giving him a cookie
   B. criticizing him

8. Fortunately, the _____ was caught.
   A. antithesis
   B. assailant

9. Most _____ are attainable if you try hard enough.
   A. people
   B. goals

10. Tyranny results in a(an) _____ human rights.
    A. loss of
    B. increase in

Exercise 3.2   Using Fewer Words

Replace the italicized words with a single word from the following list. The first one has been done for you.

| accountable | antithesis | appeasing | assailing | attainable |
| discord | perilous | unalterable | tyranny | vindicate |

1. The *cruel oppression* of Ivan the Terrible against his own citizens was finally halted.

1. _____tyranny_____

2. Although my parents sometimes argue, their love for one another is *not subject to change*.

2._____

3. Extreme sports are often *dangerous and hazardous*.

3._____

4. I didn't mean it. I was just *making concessions to* her.

4._____

5. The superstore tried to *validate and defend* its reputation for low wages by claiming that otherwise people would have no jobs at all.

5._____

6. My tall, brown-haired friend is the *exact opposite* of me in looks.

6._____

7. Even though his friends told him he'd never make it, Jorge proved that his dream of becoming a doctor was *able to be achieved*.

7._____

8. My dad complains that my loud music is always *violently attacking* his ears.

8._____

9. There is so much *conflict and incompatibility* between them; they're always fighting.

9._____

10. Being *responsible for our actions* is a mark of maturity.

10._____

Exercise 3.3 Synonyms and Antonyms

Fill in the blanks in column A with the required synonyms or antonyms, selecting them from column B. (Remember: A *synonym* is a word similar in meaning to another word. *Autumn* and *fall* are synonyms. An *antonym* is a word opposite in meaning to another word. *Beginning* and *ending* are antonyms.)

	A	B
_____	1. synonym for *responsibility*	appease
_____	2. synonym for *disagreement*	antithesis
_____	3. antonym for *provoke*	attainable
_____	4. synonym for *justify*	discord
_____	5. antonym for *safety*	assail
_____	6. synonym for *opposite*	tyranny
_____	7. synonym for *assault*	vindicate
_____	8. antonym for *unreachable*	peril
_____	9. synonym for *domination*	unalterable
_____	10. antonym for *changeable*	accountability

C. Journal Freewrite

Before you begin the reading on the next page, take out a journal or sheet of paper and spend some time responding to the following prompt.

TIP: Don't worry about grammar and spelling; just write what comes to mind. The purpose of freewriting is to explore ideas, not to produce a polished work.

Think about the rights, responsibilities, and freedoms you have as a citizen of the United States. What freedoms do you consider essential? In other words, what should everyone be free to do, no matter what? Explain.

Annual Message to the Congress, January 6, 1941

by Franklin Delano Roosevelt

About the Author

Franklin Delano Roosevelt (1882–1945) grew up at his family's estate, Hyde Park, in New York. Athletic in his youth, Roosevelt contracted polio in 1921. From that point on, he spent most of his time in a wheelchair, sometimes using leg braces and canes to walk with assistance. He refused to let his illness prevent him from fulfilling his ambitions. After serving as governor of New York, Roosevelt became the thirty-second president of the United States in 1933. It was the height of the Great Depression, and Roosevelt's New Deal programs provided relief and recovery for millions of unemployed, impoverished Americans. Roosevelt also engineered the Social Security Act and saw the country through most of World War II, although he died before the war ended. He is the only president ever elected to four terms of office.

Reader's Tip: Eleven months after this speech was given, on December 7, 1941, the Japanese bombed a U.S. naval station at Pearl Harbor in Hawaii, and the U.S. officially entered World War II.

Mr. President, Mr. Speaker, members of the 77th Congress:

I address you, the members of this new Congress, at a moment unprecedented in the history of the union. I use the word "unprecedented" because at no previous time has American security been as seriously threatened from without as it is today.

Since the permanent formation of our government under the Constitution in 1789, most of the periods of crisis in our history have related to our domestic affairs. And, fortunately, only one of these—the four-year war between the States—ever threatened our national unity. Today, thank God, 130,000,000 Americans in 48 States have forgotten points of the compass in our national unity.

It is true that prior to 1914 the United States often has been disturbed by events in other continents. We have even engaged in two wars with European nations and in a number of undeclared wars in the West Indies, in the Mediterranean and in the Pacific, for the maintenance of American rights and for the principles of peaceful commerce. But in no case had a serious threat been raised against our national safety or our continued independence.

What I seek to convey is the historic truth that the United States as a nation has at all times maintained opposition—clear, definite opposition—to any attempt to lock us in behind an ancient Chinese wall[1] while the procession of civilization went past. Today, thinking of our children and of their children, we oppose enforced isolation for ourselves or for any other part of the Americas.

That determination of ours, extending over all these years, was proved, for example, in the early days during the quarter century of wars following the French Revolution. While the

---

[1] a barrier to understanding; something that keeps people in ignorance.

Napoleonic struggles did threaten interests of the United States because of the French foothold in the West Indies and in Louisiana, and while we engaged in the War of 1812 to <u>vindicate</u> our right to peaceful trade, it is nevertheless clear that neither France nor Great Britain nor any other nation was aiming at domination of the whole world.

In like fashion, from 1815 to 1914—ninety-nine years—no single war in Europe or in Asia constituted a real threat against our future or against the future of any other American nation.

Except in the Maximilian interlude in Mexico,[2] no foreign power sought to establish itself in this hemisphere. And the strength of the British fleet in the Atlantic has been a friendly strength; it is still a friendly strength. Even when the World War broke out in 1914, it seemed to contain only small threat of danger to our own American future. But as time went on, as we remember, the American people began to visualize what the downfall of democratic nations might mean to our own democracy.

We need not overemphasize imperfections in the peace of Versailles.[3] We need not harp on failure of the democracies to deal with problems of world reconstruction. We should remember that the peace of 1919 was far less unjust than the kind of pacification which began even before Munich, and which is being carried on under the new order of <u>tyranny</u> that seeks to spread over every continent today. The American people have <u>unalterably</u> set their faces against that tyranny.

Every realist knows that the democratic way of life is at this moment being directly <u>assailed</u> in every part of the world—assailed either by arms or by secret spreading of poisonous propaganda by those who seek to destroy unity and promote <u>discord</u> in nations that are still at peace.

During sixteen long months this assault has blotted out the whole pattern of democratic life in an appalling number of independent nations, great and small. And the assailants are still on the march, threatening other nations, great and small.

Therefore, as your president, performing my constitutional duty to "give to the Congress information of the state of the union," I find it unhappily necessary to report that the future and the safety of our country and of our democracy are overwhelmingly involved in events far beyond our borders.

Armed defense of democratic existence is now being gallantly waged in four continents. If that defense fails, all the population and all the resources of Europe and Asia, and Africa and Austral-Asia will be dominated by conquerors. And let us remember that the total of those populations in those four continents, the total of those populations and their resources greatly exceed the sum total of the population and the resources of the whole of the Western Hemisphere—yes, many times over.

In times like these it is immature—and, incidentally, untrue—for anybody to brag that an unprepared America, single-handed and with one hand tied behind its back, can hold off the whole world.

---

[2]Archduke Maximilian of Austria was emperor of Mexico 1864–1867.
[3]treaty that ended World War I

No realistic American can expect from a dictator's peace international generosity, or return of true independence, or world disarmament, or freedom of expression, or freedom of religion—or even good business. Such a peace would bring no security for us or for our neighbors. "Those who would give up essential liberty to purchase a little temporary safety deserve neither liberty nor safety."

As a nation we may take pride in the fact that we are soft-hearted; but we cannot afford to be soft-headed. We must always be wary of those who with sounding brass and a tinkling cymbal preach the "ism" of <u>appeasement</u>. We must especially beware of that small group of selfish men who would clip the wings of the American eagle in order to feather their own nests.

I have recently pointed out how quickly the tempo of modern warfare could bring into our very midst the physical attack which we must eventually expect if the dictator nations win this war.

There is much loose talk of our immunity from immediate and direct invasion from across the seas. Obviously, as long as the British Navy retains its power, no such danger exists. Even if there were no British Navy, it is not probable that any enemy would be stupid enough to attack us by landing troops in the United States from across thousands of miles of ocean, until it had acquired strategic bases from which to operate.

But we learn much from the lessons of the past years in Europe—particularly the lesson of Norway, whose essential seaports were captured by treachery and surprise built up over a series of years.

The first phase of the invasion of this hemisphere would not be the landing of regular troops. The necessary strategic points would be occupied by secret agents and by their dupes—and great numbers of them are already here and in Latin America. As long as the aggressor nations maintain the offensive they, not we, will choose the time and the place and the method of their attack.

That is why the future of all the American Republics is today in serious danger.

That is why this annual message to the Congress is unique in our history.

That is why every member of the executive branch of the government and every member of the Congress face great responsibility, great <u>accountability</u>.

The need of the moment is that our actions and our policy should be devoted primarily—almost exclusively—to meeting this foreign <u>peril</u>. For all our domestic problems are now a part of the great emergency.

Just as our national policy in internal affairs has been based upon a decent respect for the rights and the dignity of all our fellow men within our gates, so our national policy in foreign affairs has been based on a decent respect for the rights and the dignity of all nations, large and small. And the justice of morality must and will win in the end.

In the future days, which we seek to make secure, we look forward to a world founded upon four essential human freedoms. The first is freedom of speech and expression—everywhere in the world. The second is freedom of every person to worship God in his own way—everywhere in the world. The third is freedom from want—which, translated into world terms, means economic understandings which will secure to every nation a healthy peacetime life for its inhabitants—everywhere in the world. The fourth is freedom from fear—which, translated into world terms, means a world-wide reduction of armaments to such a point and in such a thorough fashion that no nation will be in a position to commit an act of physical aggression against any neighbor—anywhere in the world.

That is no vision of a distant millennium. It is a definite basis for a kind of world <u>attainable</u> in our own time and generation. That kind of world is the very <u>antithesis</u> of the so-called "new order" of tyranny which the dictators seek to create with the crash of a bomb.

To that new order we oppose the greater conception—the moral order. A good society is able to face schemes of world domination and foreign revolutions alike without fear.

Since the beginning of our American history we have been engaged in change, in a perpetual, peaceful revolution, a revolution which goes on steadily, quietly, adjusting itself to changing conditions without the concentration camp or the quicklime in the ditch. The world order which we seek is the cooperation of free countries, working together in a friendly, civilized society.

This nation has placed its destiny in the hands and heads and hearts of its millions of free men and women, and its faith in freedom under the guidance of God. Freedom means the supremacy of human rights everywhere. Our support goes to those who struggle to gain those rights and keep them. Our strength is our unity of purpose.

To that high concept there can be no end save victory.

Understanding the Reading

Complete the next three exercises and see how well you understood Franklin D. Roosevelt's speech.

Exercise 3.4 Multiple-Choice Questions

Answer the following questions about the reading. Circle the letter of your answer.

TIP: *Don't try to answer the questions from memory; go back to the text as often as necessary.*

1. Which is *not* mentioned as one of the four basic freedoms?
   A. freedom from fear
   B. freedom from want
   C. freedom from war
   D. freedom of speech

2. Roosevelt probably considered the time of his speech "unprecedented" because
   A. he was a better speaker than any president in the past.
   B. the U.S. had just been attacked at Pearl Harbor.
   C. freedom means the supremacy of human rights everywhere.
   D. it was the first time that dictators in other countries were posing a real threat to the U.S.

3. Which statement about Roosevelt is *not* supported by the selection?
   A. He was not afraid to speak his mind.
   B. He urged Congress not to listen to those who advocated appeasement.
   C. He believed in human rights for all people.
   D. He thought Congress should pass laws to improve the morals of Americans.

4. The statement, "We must especially beware of that small group of selfish men who would clip the wings of the American eagle in order to feather their own nests," can best be restated as which of the following?
   A. Congress should not allow small groups to profit from war.
   B. Many of the government's problems could be solved by involving corporations.
   C. Bald eagles should not be kept as captive birds.
   D. People who are selfish are the ones who start wars.

5. Roosevelt stated that the higher moral order of a free society
   A. is the opposite of a society created by dictators.
   B. assures victory in a conflict.
   C. leads to cooperation with other free societies.
   D. has to work harder to win over tyranny.

Exercise 3.5   Short-Answer Questions

Respond to the following questions in one to two complete sentences. Go back to the text, as you did on the multiple choice.

6. In his speech, Roosevelt said, "As long as the aggressor nations maintain the offensive they, not we, will choose the time and the place and the method of their attack." What events can you think of in American history that proved the U.S. was vulnerable to surprise attack?

   _____

   _____

   _____

7. Roosevelt quoted Benjamin Franklin when he said, "Those who would give up essential liberty to purchase a little temporary safety deserve neither liberty nor safety." Why do you think he decided to use this quotation in his speech?

_____

_____

_____

8. Roosevelt said that since the beginning of American history, we have been engaged in a peaceful revolution within our own country. Explain what you think he meant.

_____

_____

_____

9. Which statement in this speech do you find most powerful or convincing? Why?

_____

_____

_____

Exercise 3.6 Extending Your Thinking

Respond to the following question in three to four complete sentences. Use details from the texts in your answer.

10. Do you think Roosevelt would agree with E. B. White's statement, "In a free country it is the duty of writers to pay no attention to duty"? Why or why not?

_____

_____

_____

_____

_____

Reading Strategy Lesson
Deciding What Is Important

Roosevelt's speech is an excellent example of good organization. In it, he introduced each topic he wanted to discuss. He elaborated on ideas related to one area before moving on to the next. His speeches were easy to follow because he wrote them and delivered them in an organized fashion, emphasizing the ideas he wanted to make sure he conveyed. He expressed main ideas, and supported them with details.

Details and examples help develop a piece of writing. They allow the writer to explain ideas and prove points. They keep you, the reader, interested enough to keep reading. Let's examine the details in a paragraph from Roosevelt's speech.

Paragraph 3

It is true that prior to 1914 the United States often has been disturbed by events in other continents. We have even engaged in two wars with European nations and in a number of undeclared wars in the West Indies, in the Mediterranean and in the Pacific, for the maintenance of American rights and for the principles of peaceful commerce. <u>But in no case had a serious threat been raised against our national safety or our continued independence.</u>

Some details are more important than others. In the example given above, you do not need to know all the information about "two wars with European nations and . . . a number of undeclared wars in the West Indies, in the Mediterranean and in the Pacific." Roosevelt gave them as **examples** of conflicts in which the U.S. was involved. The **main idea** of the paragraph is that <u>none of these conflicts threatened our national safety or independence</u>. The supporting details can be summarized briefly:

- U.S. involvement in past conflicts:
  - Europe
  - West Indies
  - Mediterranean
  - Pacific
- maintained American rights and principles of peaceful commerce

The **main idea** of this paragraph is expressed in the underlined topic sentence at the end. The details in the paragraph lead up to the main point that the U.S. has been involved in conflicts before, but never in one that threatened its independence or national safety.

When you read, finding the main idea of each paragraph can lead you to the supporting details. This is how you can decide what is important in a speech, article, story, or other piece of writing.

Exercise 3.7 Practice the Reading Strategy

On the next page are some additional paragraphs from Roosevelt's speech. Underline the topic sentence of each paragraph and briefly list the details that support the main idea expressed in the topic sentence. You do not need to write out the entire "detail" sentences. Simply jot short notes.

Armed defense of democratic existence is now being gallantly waged in four continents. If that defense fails, all the population and all the resources of Europe and Asia, and Africa and Austral-Asia will be dominated by conquerors. And let us remember that the total of those populations in those four continents, the total of those populations and their resources greatly exceed the sum total of the population and the resources of the whole of the Western Hemisphere—yes, many times over.

Details: a. _____

b. _____

c. _____

In the future days, which we seek to make secure, we look forward to a world founded upon four essential human freedoms. The first is freedom of speech and expression—everywhere in the world. The second is freedom of every person to worship God in his own way—everywhere in the world. The third is freedom from want—which, translated into world terms, means economic understandings which will secure to every nation a healthy peacetime life for its inhabitants—everywhere in the world. The fourth is freedom from fear—which, translated into world terms, means a world-wide reduction of armaments to such a point and in such a thorough fashion that no nation will be in a position to commit an act of physical aggression against any neighbor—anywhere in the world.

Details: a. _____

b. _____

c. _____

d. _____

Exercise 3.8   Apply the Reading Strategy

Identifying the main idea and details can help you understand things you read in *all* of your school subjects. Use a section of about five paragraphs from your social studies or science textbook, or another approved by your teacher. On a separate sheet of paper, analyze each paragraph as you did above. Write the topic sentence. Then list the supporting details beneath.

Writing Workshop
Organizing and Writing Topic Sentences

In the previous chapter, you learned how to gather ideas, and you made cluster maps for possible essays. In this lesson, you will choose one of those essays and organize your ideas. Finally, you will write some topic sentences.

Let's look back at the sample cluster map for "courage":

How do you find organization in a cluster of ideas like this? You'll need to look for categories within the cluster map. For example, there are three categories of things that courageous people do:

- put other people first
- stand up for a cause
- overcome personal challenges

There are also examples (subcategories) of each of these categories—and an example within each subcategory.

- Firefighters, police officers, and EMTs put other people first.

  Examples: Mr. Martinez, my neighbor, who is a firefighter; Felicia, my EMT sister

- Soldiers and activists stand up for a cause.

  Examples: my brother in Iraq; Kerri marching against wearing fur

- People with disabilities, injuries, and diseases overcome personal challenges.

  Examples: Lance Armstrong, Helen Keller

Exercise 3.9 Practice Organizing Your Ideas

Choose one of your cluster maps—the one you want to use to write an essay. Look for connections between ideas. On a separate sheet of paper, write your categories and examples, using a framework like the one that follows. Add any other ideas you think of that are not on your map. If you didn't include a lot on your cluster map, now is the time to beef it up.

Category 1:
   subcategories:
      examples:

Category 2:
   subcategories:
      examples:

Category 3:
   subcategories:
      examples:

You may have more than three categories, or a different number of subcategories.

Exercise 3.10 Practice Writing Topic Sentences

Look at your main categories for Exercise 3.9. They should suggest topic sentences. Write a topic sentence for each category.

Here is an example of a topic sentence from the sample "courage" outline:

> Turn on the TV or open a newspaper, and you're sure to find an example of an act of courage performed by someone who has put the welfare of another ahead of his or her own.

Grammar Mini-Lesson
Sticking to One Tense

> "I *address* you, the members of this new Congress, at a moment unprecedented in the history of the union."

> "That *is* no vision of a distant millennium. It *is* a definite basis for a kind of world attainable in our own time and generation."

> "The first phase of the invasion of this hemisphere *would not be* the landing of regular troops. The necessary strategic points *would be* occupied by secret agents and by their dupes . . ."

Each time you use a verb, you are using one of its **tenses**. In the first two examples above, Roosevelt is speaking about the present. In the third example, things get a little trickier because he is speaking about a future event that *could* happen. Notice the parallel use of *would not be/would be* in the two sentences.

When you write, it is important to choose one tense as your governing tense, that is, the one you will use to express most of your ideas. The most appropriate choice for a narrative (a story) is the past because you are telling about past events.

The most appropriate choice for an essay is the present, used to express ideas that you have *right now*. Using the present tense as your "main frame" allows you to introduce other tenses within your essay where they are appropriate. Make certain, though, that you maintain parallel construction (consistent tenses) within your sentences.

See if you can find the verb tense mistakes in the following sentences:
1. Courage is when you are afraid to do something but you did it anyway.
2. Good examples of courage are people who put other people first, people who stood up for a cause, and people who would overcome physical challenges.

The first verb in the first sentence, *are*, is in the present tense, but the second verb, *did*, is in the past tense. In the second sentence, *put* is in the present tense, but *stood* and *would overcome* are not parallel.

Here are revisions that align all of the verb tenses:
1. Courage is when you are afraid to do something but you *do* it anyway.
2. Good examples of courage are people who put other people first, people who *stand* up for a cause, and people who *overcome* physical challenges.

Exercise 3.11 Practice Making Tenses Consistent

On the blank line, write the correct tense of the verb in parentheses.

1. Ahead I saw a crowd, so I _____ over to see what was happening. (run, ran)

2. The driver stops the bus and _____ everybody to get off. (tells, told)

3. Just as I entered the room, someone _____ up and said "Hi." (come, came)

4. Jessie took a long lead off first and suddenly _____ toward second. (races, raced)

5. The president called the meeting to order. The secretary _____ the minutes. (reads, read)

6. Whenever I ask him to explain, he _____, "Later, not now." (said, says)

7. All of a sudden, she cried "Let's go!" and _____ my arm. (pulled, pulls)

8. As we turned onto Hudson Street, the sun _____ up. (come, came)

9. Elena starts the engine and backs out the car. In a few minutes, we _____ on the main highway. (are, were)

10. As soon as Mom heard we were going to ride the Twisted Sister roller coaster, she _____ to worry. (begins, began)

Exercise 3.12 Revise a Paragraph for Tense Consistency

The following paragraph has verb tenses that do not agree with one another. Write in your revisions to correct the errors. The first correction has been done for you.

saw
When I ~~seen~~ Rocky, I thought he was a ridiculous-looking dog.

He is half poodle and half dachshund, long and low to the

ground but he has curly black fur. He sits and glares and

growled at me. That doesn't make me want to take him home.

So then he tried wagging his tail, and he winked at me. That

done it. It is the wink that gets me. He stays like that his whole

life. Sometimes he was the glaring growler. Sometimes he is the

charming winker. He didn't know which one was working to

get him out of that cage, so he makes sure he still was doing

both.

Polish Your Spelling
Changing Nouns into Adjectives

In Chapter One, you looked closely at base words. In the second chapter, you added the suffix -*ly* to base words to form adverbs. In this chapter, we will continue to work with suffixes. This time, we will be using them to change nouns (people, places, or things) into adjectives (words that describe nouns).

Here are some ways to change nouns into adjectives.

1. Drop –*ness*.

NOUN	–	SUFFIX	=	ADJECTIVE
ripeness		ness		ripe
happiness		ness		happy

2. Drop –*ity*.

NOUN	–	SUFFIX	=	ADJECTIVE
morality		ity		moral
insanity		ity		insane

TIP: Don't forget the spelling rules you learned in Chapter One for removing suffixes. Sometimes it doesn't work to just chop off the suffix. You might need to restore certain letters, like the y *in* happy *or the* e *in* insane.

3. Add a suffix.

NOUN	+	SUFFIX	=	ADJECTIVE
peace		ful		peaceful
care		less		careless
victory		ous		victorious
health		y		healthy

4. Change a suffix.

NOUN	SUFFIX	ADJECTIVE
abundance	change *-ance* to *-ant*	abundant
urgency	change *-cy* to *-t*	urgent

Exercise 3.13 Practice the Spelling Rules

Change each noun into an adjective. Write the adjective on the blank line. (Hint: If you get stuck on one, try putting it in a sentence. Say you were given the noun *brilliance*. How would you use it as an adjective to describe a person (noun) you know? You would say, "She is *brilliant*." *Brilliant* is the adjective.)

NOUN	ADJECTIVE
1. importance	
2. friendliness	
3. glory	
4. hesitancy	
5. harm	
6. wealth	
7. self-reliance	
8. pity	
9. mercy	
10. truancy	

Unit One Review

Vocabulary Review

A. Match each word with its definition.

	DEFINITION	WORD
_____	1. ruler with complete power	a. embattled
_____	2. responsible for one's actions	b. flimsy
_____	3. easily seen or attracting attention	c. taunt
_____	4. grow strongly and vigorously	d. gainful
_____	5. to provoke with insults	e. amalgamate
_____	6. the exact reverse or opposite	f. accountable
_____	7. prepared for war	g. conspicuous
_____	8. producing profit	h. antithesis
_____	9. insubstantial or unbelievable	i. flourish
_____	10. combine into a single unit	j. despot

B. Match each word with its synonym.

	SYNONYM	WORD
_____	11. compensate for	a. votive
_____	12. assault	b. forswear
_____	13. disagreement	c. sentinel
_____	14. righteous anger	d. tyranny
_____	15. domination	e. redeem
_____	16. renounce	f. vindicate
_____	17. justify	g. indignation
_____	18. sentry	h. assail
_____	19. void	i. discord
_____	20. commemorative	j. revoke

C. Match each word with its antonym.

	ANTONYM	WORD
_____	21. provoke	a. appalled
_____	22. display	b. peril
_____	23. unreachable	c. gravely
_____	24. hindered	d. attainable

_____ 25. safety

_____ 26. delighted

_____ 27. wittily

_____ 28. changeable

_____ 29. helpful

_____ 30. lose

e. deleterious

f. conceal

g. unalterable

h. recover

i. unimpeded

j. appease

Grammar Review

The underlined portions of the paragraph below may contain errors. Check the possible rewrites in the answer choices, and circle the letter of the one that is best. If there is no error, circle D.

Eleanor Roosevelt was <u>Franklin</u>
                         (1)
<u>Roosevelt's wife. More than the first lady</u>.
             (1)
<u>Unlike other presidents' wives because she</u>
                 (2)
<u>get involved</u>. <u>She write a newspaper</u>
    (2)   (3)
<u>column. Spoke out on social issues</u>. She
              (3)
was an early opponent of racism, and was
not afraid to speak her mind. She
addressed the plight of poor people as
well. She was born into a high-society
family in New York City. <u>An orphan at</u>
                              (4)
<u>eight. Raised by her grandmother</u>. After
                (4)
she married Franklin Roosevelt, her
mother-in-law dominated their lives.

1. A. Franklin Roosevelt's wife, more than the first lady.
   B. Franklin Roosevelt's wife, but she was much more than the first lady.
   C. the wife of Franklin Roosevelt, the first lady.
   D. No change

2. A. Unlike other presidents' wives, she get involved.
   B. Unlike other presidents' wives, she got involved.
   C. She was unlike other presidents' wives, because she gets involved.
   D. No change

3. A. She wrote a newspaper column and spoke out on social issues.
   B. Writing a newspaper column and speaks out on social issues.
   C. She wrote a newspaper column, spoke out on social issues.
   D. No change

4. A. An orphan at eight, she raised by her grandmother.
   B. An orphan at eight, raised by her grandmother.
   C. Orphaned at eight, she was raised by her grandmother.
   D. No change

She volunteer as a teacher in poor areas.
(5)
Of New York. She worked with the Red
(5)
Cross in World War I. Eleanor Roosevelt was a social and political activist. Joining
(6)
the League of Women Voters. The
(6)
National Consumers' League. The
(6)
women's division of the Democratic Party.
(6)
She publish so many articles. People know
(7)
her better than her husband. Who had
(7)
polio at the time. When he was elected
(7)
governor, she was advised to be less vocal about her ideas, which angered her. She still managed to make her mark on the world. After Franklin Roosevelt dies.
(8)
Truman appoints her U.S. representative
(8)
to the UN. She fought hard for the
(8)

5. A. She was volunteering to teach in poor areas, of New York.
   B. She volunteered to teach in poor areas of New York.
   C. She volunteer as a teacher in poor areas of New York.
   D. No change

6. A. activist, joining the League of Women Voters, the National Consumers' League, and the women's division of the Democratic Party.
   B. activist, joining the League of Women Voters and the National Consumers' League. And the women's division of the Democratic Party.
   C. activist, joined the League of Women Voters, the National Consumers' League, and the women's division of the Democratic Party.
   D. No change

7. A. She publish so many articles, people know her better than her husband; who had polio at the time.
   B. She published so many articles, people knew her better than her husband, who had polio at the time.
   C. She published so many articles, people knows her better than FDR, who had polio at the time.
   D. No change

8. A. After Franklin Roosevelt dies, Truman appointed her U.S. representative to the UN.
   B. After Franklin Roosevelt died, Truman appoints her U.S. representative to the UN.
   C. After Franklin Roosevelt died, Truman appointed her U.S. representative to the UN.
   D. No change

Universal Declaration of Human Rights, and it was adopted in 1948. <u>She</u>
(9)

<u>denounced segregation and was the first</u>
(9)

<u>white person in Washington to join the</u>
(9)

<u>NAACP.</u> <u>She was a controversial figure.</u>
(9)   (10)

<u>Especially disliked by conservative men.</u>
(10)

<u>Who called her a "bleeding-heart</u>
(10)

<u>humanitarian."</u> President Truman,
(10)

however, called her "the First Lady of the World," and she is well loved by many Americans to this day.

9. A. Denouncing segregation as the first white person in Washington, she joined the NAACP.
   B. Joining the NAACP as the first white person in Washington.
   C. She denounced segregation and was the first white persons in Washington to join the NAACP.
   D. No change

10. A. She was a controversial figure, especially disliked by conservative men, who called her a "bleeding-heart humanitarian."
    B. She was a controversial figure who was especially disliked by conservative men, calling her a "bleeding-heart humanitarian."
    C. She was a controversial figure. Especially disliked by conservative men, who calls her a "bleeding-heart humanitarian."
    D. No change

Spelling Review

A. Write the base of each word listed.

WORD   BASE

  1. appallingly   _____

  2. irrevocable   _____

  3. disconnectedly   _____

  4. indefensible   _____

B. Change each adjective into an adverb.

ADJECTIVE   ADVERB

  5. affordable   _____

  6. whole   _____

  7. tragic   _____

C. Change each noun into an adjective.

NOUN	ADJECTIVE
8. necessity	_____
9. forthrightness	_____
10. independence	_____

Writing Review

Read the text of the First Amendment to the Constitution and the topics that follow, and choose one to write about. On a separate sheet of paper, plan your essay. Write your first draft, and revise and edit it. Then write your final essay. Before you begin to write:

- Be sure to identify your audience, purpose, and task.

- Use a cluster map to generate ideas for your essay.

- Organize your ideas into main ideas, subcategories, and examples.

Amendment I
Congress shall make no law respecting an establishment of religion, or prohibiting the free exercise thereof; or abridging the freedom of speech, or of the press; or the right of the people peaceably to assemble, and to petition the government for a redress of grievances.

> Discuss how one or more of the selections in this unit relate to all or part of this amendment. Give specific examples from the reading(s).

> OR

> Choose three of the freedoms outlined in the amendment and discuss what you think has actually happened in our society regarding these freedoms. Give specific examples from history, current events, or your own experience.

SPEAK/LISTEN

In Their Own Words

In groups, use the Internet or a book of famous quotations to locate a quotation by one of the authors in this unit—Langston Hughes, Ralph Waldo Emerson, E. B. White, or Franklin Delano Roosevelt. Choose a quotation that you feel reveals a great deal about the person's character or beliefs. Formulate two discussion questions that would help your class to better understand its meaning. When it is your turn, write the quotation on the board. Allow a few minutes for your classmates to study it. Then ask your questions and encourage discussion.

 EXPLORE

The Harlem Renaissance

Langston Hughes was just one of the many gifted African-Americans who participated in the Harlem Renaissance. With a partner, use the Internet to learn more about this movement and write a one-paragraph summary of your findings. Attach your summary to poster board and decorate it with a collage about some of the writers, artists, and musicians who were part of the Harlem Renaissance. Include pictures, titles, song lyrics, lines of poetry, and/or bits of information about the people. Present your posters to the class.

 WRITE

Respond to the Authors

Write a letter to E. B. White in response to the ideas he expressed in "Salt Water Farm."

OR

Write an editorial that might appear in a newspaper the day after Roosevelt's annual message to Congress in 1941.

CONNECT

Roosevelt's Contributions to Today's World

When *Time* magazine published its list of the most important 100 people of the twentieth century, Franklin Delano Roosevelt was one of them. The article about Roosevelt began, "He lifted the U.S. out of economic despair and revolutionized the American way of life. Then he helped make the world safe for democracy." Work with a group to learn more about the Great Depression and how Roosevelt's New Deal programs worked to bring prosperity and hope back to Americans. Each group should then create a brochure explaining one of the programs and encouraging people to participate.

Identity

Chapter Four

Prereading Guide
Words to know and ideas to consider before you jump into the reading.

A. Essential Vocabulary

Word	Meaning	Typical Use
avenge (v) ah-VENJ	to get even for an injury caused to another; retaliate	Ryan promised he would *avenge* the wrong done to his brother.
eclipse (n) ee-KLIPS	1. the blocking of light from one body in space by another, as when the moon eclipses the sun 2. (v) to obscure	During a full *eclipse* of the moon, it becomes extremely dark. The damage the tornado caused was *eclipsed* by that from the hurricane.
fume (v) FYOOM	to express annoyance or irritation; fret	Throughout dinner, Sydney continued to *fume* that the waiter made a mistake on her order.
immensity (n) i-MEN-si-tee	the quality of being unusually large; vastness	The *immensity* of the threat to our oceans cannot be measured.
plague (n) PLAYG	a disease or disaster affecting a large group; a curse	Some people view reality TV as a *plague* affecting the nation.
recede (v) re-SEED	to move back to a lesser or lower point; subside	They told the people they could not return to their homes until the flood waters *recede*.
rectify (v) REK-tih-fy	to remedy a situation; correct	Caleb tried to *rectify* the hurt he had caused his friend by forgetting to invite him to the party.
reparation (n) rep-uh-RAY-shun	a payment or award for damages inflicted; restitution	*Reparations* were made to Japanese-Americans who were confined in camps during World War II.
sullen (adj) SULL-un	silently angry or cross; grouchy	When her mother told her she couldn't go out until her room was clean, Melissa got a *sullen* look on her face.
tainted (adj) TAINT-ed	corrupted or decayed; spoiled	If you get involved in that scandal, you'll have a *tainted* reputation.

B. Vocabulary Practice

Exercise 4.1   Sentence Completion

Using your new vocabulary knowledge, choose the best way to complete the following sentences. Circle the letter of your answer.

1. Sean planned to avenge the _____ treatment to which his sister had been subjected.
   A. kind
   B. inconsiderate

2. The _____ eclipsed the writing on the page.
   A. magnifying glass
   B. ink stain

3. Caitlin was so _____ that she couldn't stop fuming.
   A. excited
   B. annoyed

4. The immensity of the universe is _____.
   A. difficult to comprehend
   B. one of its smallest parts

5. In the Middle Ages, many people _____ due to the plague.
   A. were saved
   B. died

6. Marisol's father is always checking to see if his _____ is receding.
   A. hairline
   B. car

7. If you hurt someone's feelings, _____ might rectify the situation.
   A. ignoring the problem
   B. a sincere apology

8. People who _____ are often told they must make reparations to their victims.
   A. commit crimes
   B. do volunteer work

9. We _____ the meat because it was tainted.
   A. enjoyed
   B. threw out

10. Cody is sullen today because he _____.
    A. is grounded
    B. got the lead role in the play

Exercise 4.2 Using Fewer Words

Replace the italicized words with a single word from the following list. The first one has been done for you.

fumed   avenging   eclipse   recede   plague

sullen   rectify   reparations   tainted   immensity

1. *Getting even for* something someone has done to you often causes even more problems.

    1. Avenging

2. Our class went outside so we could watch the *moon obscure the sun.*

    2._____

3. Grandma *expressed annoyance and irritation* over the damage done to her garden.

    3._____

4. The *unusual largeness* of the problem makes it more difficult.

    4._____

5. A flu epidemic this winter could be like a(an) *disaster affecting many*, but you can get a flu shot to protect you.

    5._____

6. In the spring, the rivers rush with water from melted snow, but later on, the levels *move back to a lower level.*

    6._____

7. My grade in math was dropping, so I took steps to *correct and improve* the situation by studying harder.

    7._____

8. The U.S. often makes *payments for damages* to those who are injured or otherwise harmed in wars.

    8._____

9. The governor's campaign was *corrupted and decayed* by the news that he had taken bribes.

    9._____

10. I couldn't figure out why my friend was so *silently angry and cross.*

    10._____

Exercise 4.3   Synonyms and Antonyms

Fill in the blanks in column A with the required synonyms or antonyms, selecting them from column B. (Remember: A *synonym* is a word similar in meaning to another word. *Autumn* and *fall* are synonyms. An *antonym* is a word opposite in meaning to another word. *Beginning* and *ending* are antonyms.)

	A	B
_____	1. synonym for *spoiled*	plague
_____	2. synonym for *retaliate*	recede
_____	3. antonym for *smallness*	eclipse
_____	4. synonym for *restitution*	fume
_____	5. antonym for *increase*	reparation
_____	6. synonym for *obscure*	tainted
_____	7. synonym for *correct*	immensity
_____	8. synonym for *fret*	sullen
_____	9. synonym for *curse*	rectify
_____	10. antonym for *cheerful*	avenge

C. Journal Freewrite

Before you begin the reading on the next page, take out a journal or sheet of paper and spend some time responding to the following prompt.

TIP: Don't worry about grammar and spelling; just write what comes to mind. The purpose of freewriting is to explore ideas, not to produce a polished work.

> Describe a time you had difficulty adjusting to a new or different environment. How did you feel like an outsider? Did you try to do anything to fit in? Explain.

Reading 5

from The Woman Warrior: Memoirs of a Girlhood Among Ghosts

by Maxine Hong Kingston

About the Author

Maxine Hong Kingston (1940–) was born in Stockton, California, the eldest daughter of Chinese immigrants. Her parents owned a laundry in Stockton's Chinatown district, and the children worked long hours there. Kingston was told not to speak to the Americans, which made it difficult for her to feel she was part of American society. Despite this barrier, however, she did well in school and earned a degree from the University of California at Berkeley. She taught math and English in California and in Hawaii. Her first book, *The Woman Warrior: Memoirs of a Girlhood Among Ghosts*, is a combination of the memories, dreams, and myths that made up Kingston's childhood and her fight to find her identity as a Chinese-American woman. She has published other award-winning books and is considered an important spokesperson for feminism and social and racial reforms.

We were working at the laundry when a delivery boy came from the Rexall drugstore around the corner. He had a pale blue box of pills, but nobody was sick. Reading the label we saw that it belonged to another Chinese family, Crazy Mary's family. "Not ours," said my father. He pointed out the name to the Delivery Ghost,[1] who took the pills back. My mother muttered for an hour, and then her anger boiled over. "That ghost! That dead ghost! How dare he come to the wrong house?" She could not concentrate on her marking and pressing. "A mistake! Huh!" I was getting angry myself. She <u>fumed</u>. She made her press crash and hiss. "Revenge. We've got to <u>avenge</u> this wrong on our future, on our health, and on our lives. Nobody's going to sicken my children and get away with it." We brothers and sisters did not look at one another. She would do something awful, something embarrassing. She'd already been hinting that during the next <u>eclipse</u> we slam pot lids together to scare the frog from swallowing the moon. (The word for "eclipse" is *frog-swallowing-the-moon.*) When we had not banged lids at the last eclipse and the shadow kept <u>receding</u> anyway, she'd said, "The villagers must be banging and clanging very loudly back home in China."

("On the other side of the world, they aren't having an eclipse, Mama. That's just a shadow the earth makes when it comes between the moon and the sun."

"You're always believing what those Ghost Teachers tell you. Look at the size of the jaws!")

"Aha!" she yelled. "You! The biggest." She was pointing at me. "You go to the drugstore."

"What do you want me to buy, Mother?" I said.

"Buy nothing. Don't bring one cent. Go and make them stop the curse."

"I don't want to go. I don't know how to do that. There are no such things as curses. They'll think I'm crazy."

---

[1]Kingston's family uses the word "ghost" to refer to a non-Chinese person

"If you don't go, I'm holding you responsible for bringing a plague on this family."

"What am I supposed to do when I get there?" I said, sullen, trapped. "Do I say, 'Your delivery boy made a wrong delivery'?"

"They know he made a wrong delivery. I want you to make them rectify their crime."

I felt sick already. She'd make me swing stinky censers around the counter, at the druggist, at the customers. Throw dog blood on the druggist. I couldn't stand her plans.

"You get reparation candy," she said. "You say, 'You have tainted my house with sick medicine and must remove the curse with sweetness.' He'll understand."

"He didn't do it on purpose. And no, he won't, Mother. They don't understand stuff like that, I won't be able to say it right. He'll call us beggars."

"You just translate." She searched me to make sure I wasn't hiding any money. I was sneaky and bad enough to buy the candy and come back pretending it was a free gift.

"Mymotherseztagimmesomecandy," I said to the druggist. Be cute and small. No one hurts the cute and small.

"What? Speak up. Speak English," he said, big in his white druggist coat.

"Tatatagimme somecandy."

The druggist leaned way over the counter and frowned. "Some free candy," I said. "Sample candy."

"We don't give sample candy, young lady," he said.

"My mother said you have to give us candy. She said that is the way the Chinese do it."

"What?"

"That is the way the Chinese do it."

"Do what?"

"Do things." I felt the weight and immensity of things impossible to explain to the druggist.

"Can I give you some money?" he asked.

"No, we want candy."

He reached into a jar and gave me a handful of lollipops. He gave us candy all year round, year after year, every time we went into the drugstore. When different druggists or clerks waited on us, they also gave us candy. They had talked us over. They gave us Halloween candy in December, Christmas candy around Valentine's day, candy hearts at Easter, and Easter eggs at Halloween. "See?" said our mother. "They understand. You kids just aren't very brave." But I knew they did not understand. They thought we were beggars without a home who lived in back of the laundry. They felt sorry for us. I did not eat their candy. I did not go inside the drugstore or walk past it unless my parents forced me to. Whenever we had a prescription filled, the druggist put candy in the medicine bag. This is what Chinese druggists normally do, except they give raisins. My mother thought she taught the Druggist Ghosts a lesson in good manners (which is the same word as "traditions"). . .

We have so many secrets to hold in. Our sixth grade teacher, who liked to explain things to children, let us read our files. My record shows that I flunked kindergarten and in first grade had no IQ—a zero IQ. I did remember the first grade teacher calling out during a test, while students marked X's on a girl or a boy or a dog, which I covered with black. First grade was when I discovered eye control; with my seeing I could shrink the teacher down to a height of one inch, gesticulating and mouthing on the horizon. I lost this power in sixth grade for lack of practice, the teacher a generous man. "Look at your family's old addresses and think about how you've moved," he said. I looked at my parents' aliases and their birthdays, which variants I knew. But when I saw Father's occupations I exclaimed, "Hey, he wasn't a farmer, he was a . . ." He had been a gambler. My throat cut off the word—silence in front of the most understanding teacher. There were secrets never to be said in front of the ghosts, immigration secrets whose telling could get us sent back to China.

Sometimes I hated the ghosts for not letting us talk; sometimes I hated the secrecy of the Chinese. "Don't tell," said my parents, though we couldn't tell if we wanted to because we didn't know. Are there really secret trials with our own judges and penalties? Are there really flags in Chinatown signaling what stowaways have arrived in San Francisco Bay, their names, and which ships they came on? "Mother, I heard some kids say there are flags like that. Are there? What colors are they? Which buildings do they fly from?"

"No. No, there aren't any flags like that. They're just talking-story. You're always believing talk-story."

"I won't tell anybody, Mother. I promise. Which building are the flags on? Who flies them? The benevolent associations?"

"I don't know. Maybe the San Francisco villagers do that; our villagers don't do that."

"What do our villagers do?"

They would not tell us children because we had been born among ghosts, were taught by ghosts, and were ourselves ghost-like. They called us a kind of ghost. Ghosts are noisy and full of air; they talk during meals. They talk about anything.

"Do we send up signal kites? That would be a good idea, huh? We could fly them from the school balcony." Instead of cheaply stringing dragonflies by the tail, we could fly expensive kites, the sky splendid in Chinese colors, distracting ghost eyes while the new people sneak in. Don't tell. "Never tell."

Occasionally the rumor went about that the United States immigration authorities had set up headquarters in the San Francisco or Sacramento Chinatown to urge wetbacks and stowaways, anybody here on fake papers, to come to the city and get their files straightened out. The immigrants discussed whether or not to turn themselves in. "We might as well," somebody would say. "Then we'd have our citizenship for real."

"Don't be a fool," somebody else would say. "It's a trap. You go in there saying you want to straighten out your papers, they'll deport you."

"No, they won't. They're promising that nobody is going to go to jail or get deported. They'll give you citizenship as a reward for turning yourself in, for your honesty."

"Don't you believe it. So-and-so trusted them, and he was deported. They deported his children too." "Where can they send us now? Hong Kong? Taiwan? I've never been to Hong Kong or Taiwan. The Big Six? Where?" We don't belong anywhere since the Revolution. The old China has disappeared while we've been away.

"Don't tell," advised my parents. "Don't go to San Francisco until they leave."

Lie to Americans. Tell them you were born during the San Francisco earthquake. Tell them your birth certificate and your parents were burned up in the fire. Don't report crimes; tell them we have no crimes and no poverty. Give a new name every time you get arrested; the ghosts won't recognize you. Pay the new immigrants twenty-five cents an hour and say we have no unemployment. And, of course, tell them we're against Communism. Ghosts have no memory anyway and poor eyesight. And the Han people won't be pinned down.

Understanding the Reading

Complete the next three exercises and see how well you understood the excerpt from *The Woman Warrior*.

Exercise 4.4   Multiple-Choice Questions

Answer the following questions about the reading. Circle the letter of your answer.

TIP: Don't try to answer the questions from memory; go back to the text as often as necessary.

1. How did the reaction of the narrator's mother differ from that of her father when the delivery boy brought medicine to the wrong house?
   A. The mother and father reacted in the same way.
   B. The father was angry, but the mother was silent.
   C. The mother had a strong reaction to the situation.
   D. The father told the mother to calm down.

2. The narrator feels herself becoming angry with her mother because
   A. she fears her mother will prevent her from avenging the wrong done to the family.
   B. she can't get her mother to see that an eclipse is a natural event.
   C. her mother is always insulting the "Ghost Teachers."
   D. she fears her mother will once again do something embarrassing.

3. The narrator is chosen to go to the drugstore because
   A. she speaks the best English.
   B. she is the oldest.
   C. it is her fault if the plague comes upon the family.
   D. she knows the delivery boy from school.

4. When the narrator speaks to the druggist, she feels *mostly* like
   A. an avenger for her family.
   B. a cute and persuasive little girl.
   C. an embarrassed beggar.
   D. a well-spoken and intelligent young lady.

5. When the narrator says she "felt the weight and immensity of things impossible to explain to the druggist," she means that
   A. there was no way she could explain Chinese traditions and culture to him.
   B. she was unable to convey to him how mad her mother would be if she came home empty-handed.
   C. no matter what she said, he would think her family was homeless.
   D. no matter how much candy he gave her, she would not be able to eat it.

Exercise 4.5   Short-Answer Questions

Respond to the following questions in one to two complete sentences. Go back to the text, as you did on the multiple choice.

6. The narrator's mother "thought she taught the Druggist Ghosts a lesson in good manners." Do you think she was right? Explain why or why not.

   _____

   _____

   _____

7. The druggists and clerks at the store continued to give candy to the family over the coming years. Why do you think they did this?

   _____

   _____

   _____

8. Why do you think the drugstore gave the family "Halloween candy in December, Christmas candy around Valentine's day, candy hearts at Easter, and Easter eggs at Halloween"?

   _____

   _____

   _____

9. Does this story strike you as humorous or serious? Or does it have elements of both? Explain your answer with examples.

_____

_____

_____

Exercise 4.6   Extending Your Thinking

Respond to the following question in three to four complete sentences. Use details from the text in your answer.

10. Remember that the theme of this unit is "Identity." How did the narrator's family circumstances and the incident described in this selection make it difficult for her to find her identity as a Chinese child in America? (Reread the author sidebar for clues.)

_____

_____

_____

_____

_____

_____

Reading Strategy Lesson
Identifying Point of View

What Is Point of View?

When you read fiction and some other types of writing, it is important to identify the author's point of view, or the vantage point from which the author "sees" the story. Authors usually choose one point of view and stick to it. The three points of view most often used are:

- **First Person:** The narrator is a character in the story and refers to herself or himself using the pronoun _I_. Here's an example:

  I don't know why the other girls in my class don't like me. I'm always careful not to say anything that would hurt anyone's feelings. I guess it's just hard to be the new person in school. My mom says that it will get easier over time.

- **Omniscient Third Person:** The narrator knows what everyone in the story is thinking and feeling at all times. The characters are referred to by name, as _he_ or _she_, or by another identifier such as "the nurse" or "the bus driver." For instance:

  Heather was a good but quiet student. She felt shy around girls who talked only about parties and clothes, shopping, and boys. They, in turn, thought Heather must consider herself too good for them. It made them uncomfortable that she was so extremely and unfairly attractive—a thought that had never once occurred to Heather herself. She always got the best scores on tests, and it seemed she did it all with no effort.

- **Limited Third Person:** The narrator knows how one character feels and thinks, and tells the story from that person's limited point of view. Look at this example:

    Something told Heather that the other girls didn't like her, but she could not understand why they didn't. It was true she could never think of anything funny or shocking to say, but she had never been mean to anyone, either. "What could be wrong?" she asked herself again and again.

Why do you need to know point of view? It is important because it affects how much you learn about the characters. If you are reading a story told in a first-person or limited third-person point of view, there are things you don't know about the other characters. In an omniscient point-of-view story, however, you know things that the other characters don't even know.

Nonfiction Points of View

When you read certain kinds of nonfiction, point of view means something a little different. Point of view is how the author sees an issue or idea, where he or she is coming from. For example, if you read a newspaper opinion column by a writer who works for a conservative or a liberal thinktank, you must take his or her political beliefs into consideration. The writer has been hired to express the views of his or her employer and is not likely to give much weight to the opposing viewpoints. Likewise, a persuasive piece of writing will try to convince you to *adopt the point of view* the author has on the subject about which he or she has written.

Informational and instructional materials are *not* usually written from a person's point of view. The authors of your trigonometry textbook do not write, "We're going to tell you our favorite way to solve this problem." Instead, they give you the information you need to know and instruct you on the steps you must take to solve the problem.

Autobiographies, however, are informational and are written in first person. Other books may also be written in first person but with a limited subject. Sample titles could be *Take Off the Pounds Without a Frown: I Did It and So Can You*, *Why My Dog Is an Agility Champ*, and *The NASCAR Life, by Those Who Live It*.

Exercise 4.7 Practice the Reading Strategy

Identify the point of view of each of the following passages.

FP = first person TPL = third person TPO = third person
limited omniscient

_____ 1. Wing Biddlebaum, forever frightened and beset by a ghostly band of doubts, did not think of himself as in any way a part of the life of the town where he had lived for twenty years. Among all the people of Winesburg but one had come close to him. (Sherwood Anderson, *Winesburg, Ohio*)

_____ 2. When this was written I had just completed the first draft of my second novel, and a natural reaction made me revel in a story wherein none of the characters need be taken seriously. And I'm afraid that I was somewhat carried away by the feeling that there was no ordered scheme to which I must conform. (F. Scott Fitzgerald, introduction to *The Jazz Age*)

_____ 3. It was a frail and blue and lonely Carol who trotted to the flat of the Johnson Marburys for Sunday evening supper. Mrs. Marbury was a neighbor and friend of Carol's sister; Mr. Marbury a traveling representative of an insurance company. They made a specialty of sand-wich-salad-coffee lap suppers, and they regarded Carol as their literary and artistic representative. She was the one who could be depended upon to appreciate the Caruso phonograph record, and the Chinese lantern which Mr. Marbury had brought back as his present from San Francisco. Carol found the Marburys admiring and therefore admirable. (Sinclair Lewis, *Main Street*)

Exercise 4.8 Apply the Reading Strategy

Now think back to *The Woman Warrior*. On a separate sheet of paper, compare Maxine Hong Kingston's first-person point of view with how the selection might have read if it had been written by a biographer detailing an incident in her life. Be specific.

Writing Workshop
Planning an Essay

In Chapter Two, you made a cluster map of ideas and grouped together categories, subcategories, and examples. In Chapter Three, you used your categories outline to write topic sentences. Now it's time to complete your planning and write a first draft.

Since you have your topic sentences, categories, and examples, you can now create paragraph plans.

Your introductory and concluding paragraph plans will differ slightly from the three (or more) plans for the body of your essay, but each one helps you to keep your ideas tightly related. Wandering off topic is one of the major mistakes student writers make, and having a careful plan can help you to avoid this pitfall.

Study the following sample plans for an essay about courage.

Introductory Paragraph:

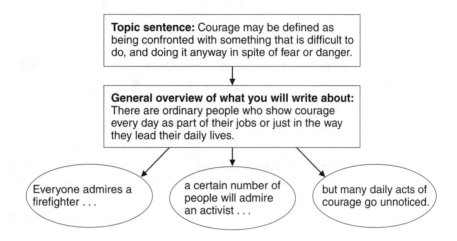

Body Paragraph:

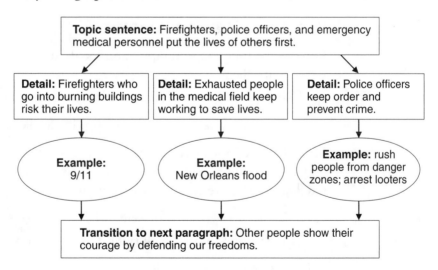

(Add more body paragraphs as necessary.)

Conclusion:

Topic sentence: Courageous people fear danger just like everyone else.

↓

Summary of your essay ideas: They put others' lives first and fight for freedoms or for what they see as right and good. They defy tests of strength, both physical and mental.

↓

Concluding sentences: Anyone may be called on without warning to save a life or to give his or her own life, to speak out against wrongs, or to overcome an obstacle. Our reactions measure our courage.

Exercise 4.9   Apply the Lesson to Your Own Writing

Following the example you just read, make paragraph plans for your own essay on a separate sheet of paper. Fill in your topic sentences, details, and examples. Be sure that each detail and example relates to the topic sentence, and work on a smooth transition to the next paragraph. Plan for the number of body paragraphs you will use. Once you have a set of completed paragraph plans, use them to write the first draft of your essay.

Grammar Mini-Lesson

Correcting Run-on Sentences

What Is a Run-on Sentence?

Look at the following examples and see if you can figure out what's wrong with them.

My laptop is working all right last week it wasn't.

The movie was scary we were afraid to walk home.

In the first example, two separate sentences are strung together with no pause or punctuation in between. This sentence needs to be fixed, and there are several ways to do it:

1. Divide it into two separate sentences:

My laptop is working all right. Last week it wasn't.

2. Use a semicolon:

My laptop is working all right; last week it wasn't.

3. Use a comma with a coordinating conjunction (*and*, *or*, *but*) or a subordinating conjunction (*although*, *because*, *whereas*, *since*, etc.):

My laptop is working all right, but last week it wasn't.

TIP: Don't forget that you can't use only *a comma—it's not strong enough to hold two sentences together. You must use it with a coordinating conjunction.*

The second sentence needs to be fixed, too. Here are several options. Which do you think sounds best?

> The movie was scary. We were afraid to walk home.
>
> The movie was scary; we were afraid to walk home.
>
> The movie was scary, and we were afraid to walk home.

As you can see, there are several ways to rewrite a run-on sentence. All of these revisions are grammatically correct, although sometimes using too many separate sentences, as in the first example, can make your writing sound choppy. The third example is particularly effective because the *and* helps emphasize the relationship between the scariness of the movie and the fear of walking home. It was scary—*and* that's why they were afraid to walk home. A person reading this sentence most likely wonders, "So what did they do? Did they walk home anyway, or did they call someone to come and get them?"

When you fix a run-on sentence, think about the message you wish to convey *and* how you want it to sound.

Exercise 4.10 Practice Fixing Run-on Sentences

The following sentences are run-ons. When you revise them for proper grammar, try to make them more interesting as well. Write your revisions on the lines.

1. Mikayla and Jordan went to the mall Saturday it was crowded.

   _____

   _____

2. Jordan tried on some shoes they were too small and Mikayla said weird looking.

   _____

   _____

3. Mikayla was looking for a new dress her brother's wedding is coming up.

   _____

   _____

4. His future wife did not ask Mikayla to be a bridesmaid she didn't like the dresses anyway.

   _____

   _____

5. Suddenly Jordan stopped and pointed at the floor there was a wallet.

   _____

   _____

6. They couldn't help looking for the money there was lots.

   _____

   _____

7. They started thinking they could buy things they wanted anything was possible.

   _____

   _____

8. "I could buy those shoes they were at the first store," said Jordan.

   _____

   _____

9. "I could buy a dress I want to look better than the bride," said Mikayla.

   _____

   _____

10. They walked toward the mall office they turned in the wallet and all the money.

   _____

   _____

Exercise 4.11 Apply the Grammar Lesson to Your Own Writing

Work with the first draft of the essay you wrote for Exercise 4.9. If you did not complete that exercise, work with another essay you wrote recently. Check your essay carefully for run-on sentences. Then use the checklist that follows to find other possible errors. You learned about these grammatical errors in Chapters One, Two, and Three.

Checklist
1. Does my essay contain any sentence fragments?
2. Do my subjects and verbs agree?
3. Are my tenses consistent?

Polish Your Spelling
Troublesome Consonants

In some words, consonants are doubled, but in others they are single. There are no rules to help you remember when a consonant is doubled or single. You can, however, study words by putting them in groups with other words of similar difficulty.

The 2 + 2 Group

Every word in this group has a troublesome DOUBLED consonant and, farther along in the word, another DOUBLED consonant.

embar*rass*   pos*sess*   as*sass*inate   as*sess*ment   Ten*nes*see

ac*comm*odate   com*mitt*ee   ag*gress*ion   mis*spell*   ac*cess*

The 2 + 1 Group

Every word in this group has a troublesome DOUBLED consonant and, farther along, a SINGLE consonant that you need to remember *not* to double.

bu*lle*tin   ap*par*el   ac*cel*erate   oc*cas*ion   ac*cum*ulate

buf*falo*   moc*cas*in   ap*pet*ite   vac*cin*ate   il*lit*erate

The 1 + 2 Group

Every word in this group has a troublesome SINGLE consonant, with a DOUBLED consonant later in the word.

ne*cess*ary   sa*tell*ite   begin*ning*   she*riff*   rebel*lion*

tar*iff*   re*comm*end   to*morr*ow   paral*lel*   Carib*bean*

Exercise 4.12 Practice the Spelling Patterns

Insert the necessary letters to complete each word.

1. I don't know what po_____e_____ed me to act like that!

2. Did you see the notice on the bu_____e_____in board?

3. Many cruises go to the Ca_____i_____ean.

4. The bu_____a_____o nearly became extinct.

5. I was emba_____a_____ed by the way my dad danced.

6. What sort of a_____a_____el are we supposed to wear to the dinner?

7. The counselor re_____o_____ends that you apply to at least three colleges.

8. I have a_____u_____ulated a lot of clothes that I no longer wear.

9. After the co_____i_____ee meets, we should have an answer.

10. I get an incredible number of stations on my sa_____e_____ite radio.

Chapter Five

Prereading Guide
Words to know and ideas to consider before you jump into the reading.

A. Essential Vocabulary

Word	Meaning	Typical Use
classism (*n*) CLASS-ism	judging people on the basis of their social rank; snobbishness	The senator, who clearly did not understand what it means to be poor, was accused of *classism*.
condescend (*v*) con-dih-SEND	to assume an air of superiority; patronize	People feel offended when someone *condescends* to them.
elusive (*adj*) ee-LOO-siv	able to avoid capture or pursuit; evasive	Fans swarmed the backstage door, but the *elusive* band members had already escaped.
fiscal (*adj*) FIS-kul	relating to money matters; monetary	The company is having *fiscal* problems and may declare bankruptcy.
genocide (*n*) JEN-uh-side	deliberate mass killing of a whole nation or group; massacre	*Genocide* in Sudan and Rwanda are tragic reminders of the inhumanity that exists in the world.
guerrilla (*n*) gur-ILL-uh	someone who engages in irregular warfare as a member of an independent unit; rebel or insurgent	You could never tell when one of the *guerrillas* would appear from nowhere with an explosive device.
indigent (*adj*) IN-di-junt	extremely poor and needy; penniless	*Indigent* people need jobs, food, housing, health care, and education.
predatory (*adj*) PRED-a-tor-ee	using another's weakness or lack of knowledge for personal gain; greedy	A *predatory* car salesman talked Kyle into a deal he cannot afford, and his car is likely to be repossessed.
urban (*adj*) UR-bun	relating to the city rather than the country or suburbs; municipal	*Urban* traffic is usually slow moving, especially at rush hour, while rural traffic is light at most times.
vetted (*v*) VET-ud	carefully investigated for reliability and trustworthiness; scrutinized	If the director of the agency had been properly *vetted*, the disaster might have been handled more efficiently.

B. Vocabulary Practice

Exercise 5.1   Sentence Completion

Using your new vocabulary knowledge, choose the best way to complete the following sentences. Circle the letter of your answer.

1. _____ must be thoroughly vetted before they are hired.
   A. CIA employees
   B. Day laborers

2. Michelle was sure she did not get the job because of classism, since a woman from _____ was hired instead.
   A. her neighborhood
   B. the "right side of town"

3. He had a condescending attitude, as if talking to us was _____.
   A. delightful
   B. a great favor

4. The tourists had hoped to see _____ from the boat, but they were elusive.
   A. whales
   B. seagulls

5. A fiscal conservative feels the nation should _____.
   A. have more social programs
   B. be careful with money

6. When her family moved to _____, it took Sarah a while to adjust to the urban lifestyle.
   A. Chicago
   B. a farm in Nebraska

7. There are numerous predatory people whose aim is to _____ unwary people.
   A. warn
   B. scam

8. The _____ is an example of genocide.
   A. World Series
   B. Holocaust

9. He was indigent, so he _____.
   A. could not pay for treatment
   B. wrote a check to the hospital

10. Guerrilla warfare is often very effective because enemies _____.
    A. wear black uniforms
    B. look like ordinary people

Exercise 5.2 Using Fewer Words

Replace the italicized words with a single word from the following list. The first one has been done for you.

classism   condescending   elusive   fiscal   genocide

guerrillas   indigent   predatory   urban   vetted

1. Police chased the burglar all over town, but   1. ___elusive___
   she was *able to avoid their grasp.*

2. *Judging people based on their social rank*   2. _____
   is a form of discrimination.

3. *Deliberate mass killing of a whole nation*   3. _____
   or group of people has unfortunately
   happened frequently throughout history.

4. Practices that are *taking advantage of*   4. _____
   another's weakness or lack of knowledge
   are increasing due to the Internet.

5. A(an) *city-related* renewal project is   5. _____
   scheduled to begin next month.

6. She was *assuming an air of superiority*   6. _____
   toward us and seemed to think we would
   never understand the issues.

7. My grandma moved in with us because   7. _____
   she has *money-related* problems and cannot
   afford a nursing home.

8. Are you sure she was *carefully investigated*   8. _____
   for reliability and trustworthiness before
   she was hired?

9. During the American Revolution, many   9. _____
   who fought for freedom were *not members*
   of the regular army.

10. If you are *extremely poor and needy*, you   10. _____
    may also be discouraged.

Exercise 5.3 Synonyms and Antonyms

Fill in the blanks in column A with the required synonyms or antonyms, selecting them from column B. (Remember: A *synonym* is a word similar in meaning to another word. *Autumn* and *fall* are synonyms. An *antonym* is a word opposite in meaning to another word. *Beginning* and *ending* are antonyms.)

	A	B
_____	1. synonym for *snobbishness*	vetted
_____	2. synonym for *massacre*	predatory
_____	3. antonym for *rural*	indigent
_____	4. synonym for *evasive*	genocide
_____	5. antonym for *respectful*	guerrilla
_____	6. synonym for *monetary*	classism
_____	7. synonym for *greedy*	urban
_____	8. antonym for *wealthy*	condescending
_____	9. synonym for *scrutinized*	elusive
_____	10. synonym for *insurgent*	fiscal

C. Journal Freewrite

Before you begin the reading on the next page, take out a journal or sheet of paper and spend some time responding to the following prompt.

TIP: Don't worry about grammar and spelling; just write what comes to mind. The purpose of freewriting is to explore ideas, not to produce a polished work.

> What social divisions are there at your school? What are the characteristics of each?

from Where We Stand: Class Matters

by bell hooks

About the Author

bell hooks (1952–), born Gloria Watkins, grew up in a segregated community in Kentucky. Her father had strong feelings about the role of women and believed they should stay at home and raise children. The family often read poetry together, and young Gloria wrote her own verses. Her early exposures to racism, sexism, and literature combined later in life as the basis of her writing career. She soon earned her bachelor's, master's, and PhD degrees in English. While writing and working as an English professor, hooks has established herself as one of America's principal African-American intellectuals, feminists, and activists. She spells her pseudonym—which is the name of her great-grandmother—in lower case letters because, in her words, "It is the substance in my books, not who is writing them, that is important."

Everywhere we turn in our daily lives in this nation we are confronted with the widening gap between rich and poor. Whether it is the homeless person we walk by as we go about daily chores in urban areas, the beggars whose cups tinkle with the sound of a few coins, the middle-class family member or friend who faces unemployment due to cutbacks, plant closings, or relocation, or the increased cost of food and housing, we are all aware of class. Yet there is no organized class struggle, no daily in-your-face critique of capitalist[1] greed that stimulates thought and action—critique, reform, and revolution.

As a nation we have become passive, refusing to act responsibly toward the more than thirty-eight million citizens who live in poverty here and the working masses who labor long and hard but still have difficulty making ends meet. The rich are getting richer. And the poor are falling by the wayside. At times it seems no one cares. Citizens in the middle who live comfortable lives, luxurious lives in relation to the rest of the world, often fear that challenging <u>classism</u> will be their downfall, that simply by expressing concern for the poor they will end up like them, lacking the basic necessities of life. Defensively, they turn their backs on the poor and look to the rich for answers, convinced that the good life can exist only when there is material affluence.[2]

More and more, our nation is becoming class-segregated. The poor live with and among the poor—confined in gated communities without adequate shelter, food, or health care—the victims of <u>predatory</u> greed. More and more poor communities all over the country look like war zones, with boarded-up bombed-out buildings, with either the evidence of gunfire everywhere or the vacant silence of unsatisfied hunger. In some neighborhoods, residents must wear name tags to gain entrance to housing projects, gated camps that are property of the nation-state. No one safeguards the interests of citizens there; they are soon to be the victims of class <u>genocide</u>. This

---

[1]related to industrial and commercial enterprises
[2]prosperity; comfort

is the passive way our country confronts the poor and <u>indigent</u>, leaving them to die from street warfare, sugar, alcohol, and drug addiction, AIDS, and/or starvation.

The rich, along with their upper-class neighbors, also live in gated communities where they zealously protect their class interests—their way of life—by surveillance, by security forces, by direct links to the police, so that all danger can be kept at bay. Strangers entering these neighborhoods who look like they do not belong, meaning that they are the wrong color and/or have the appearance of being lower class, are stopped and <u>vetted</u>. In my affluent neighborhood in Greenwich Village, I am often stopped by shopkeepers and asked where I work, whose children do I keep, the message being you must not live here—you do not look like you belong. To look young and black is to not belong. Affluence, they believe, is always white. At times when I wander around my neighborhood staring at the dark-skinned nannies, hearing the accents that identify them as immigrants still, I remember this is the world a plantation economy produces—a world where some are bound and others are free, a world of extremes.

Most folks in my predominately white neighborhood see themselves as open-minded; they believe in justice and support the right causes. More often than not, they are social liberals and <u>fiscal</u> conservatives. They may believe in recognizing multiculturalism and celebrating diversity (our neighborhood is full of white gay men and straight white people who have at least one black, Asian, or Hispanic friend), but when it comes to money and class they want to protect what they have, to perpetuate[3] and reproduce it—they want more. The fact that they have so much while others have so little does not cause moral anguish, for they see their good fortune as a sign they are chosen, special, deserving. It enhances their feeling of prosperity and well-being to know everyone cannot live as they do. They scoff at overzealous liberals who are prone to feeling guilty. Downward mobility is a thing of the past; in today's world of affluence, the message is "You got it, flaunt it."

------

[3]continue or cause to continue

Understanding the Reading

Complete the next three exercises and see how well you understood the excerpt from *Where We Stand: Class Matters.*

Exercise 5.4 Multiple-Choice Questions

Answer the following questions about the reading. Circle the letter of your answer.

TIP: Don't try to answer the questions from memory; go back to the text as often as necessary.

1. This excerpt is taken from the introduction to *Where We Stand: Class Matters*. The rest of the book will be probably be about the
   A. plight of homeless people.
   B. prevalence of crime in poor communities.
   C. conditions in corporate housing projects.
   D. widening gap between rich and poor.

2. The author believes that all of the following are true about most middle-class people *except* that they
   A. are unaware that poverty exists.
   B. are afraid to express concern for the poor.
   C. equate success with material wealth.
   D. live luxurious lives compared to most of the world's people.

3. Judging from context, hooks uses the word *poor* mostly to mean people who
   A. are on welfare.
   B. are drug addicts.
   C. work hard but cannot get ahead.
   D. live in gated communities.

4. The author likely uses the phrase "plantation economy" to describe the nation's financial system because she believes
   A. nothing has changed since before the Civil War.
   B. many hard working people earn "slave wages."
   C. blacks are not allowed in certain neighborhoods.
   D. the dark-skinned nannies in her neighborhood are immigrants.

Exercise 5.5   Short-Answer Questions

Respond to the following questions in one to two complete sentences. Go back to the text, as you did on the multiple choice.

5. Describe the two kinds of "gated communities" the author talks about.

   _____

   _____

   _____

6. How does the phrase "critique, reform, and revolution" relate to the author's message?

   _____

   _____

   _____

7. Which of the statements in this essay do you find most important? Why?

_____

_____

_____

Exercise 5.6   Extending Your Thinking

Respond to the following question in three to four complete sentences. Use details from the text in your answer.

8. After reading this selection, do you believe social class affects a
person's feelings of identity? Explain.

_____

_____

_____

_____

_____

_____

from Hunger of Memory

by Richard Rodriguez

About the Author
Richard Rodriguez (1944–) was born in San Francisco, the son of Mexican immigrants. The family spoke only Spanish in the home until Rodriguez started private Catholic school at age six. At that point, they decided to speak only English, to help him in school. He achieved success, earning a PhD in English and winning a Fulbright fellowship to study in London. Today he works as a teacher, journalist, essayist, and lecturer. He is considered somewhat controversial because he is against bilingual education and affirmative action. His book *Hunger of Memory: The Education of Richard Rodriguez* is a collection of autobiographical essays. This excerpt relates his feelings about his family.

"Your parents must be very proud of you." People began to say that to me about the time I was in sixth grade. To answer affirmatively, I'd smile. Shyly I'd smile, never betraying my sense of the irony: I was not proud of my mother and father. I was embarrassed by their lack of education. It was not that I ever thought they were stupid, though stupidly I took for granted their enormous native intelligence. Simply, what mattered to me was they were not like my teachers.

But, "Why didn't you tell us about the award?" my mother demanded, her frown weakened by pride. At the grammar school ceremony several weeks after, her eyes were brighter than the trophy I'd won. Pushing back the hair from my forehead, she whispered that I had "shown" the *gringos.*[1] A few minutes later, I heard my father speak to my teacher and felt ashamed of his labored, accented words. Then guilty for the shame. I felt such contrary feelings. (There is no simple roadmap through the heart of the scholarship boy.) My teacher was so soft-spoken and her words were edged sharp and clean. I admired her until it seemed to me that she spoke too carefully. Sensing that she was <u>condescending</u> to them, I became nervous. Resentful. Protective. I tried to move my parents away. "You both must be very proud of Richard," the nun said. They responded quickly. (They were proud.) "We are proud of all our children." Then this afterthought: "They sure didn't get their brains from us." They all laughed. I smiled.

Tightening the irony into a knot was the knowledge that my parents were always behind me. They made success possible. They evened the path. They sent their children to parochial schools because the nuns "teach better." They paid a tuition they couldn't afford. They spoke English to us.

For their children my parents wanted chances they never had—an easier way. It saddened my mother to learn that some relatives forced their children to start working right after high school. To *her* children she would say, "Get all the education you can." In schooling she recognized the key to job advancement. And with the remark she remembered her past.

---

[1] Spanish term for Americans, often used unfavorably

As a girl new to America my mother had been awarded a high school diploma by teachers too careless or busy to notice that she hardly spoke English. On her own, she determined to learn how to type. That skill got her jobs typing envelopes in letter shops, and it encouraged in her an optimism about the possibility of advancement. (Each morning when her sisters put on uniforms, she chose a bright-colored dress.) The years of young womanhood passed, and her typing speed increased. She also became an excellent speller of words she mispronounced. "And I've never been to college," she'd say, smiling, when her children asked her to spell words they were too lazy to look up in a dictionary.

Typing, however, was dead-end work. Finally frustrating. When her youngest child started high school, my mother got a full-time office job once again. (Her paycheck combined with my father's to make us—in fact—what we had already become in our imagination of ourselves—middle class.) She worked then for the (California) state government in numbered civil service positions secured by examinations. The old ambition of her youth was rekindled. During the lunch hour, she consulted bulletin boards for announcements of openings. One day she saw mention of something called an "anti-poverty agency." A typing job. A glamorous job, part of the governor's staff. "A knowledge of Spanish required." Without hesitation she applied and became nervous only when the job was suddenly hers.

"Everyone comes to work all dressed up," she reported at night. And didn't need to say more than that her co-workers wouldn't let her answer the phones. She was only a typist, after all, albeit a very fast typist. And an excellent speller. One morning there was a letter to be sent to a Washington cabinet officer. On the dictating tape, a voice referred to <u>urban</u> <u>guerrillas</u>. My mother typed (the wrong word, correctly): "gorillas." The mistake horrified the anti-poverty bureaucrats who shortly after arranged to have her returned to her previous position. She would go no further. So she willed her ambition to her children. "Get all the education you can; with an education you can do anything." (With a good education *she* could have done anything.)

When I was in high school, I admitted to my mother that I planned to become a teacher someday. That seemed to please her. But I never tried to explain that it was not the occupation of teaching I yearned for as much as it was something more <u>elusive</u>: I wanted to *be* like my teachers, to possess their knowledge, to assume their authority, their confidence, even to assume a teacher's persona.

In contrast to my mother, my father never verbally encouraged his children's academic success. Nor did he often praise us. My mother had to remind him to "say something" to one of his children who scored some academic success. But whereas my mother saw in education the opportunity for job advancement, my father recognized that education provided an even more startling possibility: It could enable a person to escape from a life of mere labor.

In Mexico, orphaned when he was eight, my father left school to work as an "apprentice" for an uncle. Twelve years later, he left Mexico in frustration and arrived in America. He had great expectations then of becoming an engineer. ("Work for my hands and my head.") He knew a

Catholic priest who promised to get him money enough to study full time for a high school diploma. But the promises came to nothing. Instead there was a dark succession of warehouse, cannery, and factory jobs. After work he went to night school along with my mother. A year, two passed. Nothing much changed, except that fatigue worked its way into the bone; then everything changed. He didn't talk anymore of becoming an engineer. He stayed outside on the steps of the school while my mother went inside to learn typing and shorthand.

Understanding the Reading

Complete the next three exercises and see how well you understood the excerpt from *Hunger of Memory*.

Exercise 5.7   Multiple-Choice Questions

Answer the following questions about the reading. Circle the letter of your answer.

TIP: Don't try to answer the questions from memory; go back to the text as often as necessary.

1. When Rodriguez says, "There is no simple road-map through the heart of the scholarship boy," he probably means
   A. it is not easy to win a scholarship.
   B. his mixed feelings were confusing.
   C. in his heart, he wished he had not won the scholarship.
   D. he had hardened his heart so he could not be hurt.

2. Which statement about the author's father is *not* supported by the reading?
   A. He did not often praise his children's success in school.
   B. Poverty prevented him from earning a high school diploma.
   C. He saw education as a way to escape all work.
   D. Fatigue sapped his energy and optimism for further education.

3. The governor's office returned the author's mother to her previous position because she
   A. could not type fast enough.
   B. did not speak English well enough to answer the phone.
   C. deliberately insulted people who lived in poor areas of town.
   D. misunderstood a homonym and embarrassed her supervisors.

4. When the author says his parents "evened the path," what does he mean?
   A. They made sure the children would not trip over a root or rock.
   B. They showed the way to success by earning diplomas and degrees.
   C. They made sacrifices so their children would receive good educations.
   D. They made frequent trips to the school to talk to the teachers.

Exercise 5.8 Short-Answer Questions

Respond to the following questions in one to two complete sentences. Go back to the text, as you did on the multiple choice.

5. Why do you think Rodriguez use the word *stupidly* when he says he took his parents' native intelligence for granted?

_____

_____

_____

6. How did the author's parents' educational experiences and attitudes differ from each other? Why do you think this was true?

_____

_____

_____

7. What is the difference between "work for the hands" and "work for the head"? Given the choice, would you prefer one over the other—or a combination? Why?

_____

_____

_____

Exercise 5.9 Extending Your Thinking

Respond to the following question in three to four complete sentences. Use details from the text in your answer.

8. As Richard Rodriguez excelled in school, he had mixed feelings about his immigrant parents. Describe some of these feelings and explain how he apparently resolved them as he accepted his own identity and better understood his parents' lives.

_____

_____

_____

_____

_____

_____

Reading Strategy Lesson

Question-Answer Relationships on Multiple-Choice Tests

What Is the QAR Technique?

When you take a quiz or a test in class or for a state assessment, you are often given a passage to read and then asked to answer multiple-choice questions and short-answer questions of a few sentences. The QAR technique helps you to answer more quickly and confidently.

QAR means "Question-Answer Relationship." When you use the technique, you determine the relationship between the question and the answer. There are three basic types of answers for multiple-choice questions.

1. Right there

To find "right there" answers, you go back to the text and find words similar to the ones in the answer choices. If it is "right there," you need look no further.

Example:

> This excerpt is taken from the introduction to *Where We Stand: Class Matters*. The rest of the book will probably be about the
> A. plight of homeless people.
> B. prevalence of crime in poor communities.
> C. conditions in corporate housing projects.
> D. widening gap between rich and poor.

When you look back at the reading, you notice that the very first sentence is, "Everywhere we turn in our daily lives in this nation we're confronted with the widening gap between rich and poor."

It is true that later on the author mentions crime in poor communities that look like "war zones." She talks about the conditions in housing projects and homelessness. These are all *examples* of the widening gap between rich and poor. The topic sentence of the first paragraph of the introduction to a book is bound to be a grabber—to let someone browsing in a bookstore or library know immediately what the book is about. These are all additional backup for your thinking that the answer is the "right there" one, answer D.

2. Think and search

A "think and search" question asks you to do exactly that: think about the question, think about the answers, and search for the information in the reading. If you've read especially carefully and comprehended well, you may only need to think about the question to choose the correct answer.

Example:

> Which statement about the author's father is *not* supported by the reading?
> A. He did not often praise his children's success in school.
> B. Poverty prevented him from earning a high school diploma.
> C. He saw education as a way to escape all work.
> D. Fatigue sapped his energy and optimism for further education.

As you think about these answer choices, you may recall that Rodriguez said something about his father never encouraging his children. You find confirmation of that in the second-to-the-last paragraph. So the reading does support that statement. How about a high school diploma? Did Rodriguez's father ever earn his? In the next paragraph (the last in the reading) you find that although he wanted to study full time for a high school diploma, he was never able to get the money he needed and had to work at boring warehouse, cannery and factory jobs during the day. Did he think education would allow him to escape work entirely? The reading tells you he wanted to be an engineer, to use his mind and not just his physical strength to make a living. The statement "He saw education as a way to escape all work" is not supported, so it is probably the answer. Just to make sure there is support for D, you read on and see that "fatigue worked its way into the bone," and that the elder Rodriguez lost hope of becoming an engineer.

3. On your own

"On your own" questions require you to evaluate what you have read and make a decision about what the author meant. You will probably need to do some skimming (see page 99) to review the reading as a whole and make your decision.

Example:

> When Rodriguez says, "There is no simple roadmap through the heart of the scholarship boy," he probably means
> A. it is not easy to win a scholarship.
> B. his mixed feelings were confusing.
> C. in his heart, he wished he had not won the scholarship.
> D. he had hardened his heart so he could not be hurt.

The answer to the question is not stated. You know it isn't easy to win a scholarship, but the author did not mention how difficult it was for him, although it might have been. You don't know if he wished he hadn't won it. He didn't say anything about hardening his heart, although that could well be true. You do know that he felt ashamed of his parents and at the same time guilty because they had worked so hard to provide him with a good education. You have to make your own determination of which answer is best. (Choice B is correct)

For short-answer questions, you are almost always on your own to make an evaluation, a judgment, or a connection, or to express your own opinions or feelings.

Example:
> Which of the statements in this essay do you find most important? Why?

You are the only person who can answer this question. You'll use scanning again and note a couple of statements that strike you as especially meaningful. Then you narrow your choice down to one and ask yourself why you chose that particular statement. Is it because you can relate it to your own life or someone else's? Perhaps you don't like the author's message, and you think one statement is simply not true. Whatever your reason, make sure to explain it.

Skimming and Scanning

Skimming can help you read quickly and find the general ideas of a piece of text. You can use skimming before you read a selection, and again to review the piece for an overall sense of the author's main ideas and meaning.

To skim:
1. Read the title along with any subtitles or subheads and any bold-faced, italicized, or footnoted words.
2. Look at any illustrations that are included. They can be clues about the passage.
3. Read the first and last sentence of each paragraph.
4. Finally, let your eyes skim over the text, taking in key words.

Skimming and **scanning** are often confused. When you **scan**, you look for specific information. For example, if you need to pick up some milk at the grocery store, you scan the store for the location of the dairy case. If you need to pick up a fact from a selection, you scan the passage for the location of the fact you want.

Use scanning when you are looking for "right there" answers and evaluating "think and search" answers. Use skimming before you read a passage and to review a passage for "on your own" multiple-choice questions and short-answer written response questions.

Exercise 5.10 Practice the Reading Strategy

Evaluate each of the questions on the next page according to QAR and indicate whether it is a "right there," a "think and search," or an "on your own" question. Also write down whether you would need to use skimming or scanning or both to find the answer.

1. The author likely uses the phrase "plantation economy" to describe the nation's financial system because she believes
   A. nothing has changed since before the Civil War.
   B. many hard working people earn "slave wages."
   C. blacks are not allowed in certain neighborhoods.
   D. the dark-skinned nannies in her neighborhood are immigrants.

   _____

   _____

2. Judging from context, hooks uses the word *poor* mostly to mean people who
   A. are on welfare.
   B. are drug addicts.
   C. work hard but cannot get ahead.
   D. live in gated communities.

   _____

   _____

3. The governor's office returned the author's mother to her previous position because she
   A. could not type fast enough.
   B. did not speak English well enough to answer the phone.
   C. deliberately insulted people who lived in poor areas of town.
   D. misunderstood a homonym and embarrassed her supervisors.

   _____

   _____

4. What is the difference between "work for the hands" and "work for the head"? Given the choice, would you prefer one over the other—or a combination? Why?

   _____

   _____

5. Did any of your answers to the questions change? If so, which ones—and why do you think you made a mistake the first time?

   _____

   _____

Exercise 5.11 Apply the Reading Strategy

On a separate sheet of paper, write a "right there," a "think and search," and an "on your own" multiple-choice question based on one of the readings in this chapter (one of each type of question). Also write an "on your own" short-answer question. Trade your questions with a partner. Answer the questions and note which kind each question is.

Writing Workshop
Using QAR for Longer Responses

In the previous section, you learned how to analyze multiple-choice questions and short-answer questions using the Question-Answer Relationship technique. When a question calls for a longer written response—a paragraph, several paragraphs, or a full-length essay—you can still use the QAR technique: determining the relationship between the question and the answer. In this case, you will be providing the answer.

You learned that questions requiring short answers almost always mean you are "on your own" when you write your responses. In other words, you need to reflect on how the selection you have read connects with the question before you can begin to write your answer.

When a longer response is called for, you need to think about the selection or the prompt in a more in-depth way. *How* you direct your thinking is where QAR comes into play. Suppose you are taking the final test on a play or novel your class has just finished studying. After answering some multiple-choice and matching questions, you see one of the following prompts:

1. Write a three-paragraph essay comparing and contrasting Tom Robinson and Boo Radley in *To Kill a Mockingbird*. Be sure to give specific details and examples from the novel.
2. Romeo and Juliet were teenagers who fell in love "at first sight" and got married immediately. Do you think this type of relationship is likely to work out in real life today? What would their parents be likely to say? Justify your response. You should write at least one paragraph of five sentences.

To use QAR, think about the relationship each question has to your eventual answer.

- The first prompt asks for *factual evidence* from the novel that shows how Tom Robinson and Boo Radley are alike and/or different. When you think about your answer, you will need to recall some *details and examples from the novel* to support your statements.

- The second prompt asks for your opinion; it relates to your own experience. There are two questions within this question: "Is a 'love at first sight' relationship likely to work out?" and "What would their parents be likely to say?" In your response, you will have to make sure you answer both of these questions. There is one more important direction in the prompt: "Justify your response." Since this is a personal-opinion question, your justification will have to come from what you have witnessed or what you imagine would happen in this situation.

Getting Started

Sometimes the hardest thing to do when you are writing under pressure is to get the first sentence on the page. Of course, before you worry about that, you need to identify your audience, purpose, and task, and plan the main ideas you will present. You will probably have a limited amount of time, so you will need to work fairly quickly on your plan.

Once your plan is complete, you can find your topic sentence right in the essay prompt. Notice how the beginning sentences of these responses go directly back to the questions.

First paragraph of a response to the first question:

> *Tom Robinson and Boo Radley were alike in more ways than they were different.* The obvious difference between them is that Tom was black and Boo was white. Both men, however, had to deal with handicaps. Neither man was fully accepted in Maycomb. Both Tom and Boo are tragic figures in the novel.

The first sentence speaks to the "compare and contrast" instructions in the prompt. The other sentences in the paragraph introduce what the writer will discuss in the remainder of the essay.

Response to the second question:

> *A quick marriage between teenagers who fall in love at first sight is unlikely to work out. If such couples would listen to their parents trying to talk them out of such an unwise move,* they could learn why the odds are against them. To begin with, "love at first sight" might be nothing more than physical attraction. They have not taken the time to find out what the other person is really like. As the first glow of love fades, they may feel the other person is holding them back from doing what they wanted to do, for example, go to college or get a job and an apartment with friends. They might have financial problems, and that will hurt their relationship. By the time they begin to discover all this, they may have started a family and run up a lot of debts. They didn't consider the consequences of getting involved too quickly.

The italicized sentence and phrase answer both of the questions posed in the prompt, and the rest of the paragraph accomplishes the "justify" task.

Exercise 5.12 Practice the Writing Lesson

Read each of the following essay prompts. Then write the topic sentence of a possible response.

1. Compare and contrast a film version of a novel with the novel itself. Did the movie do justice to the novel?

   _____

   _____

   _____

2. What adult has had the greatest influence on your life so far? What have you learned from this person? What do you admire most about the person?

   _____

   _____

   _____

3. Imagine that the school budget in your town is strained. The school board has the choice of cutting sports or music. If you were on the school board, which would you choose, and why?

   _____

   _____

   _____

4. Evaluate the following statement: "Reading is the most important skill a student can learn." Do you agree or disagree? Justify your answer.

   _____

   _____

   _____

5. Identify an invention that has been particularly harmful or helpful to society. Explain your answer.

   _____

   _____

   _____

Exercise 5.13 Apply the Lesson to Your Own Writing

Choose one of your starter sentences from the exercise above and complete a response of at least one paragraph on a separate sheet of paper.

Grammar Mini-Lesson
Concise Writing

What Is Concise Writing?

When you write a sentence, your chief objective is to communicate an idea. *Wordiness* is the use of more words than are necessary to make your point. *Conciseness* is using as few words as possible without changing or harming your meaning.

Often when students are given a specific length for an essay—say, 500 words—they become purposely wordy, just to fill up the page. They think more words will stretch the same idea farther. That's not always the case. Sometimes writing *too* much can make your main message unclear. The important thing is to cover the subject thoroughly and effectively.

Redundancy

Redundancy is closely related to wordiness, except that redundancy means conveying the same meaning more than once. "Exact same symptoms" is a redundant expression. "Same symptoms" is all that is necessary. Whole essays can be redundant as well. Perhaps you need three ideas but you really have only one. Have you ever tried to express that one idea in three different ways? That is redundancy.

Here are some examples of wordy or redundant expressions and the concise ones that should replace them. Study the table and then complete the exercises that follow.

Wordy or Redundant	Concise
adequate enough	adequate
advance planning	planning
at the present time	now
both together	both
but yet	but OR yet
contributing factor	factor
deliberate lie	lie
due to the fact that	because
during the course of	during
equally as far	as far

Wordy or Redundant	Concise
few in number	few
final outcome	outcome
for the purpose of being	to be
in spite of the fact that	although
in view of the fact that	since
in a very real sense	truly
in the not too distant future	soon
in regards to	regarding
join together	join
lack of . . . comfort, pleasure, knowledge	discomfort, displeasure, ignorance
large in size	large
my personal preference	my preference
my personal feeling	my feeling
no particular purpose	no purpose
on the part of	by
owing to the fact that	because
past history, past experience	history, experience
proceeded to . . . walk, run, laugh, etc.	walked, ran, laughed
rarely ever	rarely
refer back	refer
seldom ever	seldom
share in common	share
to the effect that	that
two different reasons	two reasons

Exercise 5.14 Practice Making Sentences Concise

Each of the sentences below contains one or more wordy or redundant expressions. Rewrite each sentence as concisely as possible.

1. In spite of the fact that the tree was large in size, it was not healthy.

   _____

2. Advance planning is rarely ever a bad idea in my personal opinion.

   _____

3. In the not too distant future we may find life on another planet.

   _____

4. Owing to the fact that I had the exact same symptoms as my brother, it looked like we had both together caught the exact same cold.

   _____

5. Mrs. Simpson was touched when she was given the bouquet that had been given to her on the part of her students.

   _____

6. For two different reasons, I love reading in a very real sense.

   _____

7. Past experience has taught me that it serves no particular purpose to tell a deliberate lie.

   _____

8. Both together we proceeded to laugh.

   _____

9. At the present time, my winter coat is adequate enough.

   _____

10. My personal preference is to have loyal friends even if they are few in number.

   _____

Exercise 5.15 Apply the Lesson and Revise a Paragraph

Rewrite the following paragraph, making it more concise.

Owing to the fact that it was cold and growing dark, I proceeded to walk as fast as I could, hoping I could get home before dark. The cold gusty wind was a contributing factor to my lack of comfort on this cold afternoon. During the course of my journey, I made phone calls to two friends of mine to see if they could come and pick me up and give me a ride home. Due to the fact that they did not answer, as they seldom ever do, I kept right on walking, faster and faster. Pretty soon I was as equally far from home as I was from school. In view of the fact that I had made adequate enough progress to believe I would make it home before it was totally and completely dark, I decided I would just relax and enjoy watching the blue sky grow pink and gold as the sun in front of me began to slowly sink down toward the horizon.

Polish Your Spelling
Homonyms

Richard Rodriguez's mother was moved out of the governor's office because she was not familiar with the **homonym** pair *gorilla/guerrilla*. Although these homonyms sound the same, their meanings are completely different.

When you write, it is important to make sure you choose the word with the meaning you intend (as Mrs. Rodriguez learned!). While you aren't likely to lose your job over a homonym, you could end up confusing people and your ideas could be misunderstood. If you use a wrong-meaning homonym in a job cover letter, résumé, or college application essay, it can send the wrong message to the people who are judging you.

Some of the most common homonym pairs and groups are *its/it's*, *their/they're/there*, *whose/who's*, *principal/principle*, and *your/you're*.

There are hundreds of homonyms in the English language, but you can often determine which one you want to use by remembering a few rules.

1. Remember that an apostrophe takes the place of missing letters in a contraction. If the homonym in question is a contraction, return it to its original words (put back the missing letters) and see if it makes sense that way. If it does, you have the right

word. If not, you want the other one—the one without the apostrophe.

Example:
Who's/whose socks are these?

Change *who's* to its original two words: *who is*.
Replace these in the sentence: *Who is* socks are these?
That obviously isn't what you want to say, so *whose* must be correct.

2. See if there is a word you know that is related to one of the homonym choices:

Example:
We need to seek legal *council/counsel*.

A guidance <u>counsel</u>or gives advice, just as a lawyer gives advice.
A council is a committee or board.
You could replace the word you need with *advice*, so the homonym you want is *counsel*.

To increase your skill with homonyms, try to increase your awareness of them as you read *anything*. You will run across homonyms everywhere!

For now, study the following list of common homonyms. Then complete the practice exercise on page 110.

.

all ready	everyone is ready
already	at this time
all together	everyone together
altogether	everything taken together
ascent	climb
assent	agreement
bare	exposed
bear	large mammal; put up with; produce
bite	sink teeth into
byte	unit of electronic memory
capital	governing city; money
capitol	a building where lawmakers meet
cent	one penny
scent	odor (*n*); to smell (*v*)
cite	to use as an example
site	location

complement	go well with; supply something that is lacking
compliment	a flattering remark
descent	a decline or climbing down
dissent	disagreement
forth	forward or onward
fourth	the ordinal of the number 4
idle	not busy
idol	much-admired figure
it's	contraction of "it is"
its	possessive of *it*
pair	two
pare	to remove the skin of a fruit or vegetable; make smaller ("pare down")
pear	a fruit
poor	with little money; not well; unfortunate
pore	tiny opening in the skin
pour	to dispense from a container or opening
principal	the most important; the main official at a school; a sum of money on which one earns or pays interest
principle	a rule of conduct or a belief
rapt	totally concentrating
rapped	talked or sang rap music
wrapped	covered
right	correct; opposite of left
rite	ceremony or custom
write	to make words
their	belonging to them
they're	contraction of "they are"
there	in that place
your	belonging to you
you're	contraction of "you are"

Exercise 5.16 Practice Choosing the Correct Homonym

Choose the homonym with the correct meaning for each sentence and write it on the blank line.

1. Planting a garden is a (rite, right, write) _____ of spring.

2. You have to choose the perfect (site, cite) _____ for the library.

3. Our garden takes up almost a (fourth, forth) _____ of an acre.

4. Planting is something our family does (altogether, all together) _____.

5. Last year we planted a (pair, pare, pear) _____ tree.

6. You put the tree in the hole and one person (poors, pours, pores) _____ in water while another one shovels dirt around the tree.

7. It won't (bear, bare) _____ fruit for about ten years.

8. Even so, (it's, its) _____ a pretty addition to our yard.

9. Our (principal, principle) _____ crop is vegetables.

10. We get a lot of thanks and (compliments, complements) _____ from our neighbors because we give away half of what we grow.

Chapter Six

Prereading Guide
Words to know and ideas to consider before you jump into the reading.

A. Essential Vocabulary

Word	Meaning	Typical Use
alignment (*n*) ah-LINE-ment	being arranged in a logical sequence; arrangement	What he says he believes is not in *alignment* with the way he acts.
connotation (*n*) con-o-TAY-shun	secondary meaning of a word; implication	Many advertisers use the word "free" because it has positive *connotations*.
dimension (*n*) dih-MEN-shun	width, depth, or height; shape; size	We need the *dimensions* of the room before we can purchase a carpet.
discretion (*n*) dis-KREH-shun	sensible forethought; caution	Use *discretion* when getting behind the wheel of a car.
dissuade (*v*) dih-SWADE	to persuade against doing something; sway	Carmela's mother *dissuaded* her from spending all her money on the expensive shoes.
exclusive (*adj*) eks-KLOO-siv	serving only a select group; special	Erik was nervous about attending the *exclusive* event, afraid he would say or do something wrong.
immaculate (*adj*) ih-MACK-yu-lut	perfectly clean and faultless; impeccable	The White House lawn and gardens are kept in *immaculate* condition.
palpitation (*n*) pal-pih-TAY-shun	rapid fluttering or beating, especially of the heart; trembling	My grandfather went to the hospital because he was having heart *palpitations*.
picturesque (*adj*) pik-shur-ESK	visually pleasing, suggesting a lovely image (normally applied to a building, landscape, or town)	The charming seacoast village, with its *picturesque* shops and restaurants, was a favorite with tourists.
tortuous (*adj*) TOR-choo-us	frequently changing direction; crooked; winding	The path up the mountain was *tortuous* and steep, but the view from the top made the climb worthwhile.

B. Vocabulary Practice

Exercise 6.1   Sentence Completion

Using your new vocabulary knowledge, choose the best way to complete the following sentences. Circle the letter of your answer.

1. The tortuous roads _____ delayed their arrival time.
   A. across the desert
   B. through the mountains

2. The politician's actions are not in _____ with the things he says in his speeches.
   A. discretion
   B. alignment

3. "Three earrings are _____," said Vanessa's mother, trying to dissuade her from further piercings.
   A. enough
   B. not enough

4. I was so _____ I think I had palpitations!
   A. depressed
   B. surprised

5. My mother insists that we keep _____ immaculate.
   A. Dad's workshop
   B. the kitchen

6. What are the _____ of the new desk you want to buy?
   A. connotations
   B. dimensions

7. The connotations of the word "_____" have changed in past decades.
   A. web
   B. three

8. It is best to use discretion when deciding _____.
   A. what kind of fruit to eat
   B. which movies to watch with children

9. The _____ was very exclusive.
   A. country club
   B. grocery store

10. Most people would agree that _____ is very picturesque.
    A. Alaska
    B. a landfill

Exercise 6.2   Using Fewer Words

Replace the italicized words with a single word from the following list. The first one has been done for you.

aligned   connotations   dimensions   discretion   dissuaded

exclusive   immaculate   palpitating   picturesque   tortuous

1. Mrs. Jenkins *arranged in a logical sequence* the desks in her classroom.

   1. __aligned__

2. After a hard and long run, Ashley's heart was *beating rapidly*.

   2._____

3. *Sensible forethought* is advisable in many situations.

   3._____

4. The *secondary meanings* of "natural" are helpful in selling many food products.

   4._____

5. What is (are) the *width, depth, and height* of your new refrigerator?

   5._____

6. Fortunately, my dad *persuaded against* me from counting solely on a football scholarship to attend college.

   6._____

7. From the prices in the boutique, we soon realized it was *only for the wealthy*, way too expensive for our meager budgets.

   7._____

8. I hope that the restaurants where I eat are *perfectly clean and faultless*.

   8._____

9. The road to the cottage was *frequently changing direction*, but that made it all the more exciting when the lake came into view around the last bend.

   9._____

10. My grandparents live in a(an) *visually pleasing* little village on the shores of Lake Huron.

    10._____

Exercise 6.3 Synonyms and Antonyms

Fill in the blanks in column A with the required synonyms or antonyms, selecting them from column B. (Remember: A *synonym* is a word similar in meaning to another word. *Autumn* and *fall* are synonyms. An *antonym* is a word opposite in meaning to another word. *Beginning* and *ending* are antonyms.)

	A	B
_____	1. antonym for *displeasing*	discretion
_____	2. synonym for *trembling*	dimension
_____	3. antonym for *straight*	dissuade
_____	4. synonym for *caution*	tortuous
_____	5. antonym for *filthy*	palpitation
_____	6. synonym for *shape*	alignment
_____	7. antonym for *encourage*	picturesque
_____	8. synonym for *implication*	exclusive
_____	9. synonym for *special*	immaculate
_____	10. synonym for *arrangement*	connotation

C. Journal Freewrite

Before you begin the reading on the next page, take out a journal or sheet of paper and spend some time responding to the following prompt.

TIP: Don't worry about grammar and spelling; just write what comes to mind. The purpose of freewriting is to explore ideas, not to produce a polished work.

> Choosing a marriage partner is a major decision that deeply affects one's life. What are some qualities and character traits you think people should look for in a spouse? What are three absolute musts?

Reading 8

from The Wedding

by Dorothy West

About the Author
Dorothy West (circa 1907–1998), the daughter of a former slave, began her writing career at the age of eighteen with a published short story. She moved from Boston to New York in the 1920s to join the Harlem Renaissance, counting Langston Hughes, Zora Neale Hurston, Countee Cullen, and Richard Wright among her friends. She was a social worker during the Depression and wrote short stories for the New York *Daily News.* In 1943, she moved to Martha's Vineyard and wrote *The Living Is Easy,* a novel about the African-American middle class. While living on Martha's Vineyard, she became acquainted with Jacqueline Kennedy Onassis, then an editor, who encouraged her to write another novel. The result was *The Wedding,* a story about the lives of upper-class African-Americans who had homes on "the Vineyard."

Reader's Tip: The author describes her characters as "colored people." It's important to understand that this was an acceptable and polite way to refer to African-Americans at the time depicted in the story.

On a morning in late August, the morning before the wedding, the sun rising out of the quiet sea stirred the Oval from its shapeless sleep and gave <u>dimension</u> and design to the ring of summer cottages.

The islanders were already astir. There was milk to deliver to the summer visitors, stores to open for their spending sprees, grass to cut for them, cars to wash for them, an endless chain of petty jobs demanding preference, particularly in the Oval, whose occupants were colored, and inclined to expect special treatment.

The Oval was a rustic stretch of flowering shrubs and tall trees, designated on the old town maps as Highland Park. The narrow dirt road that circled it was Highland Avenue. But since in no islander's memory had there ever been signposts to bring these ambitious titles to life, the area had long ago been assigned the descriptive name that better suited it.

A baker's dozen of cottages made a ring around the park. Some were small and plain of façade, others were bigger and handsomer (one, the Coles place, was called a mansion), and all of them were spruced up for summer, set back precisely on <u>immaculate</u> squares of green lawn.

They formed a fortress, a bulwark of colored society. Their occupants could boast that they, or even better their ancestors, had owned a home away from home since the days when a summer hegira[1] was taken by few colored people above the rank of servant.

Though newer comers owned cottages in other sections of the seaside town, some very splendid houses in neighborhoods customarily called white, the Ovalites still outranked them. They had been the vanguard.[2] They were now the old guard. It would sound like sour grapes to say, "So what?"

---
[1]journey, especially an escape
[2]forerunners or predecessors

Even the label "Ovalite" had acquired a <u>connotation</u> completely the contrary of its original intent. For those who had bestowed it as a bitter epithet[3] were now long gone from the scene of their failure to crash Ovalite society, and the name that was once profane had been sanctified by time and proper inflection.

The Coles house dominated the Oval. With its great glassed-in porches, against which many birds had dashed themselves to death, its ballroom, with the little gilt chairs that had hugged the walls for years now set in place for the wedding, and the undertaker's chairs in sober <u>alignment</u>, its sweep of lawns that kept the lesser cottages at a feudal[4] distance, it was the prize piece of the Oval.

Behind it were acres of <u>picturesque</u> growth that had been part of the property in the baronial era[5] of the first owner. Now they served as an effective backdrop for the Coles place, closing that end of the Oval to cars, making it a dead end.

The only means of exit from or entrance to the Oval was via a winding, rutted road. The underbrush on either side of this road forced one of two approaching cars to back to its starting place, a slow and <u>tortuous</u> procedure that often left scars on the polished hide of an oversize car that did not quite stay in the ruts.

The Ovalites could have followed established procedure and petitioned the town for a wider outlet to the highway. But this uninviting approach gave them a feeling of being as <u>exclusive</u> as the really exclusive—the really rich, the really powerful—who also lived at the end of impressively bad roads to discourage the curious.

The Clark Coleses came closest to being as real as their counterparts.[6] They had money, enough not only to spend but to save. They were college-bred, of good background. They lived graciously. Two respectful maids had served them for years, living proof that they were used to servants. If Clark and Corrine had not been with each other for years, even their daughters could not have demanded more <u>discretion</u> in their outward behavior.

Their daughters were Liz, the married one, and Shelby, the bride-to-be, both lovely, but Shelby lovelier, the image of Gram in that tinted picture of Gram as a girl, with rose-pink skin, golden hair, and dusk-blue eyes.

That Liz had married a dark man and given birth to a daughter who was tinged with her father's darkness had raised the eyebrows of the Oval. But at least she had married a man in medicine, in keeping with the family tradition that all men were created to be doctors, whose titles made introductions so easy and self-explanatory.

But how Shelby, who could have had her pick of the best of breed in her own race, could marry outside her race, outside her father's profession, and throw her life away on a nameless, faceless white

---

[3]name or label
[4]like the Middle Ages, when landholding lords granted permission to vassals to farm their land in exchange for a large percentage of the profit
[5]the 1880s, when "robber barons" made a great deal of money at the expense of others' hard labor
[6]people corresponding to them in wealthy white society

man who wrote jazz, a frivolous occupation without office, title, or foreseeable future, was beyond the Oval's understanding.

Between the dark man Liz had married and the music maker Shelby was marrying, there was a whole area of eligible men of the right colors and the right professions. For Liz and Shelby to marry so contrary to expectations affronted[7] all the subtle tenets[8] of their training.

Though Shelby might have been headstrong in her choice of a husband, at least she had let her mother <u>dissuade</u> her from following Liz's lead and eloping. Her wedding would have the Oval setting that Corinne had promised Miss Adelaide Bannister on a golden afternoon in her daughters' teens. Addie, breathing hard behind the bulging stays that tormented and squeezed the unsuitable flesh of her thin existence, had sat stuck to her chair on the glassed-in porch that drew the sun and made the heat hotter, fanning herself with the limp hand that waved in her face whenever there was nothing else to stir a breeze.

She accepted a drink that was medicinal, and the sun, and the too tight stays, and the drink, gave her <u>palpitations</u> that made her bosom heave back and forth in a rapid way that always unnerved the spineless, who did not want to see her drop dead before them. Clutching her heart to hold it in place, she confided to Corinne that her greatest hope was to live long enough to see Liz married, not that it was beyond all hope that she would live to see them both as brides.

Moved by this sad and simple confidence, Corinne made her sentimental promise that Liz would be married in the Oval, sparing Addie any tormenting trip to New York, where the unfamiliar place and people and pace might really cause Addie's untimely demise in the middle of Grand Central Station.

---

[7]disrespected
[8]principles and beliefs

Understanding the Reading

Complete the next three exercises and see how well you understood the excerpt from *The Wedding*.

Exercise 6.4   Multiple-Choice Questions

Answer the following questions about the reading. Circle the letter of your answer.

TIP: Don't try to answer the questions from memory; go back to the text as often as necessary.

1. What is the most extraordinary thing about the Ovalites?
   A. Their lawns are immaculate.
   B. Their cottages have ballrooms with gilt chairs.
   C. Some of their families have owned summer vacation homes for generations.
   D. They live on a narrow dirt road.

2. In the first sentence of paragraph 5, the word *bulwark* most likely means
   A. formation.
   B. wall.
   C. society.
   D. fortress.

3. When it was first used, the term "Ovalite" had what kinds of connotations (feelings and suggestions associated with a word)?
   A. positive ones
   B. negative ones
   C. holy ones
   D. humorous ones

4. Introducing Liz's husband is "self-explanatory" because
   A. everyone knows what a doctor is.
   B. he is a general practitioner.
   C. "doctor" means he is rich and successful.
   D. everyone knows why Liz married him.

5. From the descriptions of Gram, Liz's husband, and Shelby's fiancé, you can conclude that the Coleses are
   A. color-conscious.
   B. class-conscious.
   C. money-conscious.
   D. all of these.

Exercise 6.5   Short-Answer Questions

Respond to the following questions in one to two complete sentences. Go back to the text, as you did on the multiple choice.

6. Dorothy West uses a great deal of description in this first chapter of her novel. Which images remain most clearly in your mind?

   _____

   _____

   _____

7. From what point of view is this story told? Explain.

   _____

   _____

   _____

8. How had both Liz and Shelby fallen short of their society's expectations? Do you think they should have done what was expected? Why or why not?

   _____

   _____

   _____

9. The Ovalites were fond of the "winding, rutted road" that made it hard to get to the Oval and made them seem more exclusive. What indications of "exclusivity" do you find in the world around you?

_____

_____

_____

Exercise 6.6 Extending Your Thinking

Respond to the following question in three to four complete sentences. Use details from the text in your answer.

10. What difficulties do you think Shelby and Liz had in figuring out their identities—who they were and where they fit into society?

_____

_____

_____

_____

_____

_____

Reading Strategy Lesson
Making Inferences and Drawing Conclusions

What Is an Inference?

When you make an inference, you guess about information that the author does not state directly. You use details that *are* stated as fuel for your logical guess, or inference.

You have probably heard the phrase "read between the lines," meaning that when someone says something or writes something, you look beyond the words to see what meaning is hidden but still implied. *Reading between the lines* is what you do when you *make an inference*.

Look for the inferences you can make about the following information:

> Even the label "Ovalite" had acquired a connotation completely the contrary of its original intent. For those who had bestowed it as a bitter epithet were now long gone from the scene of their failure to crash Ovalite society, and the name that was once profane had been sanctified by time and proper inflection.

What can you infer about "those who had bestowed it as a bitter epithet"? If they referred to Ovalites bitterly, they probably didn't like them or thought they were snobbish. In fact, the paragraph states that they had failed to "crash Ovalite society." Their bitterness probably resulted from their resentment at not being included in the "in crowd."

In addition to the details the author gives us, we can add our own knowledge: that wealthy, successful people have a reputation for snubbing those they feel aren't "good enough" for them. We may have experienced that "left out" feeling ourselves.

Details that lead to inferences may be found anywhere—in characters' actions and words, in descriptions, or in story events. Always pay special attention to the words an author chooses and ask yourself *why* he or she chose them. In the example above, West says, "and the name that was once *profane* had been *sanctified* by time and *proper inflection*." The italicized words are powerful choices. *Profane* (irreverent or disrespectful) and *sanctified* (made holy) are direct opposites. *Proper inflection* means that the word "Ovalite" came to be spoken in a respectful and admiring tone of voice.

What Is a Conclusion?

You draw conclusions all day long. The grass is getting long, and you come to the conclusion that before long your mom will ask you to mow it. It's getting cold outside, so you conclude that you should get out your winter coat, hat, and gloves.

When you read, you carefully consider the facts and details the author presents. Some may be stated in a straightforward manner. You may need to infer other details. When you put the stated details and the inferences together, you can come to a conclusion.

What conclusions can you draw about the Ovalites from the paragraph we've been working with?

The paragraph is about more than just the connotations of the word. By putting together our details and inferences, we can conclude that the people who live on the Oval are members of an exclusive African-American society. They are wealthy, perhaps a bit snobbish, and definitely revered and envied as the top echelon of society.

Exercise 6.7 Practice the Reading Strategy

Read each item carefully. Then write your inference(s) in the left-hand box and your conclusions in the right-hand box.

1. The Coles house dominated the Oval. With its great glassed-in porches, against which many birds had dashed themselves to death, its ballroom, with the little gilt chairs that had hugged the walls for years now set in place for the wedding, and the undertaker's chairs

in sober alignment, its sweep of lawns that kept the lesser cottages at a feudal distance, it was the prize piece of the Oval.

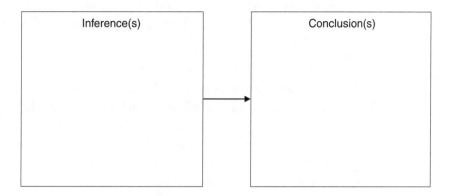

2. But how Shelby, who could have had her pick of the best of breed in her own race, could marry outside her race, outside her father's profession, and throw her life away on a nameless, faceless, white man who wrote jazz, a frivolous occupation without office, title, or foreseeable future, was beyond the Oval's understanding.

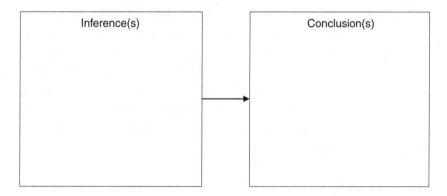

3. Their daughters were Liz, the married one, and Shelby, the bride-to-be, both lovely, but Shelby lovelier, the image of Gram in that tinted picture of Gram as a girl, with rose-pink skin, golden hair, and dusk-blue eyes.

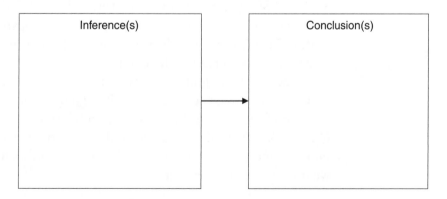

Exercise 6.8   Apply the Reading Strategy to a New Story

Read each passage carefully. Then write at least two sentences summarizing your inferences and conclusions. All of the passages are taken from "The Bride Comes to Yellow Sky," a short story by Stephen Crane.

1. A newly married pair had boarded this coach at San Antonio. The man's face was reddened from many days in the wind and sun, and a direct result of his new black clothes was that his brick-colored hands were constantly performing in a most conscious fashion. From time to time he looked down respectfully at his attire. He sat with a hand on each knee, like a man waiting in a barber's shop. The glances he devoted to other passengers were furtive and shy.

_____

_____

_____

_____

_____

2. He knew full well that his marriage was an important thing to his town. It could only be exceeded by the burning of the new hotel. His friends could not forgive him. Frequently he had reflected on the advisability of telling them by telegraph, but a new cowardice had been upon him. He feared to do it. And now the train was hurrying him toward a scene of amazement, glee, and reproach. He glanced out of the window at the line of haze swinging slowly in towards the train.

_____

_____

_____

_____

_____

3. Yellow Sky had a kind of brass band, which played painfully, to the delight of the populace. He laughed without heart as he thought of it. If the citizens could dream of his prospective arrival with his bride, they would parade the band at the station and escort them, amid cheers and laughing congratulations, to his adobe home.

   He resolved that he would use all the devices of speed and plains-craft in making the journey from the station to his house. Once within that safe citadel he could issue some sort of a vocal bulletin, and then not go among the citizens until they had time to wear off a little of their enthusiasm.

The bride looked anxiously at him. "What's worrying you, Jack?"

He laughed again. "I'm not worrying, girl. I'm only thinking of Yellow Sky."

She flushed in comprehension.

_____

_____

_____

_____

_____

Writing Workshop
Avoiding Clichés

What Is a Cliché?

We are all familiar with trite or overused expressions, known as clichés, because we hear them constantly. When you hear or see the beginning of a cliché, you already know what the rest of it will be. For example, when you hear "Last but . . .," you can already fill in ". . . not least." If a friend is telling you a story, and says "Beyond the shadow of . . .," you automatically fill in ". . . a doubt."

Dorothy West wrote:
"The Ovalites could have followed established procedure and petitioned the town for a wider outlet to the highway."

A trite way to say the same thing would be: "The Ovalites could have *fought city hall* and won a wider road."

Stephen Crane wrote:
"Frequently he had reflected on the advisability of telling them by telegraph, but a new cowardice had been upon him. He feared to do it."

He could have written, "He'd *hemmed and hawed* about telling them by telegraph, but he was *scared out of his wits*. He was *too chicken* to do it." That's three clichés in two sentences!

Clichés were original when someone first thought them up, but they have been used so much that they have almost lost their meaning, and certainly their impact. According to the Oxford English Dictionary, writer Samuel Taylor Coleridge first used the term "Achilles' heel" as a metaphor for a person's weak point. That was in 1810. Today it is considered trite to use the phrase "Achilles' heel." Author George Orwell maintained that clichés were used "because they save people the trouble of inventing phrases for themselves."

Like lack of variety in sentence structure, writing that is riddled with clichés is not likely to interest your reader for long. They are so expected that you don't really hear them when you are listening or reading. Using vivid, unique phrases when you write makes your ideas seem fresh and keeps your reader involved with what you are trying to communicate.

Recognizing Clichés

To replace clichés, you must first recognize them. While there are thousands of clichés and trite expressions, here is a list to help you identify some of the most common ones.

hard as nails	at the drop of a hat
on the road to recovery	the ladder of success
raining cats and dogs	time to kill
the bottom line	time and time again
at the crack of dawn	hook, line, and sinker
nutty as a fruitcake	needless to say
off the beaten track	fame and fortune
I'd give my right arm	

Can you think of any others?

Exercise 6.9   Practice Recognizing Clichés

See how many of these clichés you can fill in automatically. When you're done, turn to a partner to compare answers on any of the ones about which you weren't sure.

1. That's just the tip of _____.

2. Like it or _____.

3. He's one sandwich short of a _____.

4. It's a win _____ situation.

5. Let's cut to the _____.

6. She's the hostess with the _____.

7. He's a barrel of _____.

8. We got up at the crack of _____.

9. As luck would _____, the Ferris wheel was broken.

10. It's like trying to find a needle _____.

Replacing Clichés

Looking back at Exercise 6.9, what other phrases could you use to replace the worn-out ones? That's where your imagination and creativity come in.

Example:
Instead of "That's just the tip of the iceberg," you might write, "That is but one step on a harrowing journey through a forest of dishonesty and greed."

Working with a partner, choose some of the other clichés from the previous exercise and take turns creating replacements.

Exercise 6.10 Apply the Lesson to Revise Sentences

Rewrite each sentence, eliminating the cliché.

1. I can feel it in my bones that it's going to rain.

   _____

2. In fact, it looks like it's going to pour cats and dogs.

   _____

3. Looking around the room, I can see that umbrellas are scarce as hens' teeth.

   _____

4. We were making idle chitchat instead of thinking about the weather.

   _____

5. It looks like we're all in the same boat.

   _____

6. When is dinner? I'm so hungry I could eat a bear.

   _____

7. When it is finally ready, I'll probably inhale it.

   _____

8. Then my mom will have a cow.

   _____

9. She says I eat like a horse.

   _____

10. At least I'm not slow as molasses, like my sister, who gets out of clearing the table.

    _____

Grammar Mini-Lesson
Using Participles Correctly

When you describe a *rolling river*, what part of speech is *rolling*? You're using *rolling* to describe a noun, the river, so *rolling* must be an adjective, right? But isn't *to roll* an action, which would make *rolling* a verb? In fact, both thoughts are correct. *Rolling* is a verb form *acting* as an adjective, which we call a participle.

Participles

A **participle** is a **verb form acting as an adjective** and modifying (describing) a noun or pronoun. Participles help show relationships between ideas in a sentence, add details and information, and help to create sentence variety. Later in the chapter, you will see how using participles can make your writing more interesting and less choppy.

1. Present participles (like *singing* or *trotting*) are formed by adding *-ing* to the word stem (*sing, trot*), doubling the final consonant if necessary. Examine this example from *The Wedding*:

> The underbrush on either side of this road forced one of two *approaching* cars to back to its *starting* place . . .

The subject and verb in this sentence are *underbrush* and *forced*. *Approaching* describes *cars*, and *starting* modifies *place*.

Although all present participles end in *-ing*, not all words ending in *-ing* are present participles. Remember, participles function *only* like adjectives. The same *-ing* word may not be an adjective in another sentence.

Example:
> *Starting* is the first step.

Starting is the subject of this sentence, so it is not an adjective. It's another verbal form called a gerund, which functions as a noun.
> . . . the *morning* before the *wedding*

Morning and *wedding* are simply nouns that end in *-ing*.

2. A past participle is usually formed by adding *-ed*.

> Her fondest hope was to see Liz *married*.
> (*Married* describes Liz.)

> There were no seats left in the *crowded* room.
> (*Crowded* describes room.)

However, some past participles end in *-en, -d, -t,* or *-n.*

> The *frozen* pond was still not safe for skating.
> (*Frozen* describes pond—and comes from the verb *freeze.*)

> All there was to eat was *burnt* toast.
> (*Burnt* describes toast—and comes from the verb *burn.*)

Not every word that ends in *-ed, -en, -d, -t,* or *-n* is a past participle. You must look at the word's function in the sentence to determine this.

> . . . the Ovalites still *outranked* them.
> (The Ovalites did what? They *outranked* them. *Outranked* is an action, so it is a verb.)

> The Coles house *dominated* the Oval.
> (*Dominated* is a verb. The Coles house did what?)

Common Irregular Past Participles:

beaten	fallen	read	taken
begun	forgotten	risen	taught
bitten	found	seen	thought
bought	hung	shone	thrown
brought	led	spoken	told
caught	lost	stolen	wept
chosen	made	stood	worn
eaten	meant	struck	written

Exercise 6.11 Practice Using Past and Present Participles

On the blank line, write the correct past or present participle of the given verb.

Example: <u>Arriving</u> at the theater early, we easily found a parking spot. (arrive)

1. _____ by Liz's choice of a spouse, they still tried to be polite. (affront)

2. _____ driver advertisements have helped decrease DUI accidents. (designate)

3. Whenever Kayla got her hands on some money, she went on a _____ spree. (spend)

4. The children, _____ after a long day, fell asleep quickly. (exhaust)

5. _____ by time and proper inflection, the original meaning of the word "Ovalite" was lost. (sanctify)

Participial Phrases

A **participial phrase** consists of a participle plus any words modified (described) by or related to it. The whole phrase acts as an adjective—it describes a noun or pronoun. Sentences 1, 4, and 5 in Exercise 6.11 contain participial phrases.

Both past and present participles can be modified by adverbs:

I become *extremely exasperated* when I cannot do algebra.
       ADV   PAST PART.

Utterly disregarding others' feelings, Pam speaks her mind.
ADV   PRESENT PART.

Placement of Participial Phrases

To prevent confusion, place the participial phrase as close as possible to the noun or pronoun it modifies, and make sure the noun is clearly stated. Read the sentence below and see if you can figure out how to fix it.

Utterly disregarding others' feelings, Pamela's friends are often hurt.

It sounds as if Pamela's friends are the ones who disregard others' feelings, and that this causes them to be hurt. To make the meaning of the sentence clear, move the participial phrase:

Pamela, *utterly disregarding others' feelings*, often hurts her friends.

A participle in the wrong place is called a "dangling participle" and is a common grammatical error. Learning to place them correctly will help you avoid misunderstandings in your writing and speech.

Example:

Spending money like crazy, her clothes were gorgeous.

Her *clothes* were not spending money. *She* was. How would you fix this sentence?

Spending money like crazy, she bought gorgeous clothes.

See if you can tell what is wrong with these, and then fix them:

Driving home in rush-hour traffic, a light was out at a major intersection.

_____

Running up the stairs, her foot slipped and fell.

_____

Punctuating Participial Phrases

Set off a participial phrase with commas when it

- comes at the beginning of a sentence:
  Wondering which way to turn next, the puzzled driver stopped to consult his map.

- comes at the end of the sentence and is separated from the noun or pronoun it modifies:
  The puzzled driver stopped to consult his map, *wondering which way to turn next*.

- is in the interior of the sentence, but the sentence would still be complete without it:
  The puzzled driver, *wondering which way to turn next*, stopped to consult his map.

  Do not set off a participial phrase in the middle of the sentence if it is essential to the sentence's meaning:
  Drivers *wondering which way to turn next* are a traffic menace.

While "Drivers are a traffic menace" is a complete sentence, it doesn't make sense without the participial phrase. Not all drivers are traffic menaces.

Exercise 6.12 Practice Punctuating Participial Phrases

Following the rules for punctuating participial phrases, insert commas where they are needed.

1. The sundeck with its inviting view of the ocean was a popular place.

2. Working four hours after school Michael had trouble getting his homework done.

3. Alexis gave up on sleeping interrupted constantly by phone calls.

4. The wooden crates holding hundreds of shining apples sat in the cider mill yard.

5. Andrew trying hard to please his big sister brought her a bouquet of wildflowers.

6. Touched by the novel's ending Sabrina blinked back tears.

7. Stretching out on a sofa near the fire Trevor fell asleep.

8. Amanda seeing us by the window waved happily and joined us.

9. Buses delayed by heavy traffic usually run behind schedule.

10. Alarmed that I might hurt myself Dad gave me some work gloves to wear.

Polish Your Spelling

Adding the Suffix -ION

The Suffix -ION

By adding the suffix -ion, meaning "act or result of," we can change many verbs to nouns.

VERB	SUFFIX	NOUN
fascinate	+ ion	= fascination
palpitate	+ ion	= palpitation

We dropped the final *e* in these two words because -ion begins with a vowel, and we don't want two vowels together.

When a word ends with a consonant, you can add -ion without having to drop any letters.

VERB	SUFFIX	NOUN
attract	+ ion	= attraction
inflect	+ ion	= inflection

Exercise 6.13 Practice the Spelling Pattern

Change the following verbs to nouns by adding the suffix -ion correctly.

	VERB	NOUN
Example:	graduate + *ion*	graduation
	1. invent	_____
	2. humiliate	_____
	3. select	_____
	4. irritate	_____
	5. adopt	_____
	6. hesitate	_____
	7. pollute	_____
	8. operate	_____
	9. impress	_____
	10. separate	_____

Unit Two Review

Vocabulary Review

A. Match each word with its definition.

	DEFINITION	WORD
_____	1. express annoyance or irritation	a. palpitation
_____	2. exploiting weakness for gain	b. plague
_____	3. arranged in logical sequence	c. vetted
_____	4. width, depth, or height	d. connotation
_____	5. corrupted or decayed	e. fume
_____	6. rapid fluttering or beating	f. classism
_____	7. widespread disease or disaster	g. dimension
_____	8. secondary meaning of a word	h. tainted
_____	9. carefully investigated	i. aligned
_____	10. judging on basis of social rank	j. predatory

B. Match each word with its synonym.

	SYNONYM	WORD
_____	11. retaliate	a. rectify
_____	12. evasive	b. eclipse
_____	13. restitution	c. discretion
_____	14. insurgent	d. genocide
_____	15. obscure	e. fiscal
_____	16. special	f. elusive
_____	17. monetary	g. avenge
_____	18. caution	h. guerrilla
_____	19. correct	i. exclusive
_____	20. massacre	j. reparation

C. Match each word with its antonym.

ANTONYM	WORD
_____ 21. wealthy	a. urban
_____ 22. cheerful	b. immensity
_____ 23. filthy	c. tortuous
_____ 24. encourage	d. picturesque
_____ 25. increase	e. immaculate
_____ 26. straight	f. sullen
_____ 27. respectful	g. dissuade
_____ 28. smallness	h. indigent
_____ 29. displeasing	i. condescending
_____ 30. rural	j. recede

Grammar Review

Edit the paragraph below to correct run-on sentences, for conciseness, for punctuation, and to eliminate clichés. The editing job has been started for you.

          developed
Poverty in ˄ countries ~~that have been developed~~ is defined

    differently   it is
~~in a different way~~ than ~~poverty~~ in the developing world. In

undeveloped countries, ~~that is still developing~~ poverty means not

enough food or access to medical care to even survive. The average

person in the United States earns about 200 times as much money

as a person in a very poor country who is as poor as a church

mouse. In developed nations living below the poverty level means a

family's or person's income is not enough to afford decent food or

housing. And other basic needs. Some people suffering from

extreme poverty are homeless those in less poverty usually live in poor quality housing can be dangerous. Poor people are usually exposed to more crime its worse in the cities. About 20 percent of Americans live in poverty is less in Australia, Canada, Ireland, Japan, Spain, and the United Kingdom. Certain groups of people are more poor than others. Single parents and their children have the highest rates of poverty from 30% up to 50% depending on race. In the states that are in the southern part and the western part of the U.S. there are fewer good jobs equals more poverty. Exhausted they can work like a dog and never get above the poverty line. Higher percentages of African-Americans and Hispanics live below the poverty level there are many more white people in the population the number of poor whites is higher.

Spelling Review

A. Choose the correct homonym for each sentence.

1. (Descent, Dissent) _____ encourages informed discussion.
2. (It's, Its) _____ not what you think it is.
3. Please take this note to the (principal, principle) _____.

B. Circle the word in each group that is spelled correctly:

4.   comunicate   communicate   communnicate

5.   assessment   assesment   asesment

6.   embarras   embarrass   embarass

7.   apettite   appettite   appetite

C. Add *-ion* to each verb to make a noun:

8. promote   _____

9. invent   _____

10. investigate   _____

Writing Review

Choose one of the following topics. Plan your essay. Write your first draft. Then revise and edit your draft, and write your final essay. Don't forget to identify your audience, purpose, and task before you begin planning.

The theme of this unit is "Identity." What similarities can you find in the problems faced by the narrators of *The Woman Warrior* and *Hunger of Memory* as they struggle to find their identities? How are the two narrators and their families different?

OR

In *Class Matters*, bell hooks calls for "an in-your-face critique of capitalist greed" to address the problem of the widening gap between the wealthy and the poor. Explain how you believe the problem developed and offer at least two ways to begin to solve it.

SPEAK/LISTEN

Getting Deeper into a Text

Listen as your teacher or group leader reads another selection from *Where We Stand*, *Hunger of Memory*, or *The Woman Warrior*. As you listen, think about whether your feelings about the author or the subject change. Does listening to more of the book help you to better understand the selection chosen for the chapter? When you are finished listening, write a brief journal entry about what you learned or how you feel about the additional material.

 EXPLORE

Conversing with the Authors

With a partner, choose one of the authors of the four selections in this unit. Use the Internet or books from the library to find out more about the author's life. Then write a letter to the author asking him or her questions that occurred to you as you were doing research or reading what the author wrote. If the author is still alive, mail or e-mail the letter.

 WRITE

Guess Who's Coming to Dinner

Imagine that Richard Rodriguez, Maxine Hong Kingston, and bell hooks have all been invited to dinner at the Coleses' mansion in the Oval. Create a one-act play featuring the Coleses and the authors. What might they discuss? On what would they agree or disagree? Recruit classmates to read the various parts and present the play to the class.

OR

Write a short story or poem showing how it feels to be excluded from a group.

 CONNECT

The Realities of Poverty in Today's World

Work in a small group. On the Internet, find out the poverty level (also called "threshold") for a family of four in America. Assume housing and utilities cost the family 50% of that total, and that transportation, clothing, medical, and miscellaneous costs use up another 30%. Divide the remaining 20% of the total by 52 to get the amount left for one week's groceries. Obtain several supermarket ads and plan a week's menus. You must stay within the allotted amount. Share and compare with other groups. Write a paragraph reflecting on what you learned from the experience.

UNIT THREE

Love and Friendship

Chapter Seven

Prereading Guide

Words to know and ideas to consider before you jump into the reading.

A. Essential Vocabulary

Word	Meaning	Typical Use
abominable (*adj*) uh-BAHM-i-nuh-bul	deserving or causing loathing or hatred; detestable	The arrogance displayed by that actress at the awards show was *abominable*.
animosity (*n*) an-i-MOS-i-tee	a feeling of ill will; hostility	The old enemies are friends now and have put all *animosity* behind them.
defer (*v*) de-FUR	1. to give in to the wishes or opinion of another; yield 2. to postpone to another time; delay	Although Jake thought he was right, he *deferred* to his mom to avoid an argument. The final game was *deferred* due to bad weather.
diminish (*v*) dih-MIN-ish	to become or to make smaller in amount, size, or importance; lessen; decrease	My headache was bad at first, but now the pain has *diminished*.
exultation (*n*) ex-ul-TAY-shun	the act of being extremely joyful; triumphant	Having won the game, our team left the field in a mood of *exultation*.
furtive (*adj*) FUR-tiv	done in a stealthy way as if to hinder discovery; sneaky	*Furtive* looks at a classmate's answer sheet may be viewed as cheating.
petulant (*adj*) PET-yu-lunt	ill-humored and irritable	Aisha was in a *petulant* mood when she wasn't allowed to go to the party.
refuge (*n*) REF-yooj	shelter or protection from danger or harm; safe haven; protection	We took *refuge* from the storm inside a supermarket.
subsequent (*adj*) SUB-suh-kwent	still to come; later; successive	You can put half of the money down on the stereo now and pay off the rest in three *subsequent* payments.
supercilious (*adj*) soo-pur-SILL-ee-us	haughtily disdainful; contemptuous	Some high school seniors have a *supercilious* attitude toward younger students.

B. Vocabulary Practice

Exercise 7.1   Sentence Completion

Using your new vocabulary knowledge, choose the best way to complete the following sentences. Circle the letter of your answer.

1. _____, he looked furtively around before sneaking out of the meeting.
   A. Wanting everyone to notice
   B. Hoping not to be noticed

2. She was _____ because she was so petulant with customers.
   A. fired
   B. promoted

3. When Charlize _____, she didn't even try to hide her exultation.
   A. met her favorite author
   B. took out the trash

4. Taxi drivers with supercilious attitudes might get _____.
   A. better tips
   B. lower tips

5. In *Romeo and Juliet*, there is a lot of animosity between _____.
   A. Romeo and Juliet
   B. the lovers' families

6. Many people find _____ to be scary and abominable.
   A. rattlesnakes
   B. dolphins

7. She eventually deferred to her teacher, knowing that he had _____ experience on the subject.
   A. more
   B. less

8. After _____, the wind finally diminished.
   A. hardly a breeze all day
   B. blowing hard all day

9. _____ for the animals, they've made the land into a wildlife refuge.
   A. Unfortunately
   B. Fortunately

10. Writers of one _____ shape the writing of subsequent generations of writers.
    A. region
    B. literary movement

Exercise 7.2 Using Fewer Words

Replace the italicized words with a single word from the following list.

abominable	animosity	defer	diminish	exultation
furtively	petulantly	refuge	subsequent	supercilious

1. The singer has a(an) *haughty and disdainful* attitude toward noncelebrities.

   1._____

2. Shelters for the homeless and abused offer *shelter and protection.*

   2._____

3. Although loved and admired by teens, some parents found the rap album *deserving of loathing.*

   3._____

4. I don't like to cause trouble, so I usually *give in* to my sister.

   4._____

5. For some reason, Mr. Johnson bears *feelings of ill will* toward all of his neighbors.

   5._____

6. In the *still-to-come* years, the auto industry grew rapidly.

   6._____

7. A crisis can make small problems *become smaller in importance.*

   7._____

8. At the dinner table, my grandparents kept complaining *in an ill-humored way* about one thing or another.

   8._____

9. The quarterback was carried through the crowd on the shoulders of his teammates in a scene of *triumphant joy.*

   9._____

10. Security personnel closely watched a shopper who was looking around *in a stealthy way*, as if he might do something wrong.

   10._____

Exercise 7.3 Synonyms and Antonyms

Fill in the blanks in column A with the required synonyms or antonyms, selecting them from column B. (Remember: A *synonym* is a word similar in meaning to another word. An *antonym* is a word opposite in meaning to another word.)

A	B
_____ 1. synonym for *delay*	supercilious
_____ 2. synonym for *irritable*	abominable
_____ 3. antonym for *sadness*	furtive
_____ 4. synonym for *contemptuous*	diminish
_____ 5. antonym for *straightforward*	defer
_____ 6. synonym for *successive*	refuge
_____ 7. synonym for *protection*	animosity
_____ 8. antonym for *lovable*	subsequent
_____ 9. synonym for *lessen*	exultation
_____ 10. synonym for *hostility*	petulant

C. Journal Freewrite

Before you begin the reading on the next page, take out a journal or sheet of paper and spend some time responding to the following prompt.

TIP: Don't worry about grammar and spelling; just write what comes to mind. The purpose of freewriting is to explore ideas, not to produce a polished work.

> Describe a time you were ready to make up an excuse for something but wound up telling the truth. What made you decide to be honest? (If you can't think of something, write about when you think white lies are acceptable and when you think honesty is best.)

from The Adventures of Tom Sawyer

by Mark Twain

About the Author
Mark Twain (1835–1910) is the pseudonym (pen name) of Samuel Langhorne Clemens. The phrase "mark twain" was used by riverboat captains to describe water that was only two fathoms (twelve feet) deep. Twain grew up in Hannibal, Missouri, a port on the Mississippi River. He had several different jobs—printer's apprentice, steamboat pilot, Confederate cavalryman, and silver miner. One job he always had, along with the others, was writer. He wrote about his experiences as he traveled around America, and eventually he became internationally renowned. Today, his writings are still celebrated for humor, satire, memorable characters, and his disdain for hypocrisy. This is an excerpt from *The Adventures of Tom Sawyer*, published in 1876.

Reader's Tip: At this point in the novel, Tom Sawyer is on his way to school and runs into Huckleberry Finn, son of the village drunkard. The respectable boys of the town have been forbidden to associate with Huck, but that makes them enjoy Huck's company all the more. Tom has a long conversation with Huck, and, as a result, he arrives at school late.

When Tom reached the little isolated frame school-house, he strode in briskly, with the manner of one who had come with all honest speed. He hung his hat on a peg and flung himself into his seat with business-like alacrity.[1] The master, throned on high in his great splint-bottom arm-chair, was dozing, lulled by the drowsy hum of study. The interruption roused him:

"Thomas Sawyer!"

Tom knew that when his name was pronounced in full, it meant trouble.

"Sir!"

"Come up here. Now sir, why are you late again, as usual?"

Tom was about to take <u>refuge</u> in a lie, when he saw two long tails of yellow hair hanging down a back that he recognized by the electric sympathy of love; and by that form was *the only vacant place* on the girls' side of the school-house. He instantly said:

"I STOPPED TO TALK WITH HUCKLEBERRY FINN!"

The master's pulse stood still, and he stared helplessly. The buzz of study ceased. The pupils wondered if this foolhardy[2] boy had lost his mind. The master said:

"You—you did what?"

"Stopped to talk with Huckleberry Finn."

There was no mistaking the words.

"Thomas Sawyer, this is the most astounding confession I have ever listened to. No mere ferule[3] will answer for this offense. Take off your jacket."

---

[1]cheerful liveliness
[2]foolish
[3]ruler used to punish children

The master's arm performed until it was tired and the stock of switches notably <u>diminished</u>. Then the order followed:

"Now, sir, go and sit with the *girls*! And let this be a warning to you."

The titter that rippled around the room appeared to abash[4] the boy, but in reality that result was caused rather more by his worshipful awe of his unknown idol and the dread pleasure that lay in his high good fortune. He sat down upon the end of the pine bench and the girl hitched herself away from him with a toss of her head. Nudges and winks and whispers traversed the room, but Tom sat still, with his arms upon the long, low desk before him, and seemed to study his book.

By and by attention ceased from him, and the accustomed school murmur rose upon the dull air once more. Presently the boy began to steal <u>furtive</u> glances at the girl. She observed it, "made a mouth" at him and gave him the back of her head for the space of a minute. When she cautiously faced around again, a peach lay before her. She thrust it away. Tom gently put it back. She thrust it away again, but with less <u>animosity</u>. Tom patiently returned it to its place. Then she let it remain. Tom scrawled on his slate, "Please take it—I got more."

---

[4]embarrass

Understanding the Reading

Complete the next three exercises and see how well you understood the excerpt from *The Adventures of Tom Sawyer*.

Exercise 7.4 Multiple-Choice Questions

Answer the following questions about the reading. Circle the letter of your answer.

TIP: Don't try to answer the questions from memory; go back to the text as often as necessary.

1. Tom tells the truth when asked to explain why he is late because he
   A. sees it is no use to lie.
   B. wants to make the girls feel sorry for him.
   C. wants to entertain the class.
   D. wants to sit next to the yellow-haired girl.

2. At no time in the selection does
   A. the master stop watching the pupils.
   B. Tom actually study his book.
   C. the class stop paying attention to Tom.
   D. the yellow-haired girl take her eyes off Tom.

3. Judging from context, *roused* (paragraph 1) most likely means
   A. angered.
   B. annoyed.
   C. woke.
   D. made the master laugh.

4. The excerpt suggests that
   A. Tom has often been punished by the master.
   B. the pupils are absolutely silent when they study.
   C. except for Tom, the behavior of the class is perfect.
   D. Tom is usually on time for school.

Exercise 7.5   Short-Answer Questions

Respond to the following questions in one to two complete sentences. Go back to the text, as you did on the multiple choice.

5. This is an excerpt from a novel. If it were a short story, what would be a good title, and why?

   _____

   _____

   _____

6. Some people believe that schools would improve if children were punished as Tom was. Do you agree? Why or why not?

   _____

   _____

   _____

7. Twain refers to the "dread pleasure that lay in [Tom's] high good fortune." How could sitting next to the yellow-haired girl be both something he *dreaded* and a *pleasure*?

   _____

   _____

   _____

Exercise 7.6   Extending Your Thinking

Respond to the following question in three to four complete sentences. Use details from the text in your answer.

8. The theme of this unit is "Love and Friendship." Predict whether you think the peach and the note Tom wrote on his slate at the end of the story will be effective in gaining the yellow-haired girl's interest. What else might he have done and/or written?

_____

_____

_____

_____

_____

_____

from My Ántonia

by Willa Cather

About the Author
Willa Cather
(1873–1947) was born
in Virginia but moved
with her family to Red
Cloud, Nebraska, when
she was ten years old.
She graduated from the
University of Nebraska
at a time when it was
rare for women to
attend college. For a
while, she was a jour-
nalist and taught
English in Pittsburgh,
Pennsylvania. At age
32, she moved to New
York City to join the staff
of *McClure's Magazine*
and published her first
novel, *Alexander's
Bridge*. Once she was
established as a writer,
she moved to the
Southwest, an area she
felt brought out her cre-
ativity. She is known for
portraying a variety of
pioneer characters and
for lyrical descriptions
of both the harshness
and the beauty of the
land.

Reader's Tip: In this excerpt, Jim reveals that he is fond of Ántonia, a pretty immigrant girl he first noticed when they were fellow passengers on the train that brought them to the sparsely settled Nebraska Territory.

Much as I liked Ántonia, I hated a superior tone that she sometimes took with me. She was four years older than I, to be sure, and had seen more of the world; but I was a boy and she was a girl, and I resented her protecting manner. Before the autumn was over she began to treat me more like an equal and to <u>defer</u> to me in other things than reading lessons. This change came about from an adventure we had together.

One day when I rode over to the Shimerdas' I found Ántonia starting off on foot for Russian Peter's house, to borrow a spade Ambrosch needed. I offered to take her on the pony, and she got up behind me. There had been another black frost[1] the night before, and the air was clear and heady as wine. Within a week all the blooming roads had been despoiled, hundreds of miles of yellow sunflowers had been transformed into brown, rattling, burry stalks.

We found Russian Peter digging his potatoes. We were glad to go in and get warm by his kitchen stove and to see his squashes and Christmas melons, heaped in the storeroom for winter. As we rode away with the spade, Ántonia suggested that we stop at the prairie-dog town and dig into one of the holes. We could find out whether they ran straight down, or were horizontal, like mole-holes; whether they had under-ground connections; whether the owls had nests down there, lined with feathers. We might get some puppies, or owl eggs, or snake-skins.

The dog-town was spread out over perhaps ten acres. The grass had been nibbled short and even, so this stretch was not shaggy and red like the surrounding country, but gray and vel-vety. The holes were several yards apart, and were disposed with a good deal of regularity, almost as if the town had been laid out in streets and avenues. One always felt that an orderly

---

[1]frost so intense that it kills and blackens vegetation

and very sociable kind of life was going on there. I picketed Dude [his horse] down in a draw,[2] and we went wandering about, looking for a hole that would be easy to dig. The dogs were out, as usual, dozens of them, sitting up on their hind legs over the doors of their houses. As we approached, they barked, shook their tails at us, and scurried underground. Before the mouths of the holes were little patches of sand and gravel, scratched up, we supposed, from a long way below the surface. Here and there, in the town, we came on larger gravel patches, several yards away from any hole. If the dogs had scratched the sand up in excavating, how had they carried it so far? It was on one of these gravel beds that I met my adventure.

We were examining a big hole with two entrances. The burrow sloped into the ground at a gentle angle, so that we could see where the two corridors united, and the floor was dusty from use, like a little highway over which much travel went. I was walking backward, in a crouching position, when I heard Ántonia scream. She was standing opposite me, pointing behind me and shouting something in Bohemian. I whirled round, and there, on one of those dry gravel beds, was the biggest snake I had ever seen. He was sunning himself, after the cold night, and he must have been asleep when Ántonia screamed. When I turned he was lying in long loose waves, like a letter "W." He twitched and began to coil slowly. He was not merely a big snake, I thought—he was a circus monstrosity. His <u>abominable</u> muscularity, his loathsome, fluid motion, somehow made me sick. He was as thick as my leg, and looked as if millstones couldn't crush the disgusting vitality out of him. He lifted his hideous little head, and rattled. I didn't run because I didn't think of it—if my back had been against a stone wall I couldn't have felt more cornered. I saw his coils tighten—now he would spring, spring his length, I remembered. I ran up and drove at his head with my spade, struck him fairly across the neck, and in a minute he was all about my feet in wavy loops. I struck now from hate. Ántonia, barefooted as she was, ran up behind me. Even after I had pounded his ugly head flat, his body kept on coiling and winding, doubling and falling back on itself. I walked away and turned my back. I felt seasick.

Ántonia came after me, crying, "O Jimmy, he not bite you? You sure? Why you not run when I say?"

"What did you jabber Bohunk[3] for? You might have told me there was a snake behind me!" I said <u>petulantly</u>.

"I know I am just awful, Jim, I was so scared." She took my handkerchief from my pocket and tried to wipe my face with it, but I snatched it away from her. I suppose I looked as sick as I felt.

"I never know you was so brave, Jim," she went on comfortingly. You is just like big mans; you wait for him lift his head and then you go for him. Ain't you feel scared a bit? Now we take that snake home and show everybody. Nobody ain't seen in this kawn-tree so big snake like you kill."

---

[2] dry bed of a stream
[3] derogatory term for Bohemian

She went on in this strain until I began to think that I had longed for this opportunity, and had hailed it with joy. Cautiously we went back to the snake; he was still groping with his tail, turning up his ugly belly in the light. A faint, fetid smell came from him, and a thread of green liquid oozed from his crushed head.

"Look, Tony, that's his poison," I said.

I took a long piece of string from my pocket, and she lifted his head with the spade while I tied a noose around it. We pulled him out straight and measured him by my riding-quirt;[4] he was about five and half feet long. He had twelve rattles, but they were broken off before they began to taper, so I insisted that he must once have had twenty-four. I explained to Ántonia how this meant that he was twenty-four years old, that he must have been there when white men first came, left on from buffalo and Indian times. As I turned him over I began to feel proud of him, to have a kind of respect for his age and size. He seemed like the ancient, eldest Evil. Certainly his kind have left horrible unconscious memories in all warm-blooded life. When we dragged him down into the draw, Dude sprang off to the end of his tether and shivered all over—wouldn't let us come near him.

We decided that Ántonia should ride Dude home, and I would walk. As she rode along slowly, her bare legs swinging against the pony's sides, she kept shouting back to me about how astonished everybody would be. I followed with the spade over my shoulder, dragging my snake. Her exultation was contagious. The great land had never looked to me so big and free. If the red grass were full of rattlers, I was equal to them all. Nevertheless, I stole furtive glances behind me now and then to see that no avenging mate, older and bigger than my quarry, was racing up from the rear.

The sun had set when we reached our garden and went down the draw toward the house. Otto Fuchs was the first one we met. He was sitting on the edge of the cattle-pond, having a quiet pipe before supper. Ántonia called him to come quick and look. He did not say anything for a minute, but scratched his head and turned the snake over with his boot.

"Where did you run onto that beauty, Jim?"

"Up at the dog-town," I answered laconically.[5]

"Kill himself yourself? How come you to have a weepon?"

"We'd been up to Russian Peter's, to borrow a spade for Ambrosch."

Otto shook the ashes out of his pipe and squatted down to count the rattles. "It was just luck you had a tool," he said cautiously. "Gosh! I wouldn't want to do any business with that fellow myself, unless I had a fence-post along. Your grandmother's snake-cane wouldn't more than tickle him. He could stand right up and talk to you, he could. Did he fight hard?"

---

[4]horse whip
[5]concisely; using few words

Ántonia broke in: "He fight something awful! He is all over Jimmy's boots. I scream for him to run, but he just hit and hit that snake like he was crazy."

Otto winked at me. After Ántonia rode on he said: "Got him in the head first crack, didn't you? That was just as well."

We hung him up to the windmill, and when I went down to the kitchen, I found Ántonia standing in the middle of the floor, telling the story with a great deal of color.

<u>Subsequent</u> experiences with rattlesnakes taught me that my first encounter was fortunate in circumstance. My big rattler was old, and had led too easy a life; there was not much fight in him. He had probably lived there for years, with a fat prairie-dog for breakfast whenever he felt like it, a sheltered home, even an owl-feather bed, perhaps, and he had forgot that the world doesn't owe rattlers a living. A snake of his size, in fighting trim, would be more than any boy could handle. So in reality it was a mock adventure; the game was fixed for me by chance, as it probably was for many a dragon-slayer. I had been adequately armed by Russian Peter; the snake was old and lazy; and I had Ántonia beside me, to appreciate and admire.

That snake hung on our corral fence for several days; some of the neighbors came to see it and agreed that it was the biggest rattler ever killed in those parts. This was enough for Ántonia. She liked me better from that time on, and she never took a <u>supercilious</u> air with me again. I had killed a big snake—I was now a big fellow.

Understanding the Reading

Complete the next three exercises and see how well you understood the excerpt from *My Ántonia*.

Exercise 7.7 Multiple-Choice Questions

Answer the following questions about the reading. Circle the letter of your answer.

TIP: Don't try to answer the questions from memory; go back to the text as often as necessary.

1. From the first paragraph, you can infer that Jim
   A. is not very fond of Ántonia.
   B. has been teaching Ántonia to read.
   C. was in love with Ántonia.
   D. had never been anywhere but the Nebraska Territory.

2. From context, you can arrive at which definition of *picketed*? (top of page 148)
   A. protested
   B. guarded
   C. went on strike
   D. tied up

3. In the conversation with Otto,
   A. Jim boasted about killing the snake.
   B. Otto implied that the snake was harmless.
   C. Ántonia praised Jim excitedly.
   D. Otto was not impressed by the snake.

4. Jim says, "I began to think that I had longed for this opportunity" (top of page 149) because he
   A. enjoyed hearing Ántonia praise him.
   B. had always feared rattlesnakes.
   C. knew his father would be proud of him.
   D. knew the whole town would hear about his bravery.

Exercise 7.8   Short-Answer Questions

Respond to the following questions in one to two complete sentences. Go back to the text, as you did on the multiple choice.

5. How did this incident make Jim feel about himself?

   _____

   _____

   _____

6. In your opinion, should Jim have killed the snake—or just walked away? Explain.

   _____

   _____

   _____

7. What pictures remain in your mind after having read this excerpt? Why?

   _____

   _____

   _____

Respond to the following question in three to four complete sentences. Use details from the text in your answer.

8. How does the incident Jim describes change the relationship between him and Ántonia?

_____

_____

_____

_____

_____

_____

Reading Strategy Lesson
Activating Your Prior Knowledge

In the About the Author, you read that *Tom Sawyer* was published in 1876. What does this fact tell you about the lives of the characters? What can you add from your own experience, from your knowledge of American history, and from other literature you've read or films you have seen? Activating your prior knowledge is especially helpful in understanding and enjoying literature set in an earlier time period and in a specific place.

Let's take a closer look at *Tom Sawyer*.

History

You've probably heard about the one-room schoolhouses that were common in the 1800s. You may have learned that children used slates instead of paper because paper was not as easily available as it is today. Today, Tom Sawyer might have passed a note to the yellow-haired girl, sent her an e-mail, or called her on his cell phone. Corporal (physical) punishment was widely accepted as a form of discipline in schools until recent decades, and being late for school was a serious offense, so it's not surprising that the master beat Tom.

Personal Experience

The Reader's Tip tells us, "The respectable boys of the town have been forbidden to associate with Huck, but that makes them enjoy Huck's company all the more." You can probably understand from your own experience how forbidding something often makes it seem more attractive and exciting.

Literature

Perhaps you've read *The Adventures of Tom Sawyer* or *The Adventures of Huckleberry Finn*. If so, you know that Tom was noted for his cleverness, and that the yellow-haired girl is Becky Thatcher. You might recall that all three lived near the Mississippi River. You'll remember that Huck ran away with Jim, and that the two had a number of interesting encounters as they floated down the river on a raft. You also know *why* parents told their children not to associate with Huck.

Movies

If you haven't seen movies about Huck or Tom, you have probably seen TV shows or films that showed one-room schoolhouses and small towns like the ones in this story. This can help you picture the scene.

Exercise 7.10 Practice the Reading Strategy

We went through the strategy of activating prior knowledge with *Tom Sawyer*; now you're ready to try it with *My Ántonia*. The Reader's Tip tells us that Jim met Ántonia on a train going to the Nebraska Territory. Combine this tip with your own personal experience, knowledge of history and geography, and other literature you've read or films you've seen about the American West. The following paragraph will help you with the historical and geographical background. Read it and then answer the questions.

> In the Homestead Act of 1862, the U.S. government gave 160 acres of land to settlers who farmed the land for five years. The same year, construction began on the Union-Pacific Railroad, which passed through the Nebraska Territory and was completed in 1869. The government gave the railroad companies huge amounts of land as an incentive to build the railroads. They in turn sold land cheaply to settlers. This provided money for railroad construction and encouraged immigration to the West and a continuing need for goods that would be shipped in by the railroad. Livestock and farm crops would go east on the return trip. Many immigrants came from Germany, Sweden, and countries in northern and central Europe, attracted by the cheap or free land.

1. The Nebraska Territory was "sparsely settled" at the time Jim and Ántonia met. What can you assume about the time frame during which their families arrived?

   _____

   _____

   _____

2. Why did Ántonia's family probably come to America?

_____

_____

_____

3. How might Ántonia's family have obtained their land?

_____

_____

_____

4. What are some features of the Nebraska countryside?

_____

_____

_____

5. How did early Nebraska pioneer families like Jim's and Ánto-nia's get things they needed from the East?

_____

_____

_____

Exercise 7.11 Apply the Reading Strategy

Here is a portion of an article that appeared in the *St. Edward Advance* (a newspaper in St. Edward, Nebraska) in December of 1931. Read the article. Then activate your prior knowledge (including what you have just learned about Nebraska). Write a two- to three-sentence answer to each question.

Mrs. J. W. Currier Called to Final Rest

Adella Lovejoy Currier was born at Markesan, Wisconsin, February 12, 1864, and passed away at her home in St. Edward, Nebraska, December 24, 1931. She was the eldest of a family of five daughters of Edwin S. and Mary Lovejoy. Her father was a scholar and writer of ability and her mother, a gentlewoman of English birth.

Adella received her education in the schools of Wisconsin. She was united in marriage to John W. Currier at Markesan, Wis. on March 11, 1884. Immediately after their marriage they came to Nebraska and located in Platte County, a few miles southeast of St. Edward, their home being known as "Clover Hill."

Here the young couple labored and lived the life of pioneers, here were born their five children, of whom Henry, Edwin, Mary and Robert, with their father, are left to mourn their great loss. One son, Benjamin Merrill, passed away in infancy.

The scenes and the years of happiness in this home, where her family grew up to take their places in the world, were the inspiration for her books, "Clover Bloom" and "Candle Light." Her poems are typical of Nebraska and Nebraska home life and contain deep pathos, rare humor and a wonderful insight to the heartaches of human nature.

1. What are two ways John and Adella Currier might have obtained their farm in Nebraska?

_____

_____

_____

2. What did Adella and John Currier have in common with Ántonia and Jim?

_____

_____

_____

3. What did Adella Currier have in common with Willa Cather?

_____

_____

_____

4. Why do you think the article is written in such old-fashioned language? Give a specific example and explain what it means today.

_____

_____

_____

Writing Workshop
Using Strong Adjectives and Adverbs

GRAMMAR REFRESHER:

An **adjective** describes a noun, a pronoun, or another part of a sentence that functions as a noun.
   Example: The *hungry* student wolfed down his sandwich.
   Hungry is the adjective that describes the noun *student*.

An **adverb** modifies (describes) a verb, an adjective, or another adverb.
   Example: José responded *nervously* to her question.
   Nervously is the adverb that describes the verb *responded*.
   It tells us *how* he responded.

Adjectives and adverbs are always subordinate to other elements in a sentence. That means they need the other words in the sentence to work grammatically. Take this sentence:

Jackie walked very slowly.

You could write, "Jackie walked." It would not be an interesting sentence, but it would be grammatically correct. But if you just wrote "Very slowly" as a sentence it would not be correct and would leave the reader baffled.

How Adjectives and Adverbs Improve Your Writing

Helpless as they may be on their own, adjectives and adverbs can be strong additions to your sentences and greatly improve your writing style. Adjectives and adverbs help you to be more precise in what you convey, and they lend vividness to your ideas and descriptions.

Let's start with a simple sentence and see what we can do to improve it:

They stayed home.

They stayed home this year.

They stayed home this year because of gas prices.

Unhappily, the Parkers did not go away this year because of rising gas prices.

Unable to go away this year due to soaring gas prices, the Parkers dejectedly stayed home.

By the fifth version of this sentence, you know who stayed home, when, what they stayed home from, the reason why, and how they felt about it. They weren't just unhappy. They stayed home *dejectedly*, a much stronger adverb than *unhappily*.

Look at the difference between *rising* gas prices and *soaring* gas prices. Which adjective do you think is stronger? Why?

Exercise 7.12 Practice the Writing Lesson

Do the following exercise in a small group of three or four, or on your own, per your teacher's guidelines. Write each sentence on a sheet of paper. If you're in a group, pass the paper around. Each group member adds or changes words until you all agree you have a sentence that is precise, interesting, and vivid, with strong adjectives and adverbs. If you do this exercise on your own, you can still use the "pyramid" method of building the sentences, as in the example above.

1. The puppies cried.
2. The car raced.
3. She gave up.
4. The tree fell.

5. We shared.
6. They sing.
7. They dance.
8. Rain falls.
9. The children laughed.
10. The boys studied.

Exercise 7.13 Apply the Writing Lesson to Revise a Paragraph

The following paragraph is not very interesting. Rewrite it on a separate sheet of paper, using strong adjectives and adverbs as well as any other words you want to add or change.

> The sun shone. It was hot. We could see the boat. We couldn't wait. Dad was taking us fishing. We might not catch any. We didn't care. We wanted to get away. The city was hot. We wanted to go swimming. That would cool us off. Dad rented the boat. The motor didn't start. A man came to look. Then we got going. There was a breeze on the lake. We were all smiling.

Grammar Mini-Lesson
Writing Complex Sentences

What Is a Complex Sentence?

A complex sentence consists of one **independent** clause and one or more **dependent** clauses.

<u>Although Jim liked Ántonia,</u> <u>he hated her superior tone</u>.
      DEP. CLAUSE   INDEP. CLAUSE

The first part is called a **dependent** clause because it cannot stand by itself as a sentence:

Although Jim liked Ántonia

The second part is called an **independent** clause because it *can* stand on its own as a sentence:

He hated her superior tone.

When you link a dependent clause to an independent one, you have a complex sentence.

The table on the next page gives you additional examples of complex sentences, broken down into their different clauses.

Complex Sentence	Independent Clause	Dependent Clause(s)
When Tom reached the little isolated frame school-house, he strode in briskly, with the manner of one who had come with all honest speed.	he strode in briskly	When Tom reached the little isolated frame school-house with the manner of one who had come with all honest speed
As we approached, they barked, shook their tails at us, and scurried underground.	they barked, shook their tails at us, and scurried underground	As we approached

Notice that the dependent clauses usually begin with a word such as *although*, *when*, or *as*. These words are often referred to as subordinating conjunctions, because they make that clause subordinate, or dependent.

Exercise 7.14 Practice Identifying the Parts of a Complex Sentence

Break down the following sentences into their dependent and independent clauses. Write your answers in the table, as in the previous example.

Complex Sentence	Independent Clause	Dependent Clause(s)
1. When she cautiously faced around again, a peach lay before her.		
2. The sun had set when we reached our garden and went down the draw toward the house.		
3. By and by attention ceased from him, and the accustomed school murmur rose upon the dull air once more.		
4. We decided that Ántonia should ride Dude home, and I would walk.		

Complex Sentence	Independent Clause	Dependent Clause(s)
5. Nudges and winks and whispers traversed the room, but Tom sat still, with his arms upon the long, low desk before him, and seemed to study his book.		

Why Write Complex Sentences?

Like strong adjective and adverb choices, complex sentences help you express your ideas with more precision. The following sentence shows the connection between Jim and Ántonia's advance on the prairie dog town and the reaction of the prairie dogs. It tells *why* they scurried underground.

> *As we approached*, they barked, shook their tails at us, and scurried underground.

Complex sentences help you vary your style and make your essays, stories, letters, articles—*everything* you write—more interesting to read.

Punctuating Complex Sentences

- A comma usually follows a dependent clause that introduces a sentence.

  Although Jackson was far behind, he did not drop out of the race.
  DEP. CLAUSE   INDEP. CLAUSE

- No comma is usually necessary when an independent clause introduces a sentence.

  Angelina did not order the copier *because it was too expensive*.
  INDEP. CLAUSE   DEP. CLAUSE

Exercise 7.15 Apply the Grammar Lesson: Forming Complex Sentences

Combine each pair of sentences into a complex sentence. Do this by changing the italicized sentence into a dependent clause beginning with one of these conjunctions. The first one has been done for you.

after	as if	before	so that	while
although	because	if	when	until

1. Turn on the light. *You can see where you are going.*
   Turn on the light, so that you can see where you are going.

2. *Alison was not well*. She came to take the exam.

_____

_____

3. *You do not have the fare*. You won't be allowed on the bus.

_____

_____

4. It is futile to shut the barn door. *The horses have already run away*.

_____

_____

5. *Spring arrives*. We begin to spend more time outdoors.

_____

_____

6. She asked me to hold her books. *She tried to unlock the door*.

_____

_____

7. Cashiers are on duty daily from 9 A.M. *The shop closes at 7 P.M.*

_____

_____

8. I have to go now. *My class is about to start*.

_____

_____

9. *We go to school*. We should eat a good breakfast.

_____

_____

10. You glided through the water effortlessly. *You were a fish*.

_____

_____

Polish Your Spelling
Adding the Suffixes -OR and -ER

The suffixes *-or* and *-er* have the same meaning: "one who."
imitate + or = imitator (one who imitates)
observe + er = observer (one who observes)

Let's say you wanted to describe Tom Sawyer *as one who creates mischief*. Is there a way to tell whether the noun for *one who creates* should end in *-or* or *-er*?

1. If you can trace the noun to a verb of at least two syllables ending in *ate*, use *-or* with that noun. *Create* ends in *ate*, so you would say that Tom Sawyer is often the *creator* of mischief.

Here are some other examples:

imitate	imitator
demonstrate	demonstrator
investigate	investigator

(Exception: debate → debater)

2. Aside from the above clue, there is no easy way to tell whether a noun ends in *-or* or *-er*. That is why you need to study the most frequently used *-or* and *-er* nouns.

-OR		-ER	
ambassador	mayor	adventurer	organizer
author	monitor	buyer	owner
contributor	possessor	defender	pleader
creditor	professor	interpreter	pretender
debtor	senator	invader	printer
governor	supervisor	laborer	reporter
janitor	tailor	manufacturer	supporter
juror	vendor	offender	writer

3. Also study these few nouns that end in *-ar*:

beggar   burglar   liar   scholar

Exercise 7.16 Practice the Spelling Rules: -OR or -ER?

Change each word below by adding *-or*, *-er*, or *-ar*. Write the complete word on the line.

1. ambassad____ _____

2. govern____ _____

3. manufactur____ _____

4. monit____ _____

5. schol____ _____

6. may____ _____

7. support____   _____

8. senat____   _____

9. labor____   _____

10. credit____   _____

Chapter Eight

Prereading Guide
Words to know and ideas to consider before you jump into the reading.

A. Essential Vocabulary

Word	Meaning	Typical Use
disquieting (*adj*) dis-KWY-uh-ting	disturbing or alarming	The teacher's comments on the new promotinal requirements were *disquieting*.
evoke (*v*) ee-VOKE	to bring out; elicit	Grandpa's stories about the Old Country *evoked* both laughter and tears.
impudent (*adj*) IM-pew-dunt	boldly disrespectful and causing irritation to others; rude	"I refuse to apologize for calling you that," he said in an *impudent* manner.
incisive (*adj*) in-SY-siv	penetrating and sharp; biting	The newspaper's editor made some *incisive* remarks about the proposed reforms.
latent (*adj*) LAYT-unt	present but not yet evident; dormant	His *latent* gift for music blossomed once his mother bought him a guitar.
panorama (*n*) pan-or-AM-uh	1. a long series of passing events; overview 2. a wide view of something; vista	We watched a movie that discussed the interesting *panorama* of American history. A *panorama* of mountains and lakes lay below them.
poignant (*adj*) POIN-yunt	extremely moving or emotional; touching	Movies known as tear-jerkers usually have several *poignant* moments.
revelry (*n*) REV-ul-ree	noisy partying; merrymaking	After the *revelry* of the holidays, many people make New Year's resolutions.
sardonic (*adj*) sar-DON-ik	scornful or mocking; cynical	Gary Larson's "Far Side" cartoons are often *sardonic*.
self-effacement (*n*) self-ih-FACE-ment	the tendency not to draw attention to oneself; modesty	"Oh, I didn't do much," said my mother with *self-effacement*, although she had created a delicious buffet.

B. Vocabulary Practice

Exercise 8.1   Sentence Completion

Using your new vocabulary knowledge, choose the best way to complete the following sentences. Circle the letter of your answer.

1. The thought of _____ is disquieting to many scientists and citizens of the world.
   A. global warming
   B. preserving forests

2. "Maria _____," said Kelsey self-effacingly.
   A. deserves all the credit
   B. hardly did anything

3. The new town curfew _____ angry reactions from some teenagers.
   A. evoked
   B. promoted

4. Kevin has a sardonic sense of humor; sometimes his jokes can seem a little too _____.
   A. innocent
   B. cruel

5. "Because of your impudence, I'm going to _____," the mother told the child.
   A. forget about buying you that toy
   B. let you skip tonight's chores

6. Revelry on _____ is the norm in New York's Times Square.
   A. weekdays
   B. New Year's Eve

7. "And now, for an incisive _____, we go to Hollywood."
   A. look at the movie
   B. search for celebrities

8. It was a _____ moment when the family reunited after ten years.
   A. sardonic
   B. poignant

9. His artistic abilities have lain latent for years, but now they _____.
   A. show in his sculpture
   B. have declined

10. The panorama of the _____ is something that cannot be described or even seen in pictures.
    A. Grand Canyon
    B. Statue of Liberty

Exercise 8.2 Using Fewer Words

Replace the italicized words with a single word from the following list.

disquieting   evoke   impudent   incisive   latent

panorama   poignant   revelry   sardonic   self-effacement

1. Jason's *present but not yet evident* talents as   1._____
   a chef are beginning to be seen in his delicious
   creations.

2. Pedro, who had always lived in the city,   2._____
   found the silence of the forest *disturbing*
   and upsetting.

3. The *wide view* from the top of Birch   3._____
   Mountain is worth the hike.

4. My humble sister is the very definition of   4._____
   not wanting to draw attention to herself.

5. The sentimental cards I give my mother   5._____
   always *bring out* tears of happiness.

6. The sportscaster's *penetrating and sharp*   6._____
   analysis of the game made it easier to
   understand everything that was happening.

7. I loved that movie! The ending was so   7._____
   touching and emotional.

8. Some comedians' *scornful and mocking*   8._____
   routines are tiresome.

9. My little brother drives me nuts sometimes!   9._____
   He's so *boldly disrespectful and irritating*!

10. "I don't know why the neighbors called   10._____
    the police," Halley said. "What's wrong
    with a little *noisy merrymaking?*"

Exercise 8.3 Synonyms and Antonyms

Fill in the blanks in column A with the required synonyms or antonyms, selecting them from column B. (Remember: A *synonym* is a word similar in meaning to another word. An *antonym* is a word opposite in meaning to another word.)

	A	B
_____	1. synonym for *elicit*	incisive
_____	2. synonym for *touching*	latent
_____	3. antonym for *polite*	revelry
_____	4. synonym for *overview*	self-effacement
_____	5. antonym for *evident*	disquieting
_____	6. synonym for *biting*	impudent
_____	7. antonym for *immodesty*	panorama
_____	8. synonym for *partying*	sardonic
_____	9. synonym for *alarming*	poignant
_____	10. antonym for *optimistic*	evoke

C. Journal Freewrite

Before you begin the reading on the next page, take out a journal or sheet of paper and spend some time responding to the following prompt.

TIP: Don't worry about grammar and spelling; just write what comes to mind. The purpose of freewriting is to explore ideas, not to produce a polished work.

> Describe how you would feel if someone you were close to (friend, boyfriend or girlfriend) suddenly seemed closer to or interested in someone else. How would you confront him or her or express your feelings?

from Ethan Frome

by Edith Wharton

About the Author
Edith Wharton
(1862–1937) is the author of more than 40 books that include novels, short stories, poetry, and nonfiction. She was born during the American Civil War to an upper-class family that encouraged her intellectual development. Wharton married at age 23 and got divorced 30 years later, deciding to move to Paris. There, she mingled with the "Lost Generation"—a group of Americans who had become disillusioned with how materialism and industrialism were affecting America. This outlook is often present in her writings. Her best-known works center on how social conventions restrict individuals and trap them into situations they find inescapable. *Ethan Frome* takes place in New England and tells the tragic story of a man ensnared by his emotions.

Frome's heart was beating fast. He had been straining for a glimpse of the dark head under the cherry-coloured scarf and it vexed him that another eye should have been quicker than his. The leader of the reel,[1] who looked as if he had Irish blood in his veins, danced well, and his partner caught his fire. As she passed down the line, her light figure swinging from hand to hand in circles of increasing swiftness, the scarf flew off her head and stood out behind her shoulders, and Frome, at each turn, caught sight of her laughing panting lips, the cloud of dark hair about her forehead, and the dark eyes which seemed the only fixed points in a maze of flying lines.

The dancers were going faster and faster, and the musicians, to keep up with them, belaboured[2] their instruments like jockeys lashing their mounts on the home-stretch; yet it seemed to the young man at the window that the reel would never end. Now and then he turned his eyes from the girl's face to that of her partner, which, in the exhilaration of the dance, had taken on a look of almost <u>impudent</u> ownership. Denis Eady was the son of Michael Eady, the ambitious Irish grocer, whose suppleness and effrontery[3] had given Starkfield its first notion of "smart" business methods, and whose new brick store testified to the success of the attempt. His son seemed likely to follow in his steps, and was meanwhile applying the same arts to the conquest of the Starkfield maidenhood. Hitherto Ethan Frome had been content to think him a mean fellow; but now he positively invited a horse-whipping. It was strange that the girl did not seem aware of it: that she could lift her rapt face to her dancer's, and drop her hands into his, without appearing to feel the offence of his look and touch.

Frome was in the habit of walking into Starkfield to fetch home his wife's cousin, Mattie Silver, on the rare evenings when some chance of amusement drew her to the village. It was his wife who had suggested, when the girl came to live

---

[1] a group dance
[2] attacked
[3] insolence; nerve

with them, that such opportunities should be put in her way. Mattie Silver came from Stamford, and when she entered the Fromes' household to act as her cousin Zeena's aid it was thought best, as she came without pay, not to let her feel too sharp a contrast between the life she had left and the isolation of a Starkfield farm. But for this— as Frome <u>sardonically</u> reflected—it would hardly have occurred to Zeena to take any thought for the girl's amusement.

When his wife first proposed that they should give Mattie an occasional evening out he had inwardly demurred at having to do the extra two miles to the village and back after his hard day on the farm; but not long afterward he had reached the point of wishing that Starkfield might give all its nights to <u>revelry</u>.

Mattie Silver had lived under his roof for a year, and from early morning till they met at supper he had frequent chances of seeing her; but no moments in her company were comparable to those when, her arm in his, and her light step flying to keep time with his long stride, they walked back through the night to the farm. He had taken to the girl from the first day, when he had driven over to the Flats to meet her, and she had smiled and waved to him from the train, crying out, "You must be Ethan!" as she jumped down with her bundles, while he reflected, looking over her slight person: "She don't look much on housework, but she ain't a fretter, anyhow." But it was not only that the coming to his house of a bit of hopeful young life was like the lighting of a fire on a cold hearth. The girl was more than the bright serviceable creature he had thought her. She had an eye to see and an ear to hear: he could show her things and tell her things, and taste the bliss of feeling that all he imparted left long reverberations and echoes he could wake at will.

It was during their night walks back to the farm that he felt most intensely the sweetness of this communion. He had always been more sensitive than the people about him to the appeal of natural beauty. His unfinished studies had given form to this sensibility and even in his unhappiest moments field and sky spoke to him with a deep and powerful persuasion. But hitherto the emotion had remained in him as a silent ache, veiling with sadness the beauty that <u>evoked</u> it. He did not even know whether any one else in the world felt as he did, or whether he was the sole victim of this mournful privilege. Then he learned that one other spirit had trembled with the same touch of wonder: that at his side, living under his roof and eating his bread, was a creature to whom he could say: "That's Orion down yonder; the big fellow to the right is Aldebaran, and the bunch of little ones—like bees swarming—they're the Pleiades . . ." or whom he could hold entranced before a ledge of granite thrusting up through the fern while he unrolled the huge <u>panorama</u> of the ice age, and the long dim stretches of succeeding time. The fact that admiration for his learning mingled with Mattie's wonder at what he taught was not the least part of his pleasure. And there were other sensations, less definable but more exquisite, which drew them together with a shock of silent joy: the cold red of sunset behind winter hills, the flight of cloud-flocks over slopes of golden stubble, or the intensely blue shadows of hemlocks on sunlit snow. When she said to him once: "It looks just as if it was painted!" it seemed to Ethan that the art of definition could go no farther, and that words had at last been found to utter his secret soul. . . .

As he stood in the darkness outside the church these memories came back with the poignancy of vanished things. Watching Mattie whirl down the floor from hand to hand he wondered how he could ever have thought that his dull talk interested her. To him, who was never gay but in her presence, her gaiety seemed plain proof of indifference. The face she lifted to her dancers was the same which, when she saw him, always looked like a window that has caught the sunset. He even noticed two or three gestures which, in his fatuity,[4] he had thought she kept for him: a way of throwing her head back when she was amused, as if to taste her laugh before she let it out, and a trick of sinking her lids slowly when anything charmed or moved her.

The sight made him unhappy, and his unhappiness roused his latent fears. His wife had never shown any jealousy of Mattie, but of late she had grumbled increasingly over the house-work and found oblique[5] ways of attracting attention to the girl's inefficiency. Zeena had always been what Starkfield called "sickly," and Frome had to admit that, if she were as ailing as she believed, she needed the help of a stronger arm than the one which lay so lightly in his during the night walks to the farm. Mattie had no natural turn for housekeeping, and her training had done nothing to remedy the defect. She was quick to learn, but forgetful and dreamy, and not disposed to take the matter seriously. Ethan had an idea that if she were to marry a man she was fond of the dormant instinct would wake, and her pies and biscuits become the pride of the county; but domesticity in the abstract did not interest her. At first she was so awkward that he could not help laughing at her; but she laughed with him and that made them better friends. He did his best to supplement her unskilled efforts, getting up earlier than usual to light the kitchen fire, carrying in the wood overnight, and neglecting the mill for the farm that he might help her about the house during the day. He even crept down on Saturday nights to scrub the kitchen floor after the women had gone to bed; and Zeena, one day, had surprised him at the churn and had turned away silently, with one of her queer looks.

Of late there had been other signs of her disfavour, as intangible but more disquieting. One cold winter morning, as he dressed in the dark, his candle flickering in the draught of the ill-fitting window, he had heard her speak from the bed behind him.

"The doctor don't want I should be left without anybody to do for me," she said in her flat whine.

He had supposed her to be asleep, and the sound of her voice had startled him, though she was given to abrupt explosions of speech after long intervals of secretive silence.

---

[4]foolishness
[5]indirect or devious

He turned and looked at her where she lay indistinctly outlined under the dark calico quilt, her high-boned face taking a grayish tinge from the whiteness of the pillow.

"Nobody to do for you?" he repeated.

"If you say you can't afford a hired girl when Mattie goes."

Frome turned away again, and taking up his razor stooped to catch the reflection of his stretched cheek in the blotched looking-glass above the wash-stand.

"Why on earth should Mattie go?"

"Well, when she gets married, I mean," his wife's drawl came from behind him.

"Oh, she'd never leave us as long as you needed her," he returned, scraping hard at his chin.

"I wouldn't ever have it said that I stood in the way of a poor girl like Mattie marrying a smart fellow like Denis Eady," Zeena answered in a tone of plaintive <u>self-effacement</u>.

Ethan, glaring at his face in the glass, threw his head back to draw the razor from ear to chin. His hand was steady, but the attitude was an excuse for not making an immediate reply.

"And the doctor don't want I should be left without anybody," Zeena continued. "He wanted I should speak to you about a girl he's heard about, that might come—"

Ethan laid down the razor and straightened himself with a laugh.

"Denis Eady! If that's all, I guess there's no such hurry to look round for a girl."

"Well, I'd like to talk to you about it," said Zeena obstinately.

He was getting into his clothes in fumbling haste. "All right. But I haven't got the time now; I'm late as it is," he returned, holding his old silver turnip-watch to the candle.

Zeena, apparently accepting this as final, lay watching him in silence while he pulled his suspenders over his shoulders and jerked his arms into his coat; but as he went toward the door she said, suddenly and <u>incisively</u>: "I guess you're always late, now you shave every morning."

That thrust had frightened him more than any vague insinuations about Denis Eady. It was a fact that since Mattie Silver's coming he had taken to shaving every day; but his wife always seemed to be asleep when he left her side in the winter darkness, and he had stupidly assumed that she would not notice any change in his appearance. Once or twice in the past he had been faintly disquieted by Zenobia's way of letting things happen without seeming to remark them, and then, weeks afterward, in a casual phrase, revealing that she had all along taken her notes and drawn her inferences. Of late, however, there had been no room in his thoughts for such vague apprehensions. Zeena herself, from an oppressive reality, had faded into an insubstantial shade. All his life was lived in the sight and sound of Mattie Silver, and he could no longer conceive of its being otherwise. But now, as he stood outside the church, and saw Mattie spinning down the floor with Denis Eady, a throng of disregarded hints and menaces wove their cloud about his brain. . . .

Understanding the Reading

Complete the next three exercises and see how well you understood the excerpt from *Ethan Frome*.

Exercise 8.4 Multiple-Choice Questions

Answer the following questions about the reading. Circle the letter of your answer.

TIP: Don't try to answer the questions from memory; go back to the text as often as necessary.

1. Frome watches Mattie and Denis Eady dance from
   A. the sidelines in the barn.
   B. his place as fiddler in the band.
   C. the window of the church.
   D. the dance floor.

2. From context, you can conclude that *demurred* (paragraph 4) most likely means
   A. was furious about.
   B. took exception to.
   C. looked forward to.
   D. could not understand.

3. Which statement about Zeena is *not* supported by the reading?
   A. She is suspicious that Ethan has feelings for Mattie.
   B. She enjoys believing she is sicker than she really is.
   C. She taunts Ethan with the thought that Mattie will marry Denis Eady.
   D. She blames Ethan for the accident that left her paralyzed.

4. Ethan is attracted to Mattie *mostly* because she
   A. is young and attractive.
   B. feels as he does about natural beauty.
   C. is an excellent cook and is kind to Zeena.
   D. is the best dancer in the county.

5. At the end of the selection, the author focuses on Ethan's
   A. fear that Zeena knows about Mattie, and Mattie will leave.
   B. guilt and shame over his betrayal of Zeena.
   C. love and concern for Zeena's health.
   D. anger and jealousy toward Denis Eady.

Exercise 8.5 Short-Answer Questions

Respond to the following questions in one to two complete sentences. Go back to the text, as you did on the multiple choice.

6. The author writes, "'I wouldn't ever have it said that I stood in the way of a poor girl like Mattie marrying a smart fellow like

Denis Eady,' Zeena answered in a tone of plaintive self-effacement" (page 170). How do Zeena's choice of words and tone of voice affect Ethan?

_____

_____

_____

7. Ethan is upset to see that Mattie looks at all her dance partners the same way she looks at him. What light does this shed on Mattie's character?

_____

_____

_____

8. Imagine that you are Ethan Frome. What would you like to say to Mattie on the walk home?

_____

_____

_____

9. Do you think it is wrong for Ethan Frome to allow himself to be attracted to Mattie when he is married to Zeena? Why or why not?

_____

_____

_____

Exercise 8.6 Extending Your Thinking

Respond to the following question in three to four complete sentences. Use details from the text in your answer.

10. Jealousy often plays a part in both love and friendships. What part does it play in the relationships portrayed in this reading?

_____

_____

_____

_____

_____

_____

Reading Strategy Lesson
Identifying Setting and Characters

Setting

The first step some writers take in creating a story is deciding on the setting—*where* and *when* it will take place. Some settings lend themselves better than others to stories. If a story is set in 1830, the characters will be writing letters or sending messages by foot or horse to one another, not sending e-mails or telephoning as they might in a story set in today's world. A story that takes place in a spaceship is going to be much different from one that takes place on a wagon train bound west or a steamboat on the Mississippi.

As the reader, you need to picture the setting to fully understand the *what* and the *how* of the story. To do this, you once again bring your prior knowledge and imagination into play. For example, this excerpt from *Ethan Frome* takes place in rural New England. The very name Starkfield evokes a bleak scene, and the author mentions "the isolation of a Starkfield farm." We can guess that the story takes place sometime in the past, perhaps around 1900. There are trains (Mattie arrived on one) but apparently no cars, since Ethan and Mattie walk to and from the village. Other clues to the time are Michael Eady's "smart business methods" and "new brick store," and Ethan's desire to give Denis a "horse-whipping."

A novel or story can have several more specific settings—places where events in the story occur. The best way to understand this is to think of a movie. It takes place in a certain town—let's say a small town in Idaho. Within that small town are a number of "scenes" where events take place: the hospital where the main character was born 15 years prior to the movie's main action, a church, a grocery store, a post office, various people's houses and cars, and so forth. These are all more specific settings within the main one of "small Idaho town, present time."

Characters

Characters are the people in the story. **Characterization** is the technique the author uses to make the characters seem real to you. The author tells you or shows you how a character feels, thinks, and acts so that you can picture the character in your mind. Tone of voice, body language, how the character dresses, and his or her choice of words all help you form a mental picture of a character.

Just how alive can a character be? Characters created by Mark Twain, Laura Ingalls Wilder, F. Scott Fitzgerald, and many other authors have lived on far past their creators' deaths. We still laugh at Tom and Huck's shenanigans, learn moral lessons with Laura and Mary Ingalls, and hope that at some point Tom and Daisy Buchanan will have to pay for the way they treat others.

The two main types of characters are the **protagonist** (the person we side with) and the **antagonist** (the person who opposes the protagonist).

Another type of character is the **antihero**. The antihero is a protagonist who is flawed in some way. He or she does not have the characteristics we expect to find in a hero, but we still hope things will turn out well for him or her. Perhaps the antihero will even change in some dramatic way by the end of the story.

Exercise 8.7   Practice the Reading Strategy

Use the organizer below to take notes about Ethan and the setting. You may need to add some details that you infer or bring to the story from your knowledge or imagination.

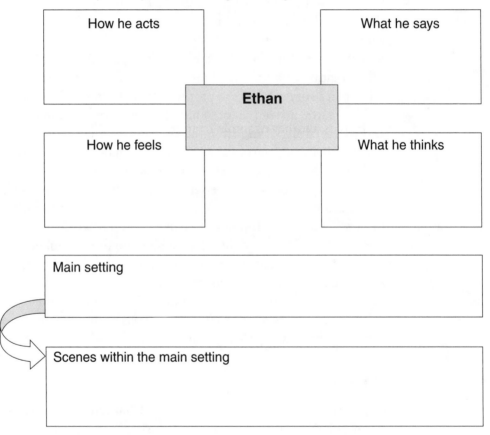

Exercise 8.8   Apply the Reading Strategy

On a separate sheet of paper, make character maps, like the one above, but now for Mattie and Zeena. Then, judging from the information in this reading, list some other scenes within the main setting that you think might appear in the novel. (There is no right or wrong answer to this part—just use your imagination.)

Writing Workshop
Using Words That Appeal to the Senses

The Five Senses

Using words that appeal to *all* of the senses—sight, hearing, touch, smell, and taste—helps writers connect with their readers and create **sensual imagery**—that is, a mental picture of what is being described, the sound of a noise, or the feel, taste, or smell of something.

When Edith Wharton describes the dance at the beginning of this excerpt, you can almost see the dancers flying across the floor and hear the musicians playing faster and faster. What senses come into play when you read the following sentence?

> One cold winter morning, as he dressed in the dark, his candle flickering in the draught of the ill-fitting window, he had heard her speak from the bed behind him.

You can feel the cold draft slipping around the edge of the window, see the flickering light of the candle, and hear Zeena's voice. Three of your senses are involved in just one sentence.

Here is another example from the selection:

> But it was not only that the coming to his house of a bit of hopeful young life was like the lighting of a fire on a cold hearth. The girl was more than the bright serviceable creature he had thought her. She had an eye to see and an ear to hear: he could show her things and tell her things, and taste the bliss of feeling that all he imparted left long reverberations and echoes he could wake at will.

You can hear and see the fire crackling to life, and understand how Mattie was like that fire for Ethan. You can see the things Ethan showed Mattie and told her, and you can feel the bliss he "tasted" and know what is meant by "long reverberations and echoes."

Wharton could have written something rather uninteresting that would still get the point across. For example:

Mattie's youthfulness brought hope to Ethan. She was smarter than he had thought. She caught on to whatever he said right away, and that made him happy.

Comparing the two paragraphs, you can see the difference between using language that appeals to the senses and language that *only tells the facts*.

Exercise 8.9   Practice the Writing Lesson

Read these paragraphs from other parts of *Ethan Frome*. What can you see, hear, feel, touch, and taste? Fill in the sensory image table below the paragraph by jotting down the words that create the image for you and then checking the type of image created. Look into your own senses to add sensory images that may not be specifically expressed in the paragraphs.

They went back to the kitchen, and he fetched the coal and kindlings and cleared out the stove for her, while she brought in the milk and the cold remains of the meat-pie. When warmth began to radiate from the stove, and the first ray of sunlight lay on the kitchen floor, Ethan's dark thoughts melted in the mellower air. The sight of Mattie going about her work as he had seen her on so many mornings made it seem impossible that she should ever cease to be a part of the scene. He said to himself that he had doubtless exaggerated the significance of Zeena's threats, and that she too, with the return of daylight, would come to a saner mood . . .

Ethan drove on in silence till they reached a part of the wood where the pines were more widely spaced, then he drew up and helped Mattie to get out of the sleigh. They passed between the aromatic trunks, the snow breaking crisply under their feet, till they came to a small sheet of water with steep wooded sides. Across its frozen surface, from the farther bank, a single hill rising against the western sun threw the long conical shadow which gave the lake its name. It was a shy secret spot, full of the same dumb melancholy that Ethan felt in his heart.

Words That Create the Image	Sight	Hearing	Touch	Smell	Taste

Exercise 8.10 Apply the Writing Lesson

Close your eyes and take a few minutes to think about a scene with which you are very familiar. Put yourself in the scene and try to identify all of the senses you use when you are in this scene. Then, on a separate sheet of paper, write a descriptive paragraph about the scene, using as many sensory images as you can.

Grammar Mini-Lesson
Active and Passive Voice

Active and Passive Verbs

1. An **active verb** describes an action done **by** its subject.

   The weather bureau *forecast* sun.
   (The verb *forecast* is active because it describes an action done by the weather bureau. The *weather bureau* is the subject of this sentence.)

2. A **passive verb** describes an action done **to** its subject.

   Sun *was forecast* by the weather bureau.
   (The verb *was forecast* is passive because it describes an action done *to the sun*. *Sun* is the subject of this sentence.)

When you use an active verb, you are writing in the active voice. When you use a passive verb, you are writing in the passive voice. Here are some additional examples of active and passive verbs:

   Active: Carelessness *causes* accidents.
   Passive: Accidents *are caused* by carelessness.

   Active: She *will write* the letter.
   Passive: The letter *will be written* by her.

   Active: The children *ate* the chocolates.
   Passive: The chocolates *were eaten* by the children.

Which voice sounds more clear, brief, and natural? The active voice is generally your better choice. (It is particularly essential in news writing, when you want an article to sound lively and current.)
   Compare these sentences:

   Passive: The dog was washed by us.
   Active: We washed the dog.

The second sentence uses fewer words and states the action clearly and simply. The use of the passive verb in the first sentence makes the sentence unnatural sounding and awkward. Think about it. If you gave the family dog a bath, would you say. "Guess what! The dog was washed by me!"?
   Active verbs are far more common in English than are passive verbs. You should use the active voice whenever possible, especially when the passive voice sounds awkward.
   Passive verbs can come in handy at times, however. One good use of passive verbs is to help you avoid the vague pronoun *they*.

Poor: *They* grow oranges in Florida.
           (Who are *they*? The sentence is not clear on this point. *They* could refer to the people who own a particular orange grove or to all of the orange growers in Florida.)

Better: Oranges *are grown* in Florida.

The focus is on *oranges,* where it belongs—not on who grows them.

You can form the passive by adding some form of the verb *to be* to the past participle of a verb. Forms of the verb *to be* are *is, was, will be, has been,* etc. Examples:

is broken	*has been collected*	*was introduced*
will be told	*are being sent*	*were misplaced*

Exercise 8.11 Apply the Grammar Lesson to Revise Sentences

Improve each of the following sentences by rewriting it with an active or a passive verb, as needed.

Example: An agreement will be entered into by us.
We will enter into an agreement.

1. Three pictures were painted by my sister.

2. A second look at Amber was stolen by Justin.

3. Your help could definitely be used by me.

4. They grow excellent apples in Massachusetts.

5. A good time will be had by everyone.

6. Their new uniforms were received by the football players.

7. Diamond earrings were worn by Alina.

8. They arrest people who break the curfew in this town.

9. The moon was jumped over by the cow.

10. The car was hidden by the trees.

Polish Your Spelling
Silent Letters

Reread the following sentence from *Ethan Frome*:

> Now and then he turned his eyes from the girl's face to that of her partner, which, in the exhilaration of the dance, had taken on a look of almost impudent ownership.

When you read the sentence to yourself, you automatically knew not to pronounce the *h* in *exhilaration*. It is a silent letter, like the *t* in *listen*, or the *k* in *knee*. However, silent letters can be tricky when it comes to spelling. If you're not used to pronouncing the letters, it's easy to forget to write them in. This lesson will help you review some of the more common silent letters.

First, say each of the following words to yourself, leaving out the silent letters. Then go through the *spelling* of each word, paying close attention to *every* letter in the word. Practice writing the ones with which you have difficulty on a separate sheet of paper.

SILENT *b*

bom*b*	crum*b*	dou*b*t
clim*b*	de*b*t	dum*b*
com*b*		

SILENT *c*

des*c*end	mus*c*le	a*c*quire
fas*c*inate	s*c*issors	(all other *acq* words)

SILENT *d*

han*d*kerchief	a*d*just	(all other *adj* words)

SILENT *g*

desi*g*n	*g*naw	si*g*n

SILENT *h*

ex*h*aust	*g*host	*h*erb
ex*h*ibit	*h*eir	ve*h*icle

SILENT *k*

ac*k*nowledge	*k*nee	*k*nob
*k*nack	*k*night	(all other *kn* words)

SILENT *l*

a*l*mond	fo*l*k	sa*l*mon
ca*l*m	pa*l*m	yo*l*k

SILENT *n*

autum*n*	colum*n*	hym*n*

SILENT *p*

*p*neumonia	*p*sychology	recei*p*t

SILENT *s*

ai*s*le	i*s*land	i*s*le

SILENT *t*

bankrup*t*cy	lis*t*en	sof*t*en
Chris*t*mas	mor*t*gage	wres*t*le (the *w* is silent, too)

SILENT *w*

ans*w*er	s*w*ord	*w*rap
play*w*right	*w*hole	(all other *wr* words)

Exercise 8.12 Practice Spelling Words with Silent Letters

One word in each line is missing its silent letter. Write that word correctly on the blank line.

1. unknown, climber, ajoin, plumber   _____

2. adjusted, exausted, folk, descended   _____

3. almond, fasinating, doubtful, bombshell   _____

4. hym, wrestler, salmon, acknowledge   _____

5. whole, knee, condem, isle   _____

6. ghost, herb, knack, aquired   _____

7. scissors, crumb, receit, bankruptcy   _____

8. aquainted, dumb, knuckle, Christmas   _____

9. yolk, neumonia, writer, column   _____

10. playright, palm, muscle, shepherd   _____

Chapter Nine

Prereading Guide
Words to know and ideas to consider before you jump into the reading.

A. Essential Vocabulary

Word	Meaning	Typical Use
dilapidated (*adj*) dil-AP-ih-day-tud	fallen into disrepair; run-down	The house was *dilapidated*, but plans were under way to remodel it.
distraught (*adj*) dist-RAWT	extremely anxious or upset; distressed	Don't be *distraught* over one bad quiz grade. Work hard and do better next time!
eerie (*adj*) EAR-ee	peculiar and mysterious	The trees bent in the wind, and in the moonlight they looked *eerie*.
elation (*n*) ee-LAY-shun	a feeling of pleasure and happiness; joy	The *elation* she felt when he smiled at her was obvious from her joyful look.
enthralled (*adj*) en-THRAWLD	fascinated or charmed; captivated	*Enthralled* by the latest *Harry Potter* novel, Connor had to be reminded to eat dinner.
humiliation (*n*) hew-mil-ee-AY-shun	the feeling of being ashamed or disgraced; embarrassment	Until the *humiliation* of the talent contest, he had thought he was quite a good singer.
infatuated (*adj*) in-FATCH-ew-ATE-ud	very attracted to another (often foolishly so); lovesick	When you're *infatuated* with someone, it is difficult to see his or her flaws.
intently (*adv*) in-TENT-lee	with focus and concentration; attentively	When I practice piano, I have to think very hard and stare *intently* at the music.
solace (*n*) SAHL-us	consolation and support; comfort	The only *solace* the firefighters could offer the family was that at least they had saved their dog.
vigilant (*adj*) VIDG-uh-lunt	watchful and observant; on guard	The flu is going around, so be *vigilant* for any signs that you are becoming ill.

B. Vocabulary Practice

Exercise 9.1 Sentence Completion

Using your new vocabulary knowledge, choose the best way to complete the following sentences. Circle the letter of your answer.

1. I am so infatuated with Malik that I _____ to see him.
   A. go out of my way
   B. can't stand

2. The babysitter was not very vigilant. She often let the children _____.
   A. out of her sight
   B. nap an extra half hour

3. Early filmgoers were enthralled by the first _____.
   A. video cameras
   B. moving pictures

4. Martin Luther King's _____ left his audiences feeling elated.
   A. assistants
   B. speeches

5. My neighbor was distraught after her _____.
   A. rent doubled
   B. plant died

6. American troops left _____ in humiliation.
   A. the parade field
   B. Vietnam

7. The Fords are eager to _____ the dilapidated house down the road.
   A. move into
   B. fix up

8. Caitlin and Ashley were _____ by the eerie sound outside their window.
   A. amused
   B. frightened

9. Damion listened to his father intently and _____ how to repair a car.
   A. learned
   B. missed the explanation on

10. Clifford found solace in the hours he spent _____.
    A. working at the restaurant
    B. running in the park

Exercise 9.2   Using Fewer Words

Replace the italicized words with a single word from the following list.

dilapidated	distraught	eerie	elation	enthralled
humiliation	infatuated	intently	solace	vigilant

1. Poverty can be a daily source of *feelings of shame and disgrace.*

   1._____

2. Their friends hurried to the hospital after the accident to offer *consolation and support* to the victims.

   2._____

3. She is *foolishly attracted* with him, and no one can make her see what he is really like.

   3._____

4. My brother kicked the winning goal in the last few seconds of the game and ran off the field to the sounds of the fans' *pleasure and happiness.*

   4._____

5. I can't understand why my parents bought a house that is so *fallen into disrepair.*

   5._____

6. I was *extremely anxious and upset* when I found out I would have to change schools.

   6._____

7. As *watchful and observant* as the police are about preventing it, some crime seems unavoidable.

   7._____

8. The story *fascinated and charmed* the preschoolers.

   8._____

9. The cat watched the bird *with focus and concentration.*

   9._____

10. There was a(an) *peculiar and mysterious* feeling in the old house.

    10._____

Exercise 9.3   Synonyms and Antonyms

Fill in the blanks in column A with the required synonyms or antonyms, selecting them from column B. (Remember: A *synonym* is a word similar in meaning to another word. An *antonym* is a word opposite in meaning to another word.)

	A	B
_____	1. synonym for *lovesick*	elation
_____	2. synonym for *mysterious*	distraught
_____	3. antonym for *neglectful*	dilapidated
_____	4. synonym for *joy*	solace
_____	5. antonym for *bored*	humiliation
_____	6. synonym for *attentively*	infatuated
_____	7. antonym for *new*	enthralled
_____	8. synonym for *embarrassment*	intently
_____	9. synonym for *comfort*	vigilant
_____	10. antonym for *delighted*	eerie

C. Journal Freewrite

Before you begin the reading on the next page, take out a journal or sheet of paper and spend some time responding to the following prompt.

TIP: Don't worry about grammar and spelling; just write what comes to mind. The purpose of freewriting is to explore ideas, not to produce a polished work.

> What are some things that you might find out about a person that would make you think twice about getting to know him or her?

from American History

by Judith Ortiz Cofer

About the Author
Judith Ortiz Cofer
(1952–) was born in
Puerto Rico and moved
with her parents to
Paterson, New Jersey,
when she was four. She
earned a bachelor's
degree in English litera-
ture at Augusta College
and a master's degree at
Florida Atlantic
University. In 1984,
Cofer became an
English professor at the
University of Georgia.
She is one of the most
prominent Latina writ-
ers in the United States.
She gives lectures and
speeches that celebrate
the literature of the
many cultures within
the United States. Her
characters are often
Puerto Rican women or
teens who are facing
bicultural issues. *The
Latin Deli*, from which
this story excerpt is
taken, is a collection of
essays, short fiction, and
poetry. Cofer has won
numerous awards for
her work.

On the day that President Kennedy was shot, my ninth grade
class had been out in the fenced playground of Public School
Number 13. We had been given "free" exercise time and had
been ordered by our P.E. teacher, Mr. DePalma, to "keep
moving." That meant that the girls should jump rope and the
boys toss basketballs through a hoop at the far end of the
yard. He in the meantime would "keep an eye" on us from
just inside the building.

It was a cold gray day in Paterson. The kind that warns of
early snow. I was miserable, since I had forgotten my gloves
and my knuckles were turning red and raw from the jump
rope. I was also taking a lot of abuse from the black girls for
not turning the rope hard and fast enough for them.

"Hey, Skinny Bones, pump it, girl. Ain't you got no
energy today?" Gail, the biggest of the black girls who had
the other end of the rope, yelled, "Didn't you eat your rice
and beans and pork chops for breakfast today?"

The other girls picked up the "pork chop" and made it
into a refrain: "pork chop, pork chop, did you eat your pork
chop?" They entered the double ropes in pairs and exited
without tripping or missing a beat. I felt a burning on my
cheeks, and then my glasses fogged up so that I could not
manage to coordinate the jump rope with Gail. The chill was
doing to me what it always did, entering my bones, making
me cry, humiliating me. I hated the city, especially in winter. I
hated Public School Number 13. I hated my skinny flat-
chested body, and I envied the black girls who could jump
rope so fast that their legs became a blur. They always
seemed to be warm while I froze.

There was only one source of beauty and light for me that
school year. The only thing I had anticipated at the start of
the semester. That was seeing Eugene. In August, Eugene and
his family had moved into the only house on the block that
had a yard and trees. I could see his place from my window
in El Building. In fact, if I sat on the fire escape I was literally
suspended above Eugene's backyard. It was my favorite spot
to read my library books in the summer. Until that August
the house had been occupied by an old Jewish couple. Over

the years I had become part of their family, without their knowing it, of course. I had a view of their kitchen and their backyard, and though I could not hear what they said, I knew when they were arguing, when one of them was sick, and many other things. I knew all this by watching them at mealtimes. I could see their kitchen table, the sink and the stove. During good times, he sat at the table and read his newspapers while she fixed the meals. If they argued, he would leave and the old woman would sit and stare at nothing for a long time. When one of them was sick, the other would come and get things from the kitchen and carry them out on a tray. The old man had died in June. The last week of school I had not seen him at the table at all. Then one day I saw that there was a crowd in the kitchen. The old woman had finally emerged from the house on the arm of a stocky middle-aged woman whom I had seen there a few times before, maybe her daughter. Then a man had carried out suitcases. The house had stood empty for weeks. I had had to resist the temptation to climb down into the yard and water the flowers the old lady had taken such good care of.

By the time Eugene's family moved in, the yard was a tangled mass of weeds. The father had spent several days mowing, and when he finished, I didn't see the red, yellow, and purple clusters that meant flowers to me from where I sat. I didn't see this family sit down at the kitchen table together. It was just the mother, a red-headed tall woman who wore a white uniform—a nurse's, I guessed it was; the father was gone before I got up in the morning and was never there at dinner time. I only saw him on weekends when they sometimes sat on lawn chairs under the oak tree, each hidden behind a section of the newspaper; and there was Eugene. He was tall and blond, and he wore glasses. I liked him right away because he sat at the kitchen table and read books for hours. That summer, before we had even spoken one word to each other, I kept him company on my fire escape.

Once school started I looked for him in all my classes, but P.S. 13 was a huge, overpopulated place and it took me days and many discreet questions to discover that Eugene was in honors classes for all his subjects; classes that were not open to me because English was not my first language, though I was a straight A student. After much maneuvering I managed "to run into him" in the hallway where his locker was—on the other side of the building from mine—and in study hall at the library, where he first seemed to notice me but did not speak; and finally, on the way home after school one day when I decided to approach him directly, though my stomach was doing somersaults.

I was ready for rejection, snobbery, the worst. But when I came up to him, practically panting in my nervousness, and blurted out: "You're Eugene. Right?" He smiled, pushed his glasses up on his nose, and nodded. I saw then that he was blushing deeply. Eugene liked me, but he was shy. I did most of the talking that day. He nodded and smiled a lot. In the weeks that followed, we walked home together. He would linger at the corner of El Building for a few minutes then walk down to his two-story house. It was not until Eugene moved into that house that I noticed that El Building blocked most of the sun and that the only spot that got a little sunlight during the day was the tiny square of earth the old woman had planted with flowers.

I did not tell Eugene that I could see inside his kitchen from my bedroom. I felt dishonest, but I liked my secret sharing of his evenings, especially now that I knew what he was reading, since we chose our books together at the school library.

One day my mother came into my room as I was sitting on the windowsill staring out. In her abrupt way she said: "Elena, you are acting 'moony.'" *Enamorada* was what she really said—that is, like a girl stupidly <u>infatuated</u>. Since I had turned fourteen and started menstruating my mother had been more <u>vigilant</u> than ever. She acted as if I was going to go crazy or explode or something if she didn't watch me and nag me all the time about being a señorita now. She kept talking about virtue, morality, and other subjects that did not interest me in the least. My mother was unhappy in Paterson, but my father had a good job at the blue jeans factory in Passaic, and soon, he kept assuring us, we would be moving to our own house there. Every Sunday we drove out to the suburbs of Paterson, Clifton, and Passaic, out to where people mowed grass on Sundays in the summer and where children made snowmen in the winter from pure white snow, not like the gray slush of Paterson, which seemed to fall from the sky in that hue. I had learned to listen to my parents' dreams, which were spoken in Spanish, as fairy tales, like the stories about life in the island paradise of Puerto Rico before I was born. I had been to the Island once as a little girl, to grandmother's funeral, and all I remembered was wailing women in black, my mother becoming hysterical and being given a pill that made her sleep two days, and me feeling lost in a crowd of strangers all claiming to be my aunts, uncles, and cousins. I had actually been glad to return to the city. We had not been back there since then, though my parents talked constantly about buying a house on the beach someday, retiring on the island—that was a common topic among the residents of El Building. As for me, I was going to go to college and become a teacher.

But after meeting Eugene I began to think of the present more than of the future. What I wanted now was to enter that house I had watched for so many years. I wanted to see the other rooms where the old people had lived and where the boy I liked spent his time. Most of all, I wanted to sit at the kitchen table with Eugene like two adults, like the old man and his wife had done, maybe drink some coffee and talk about books. I had started reading *Gone with the Wind*. I was <u>enthralled</u> by it, with the daring and the passion of the beautiful girl living in a mansion, and with her devoted parents and the slaves who did everything for them. I didn't believe such a world had ever really existed, and I wanted to ask Eugene some questions, since he and his parents, he had told me, had come up from Georgia, the same place where the novel was set. His father worked for a company that had transferred him to Paterson. His mother was very unhappy, Eugene said, in his beautiful voice that rose and fell over words in a strange, lilting way. The kids at school called him the Hick and made fun of the way he talked. I knew I was his only friend so far, and I liked that, though I felt sad for him sometimes. Skinny Bones and the Hick, was what they called us at school when we were seen together.

The day Mr. DePalma came out into the cold and asked us to line up in front of him was the day that President Kennedy was shot. Mr. DePalma, a short muscular man with slicked-down black hair, was the science teacher, P.E. coach, and disciplinarian at P.S. 13. He was the teacher to whose homeroom you got assigned if you were a troublemaker, and the man called out to break up playground fights, and to escort violently angry teenagers to the office. And Mr. DePalma was the man who called your parents in for "a conference."

That day, he stood in front of two rows of mostly black and Puerto Rican kids, brittle from their efforts to "keep moving" on a November day that was turning bitter cold. Mr. DePalma, to our complete shock, was crying. Not just silent adult tears, but really sobbing. There were a few titters from the back of the line where I stood shivering.

"Listen," Mr. DePalma raised his arms over his head as if he were about to conduct an orchestra. His voice broke, and he covered his face with his hands. His barrel chest was heaving. Someone giggled behind me.

"Gross," someone said and there was a lot of laughter.

"The president is dead, you idiots. I should have known that wouldn't mean anything to a bunch of losers like you kids. Go home." He was shrieking now. No one moved for a minute or two, but then a big girl let out a "yeah!" and ran to get her books piled up with the others against the brick wall of the school building. The others followed in a mad scramble to get to their things before somebody caught on. It was still an hour to the dismissal bell.

A little scared, I headed for El Building. There was an <u>eerie</u> feeling on the streets. I looked into Mario's drugstore, a favorite hangout for the high school crowd, but there were only a couple of old Jewish men at the soda bar, talking with the short order cook in tones that sounded almost angry, but they were keeping their voices low. Even the traffic on one of the busiest intersections in Paterson—Straight Street and Park Avenue—seemed to be moving slower. There were no horns blasting that day. At El Building, the usual little group of unemployed men were not hanging out on the front stoop, making it difficult for women to enter the front door. No music spilled out from open doors in the hallway. When I walked into our apartment, I found my mother sitting in front of the grainy picture of the television set.

She looked up at me with a tear-streaked face and just said: "Dios mío," turning back to the set as if it were pulling at her eyes. I went into my room.

Though I wanted to feel the right thing about President Kennedy's death, I could not fight the feeling of <u>elation</u> that stirred in my chest.

Today was the day I was to visit Eugene in his house. He had asked me to come over after school to study for an American history test with him. We had also planned to walk to the public library together. I looked down into his yard. The oak tree was bare of leaves, and the ground looked gray with ice. The light through the large kitchen window of his house told me El Building blocked the sun to such an extent that they had to turn lights on in the middle of the day. I felt ashamed about it. But the white kitchen table with the lamp hanging just above it looked cozy and inviting. I would soon sit there, across from Eugene, and I would tell him about my perch just above his house. Maybe I would.

In the next thirty minutes I changed clothes, put on a little pink lipstick, and got my books together. Then I went in to tell my mother that I was going to a friend's house to study. I did not expect her reaction.

"You are going out *today*?" The way she said "today" sounded as if a storm warning had been issued. It was said in utter disbelief. Before I could answer, she came toward me and held my elbows as I clutched my books.

"*Hija*, the president has been killed. We must show respect. He was a great man. Come to church with me tonight."

She tried to embrace me, but my books were in the way. My first impulse was to comfort her, she seemed so distraught, but I had to meet Eugene in fifteen minutes.

"I have a test to study for, Mama. I will be home by eight."

"You are forgetting who you are, Niña. I have seen you staring down at that boy's house. You are heading for humiliation and pain. My mother said this in Spanish and in a resigned tone that surprised me, as if she had no intention of stopping me from "heading for humiliation and pain." I started for the door. She sat in front of the TV holding a white handkerchief to her face.

I walked out to the street and around the chain-link fence that separated El Building from Eugene's house. The yard was neatly edged around the little walk that led to the door. It always amazed me how Paterson, the inner core of the city, had no apparent logic to its architecture. Small, neat, single residences like this one could be found right next to huge, dilapidated apartment buildings like El Building. My guess was that the little houses had been there first, then the immigrants had come in droves, and the monstrosities had been raised for them—the Italians, the Irish, the Jews, and now us, the Puerto Ricans, and the blacks. The door was painted a deep green: *verde*, the color of hope. I had heard my mother say it: Verde-Esperanza.

I knocked softly. A few suspenseful moments later the door opened just a crack. The red, swollen face of a woman appeared. She had a halo of red hair floating over a delicate ivory face—the face of a doll—with freckles on the nose. Her smudged eye makeup made her look unreal to me, like a mannequin seen through a warped store window.

"What do you want?" Her voice was tiny and sweet-sounding, like a little girl's, but her tone was not friendly.

"I'm Eugene's friend. He asked me over. To study." I thrust out my books, a silly gesture that embarrassed me almost immediately.

"You live there?" She pointed up to El Building, which looked particularly ugly, like a gray prison with its many dirty windows and rusty fire escapes. The woman had stepped halfway out, and I could see that she wore a white nurse's uniform with "St. Joseph's Hospital" on the name tag.

"Yes, I do."

She looked <u>intently</u> at me for a couple of heartbeats, then said as if to herself, "I don't know how you people do it." Then directly to me: "Listen. Honey. Eugene doesn't want to study with you. He is a smart boy. Doesn't need help. You understand me. I am truly sorry if he told you you could come over. He cannot study with you. It's nothing personal. You understand? We won't be in this place much longer, no need for him to get close to people; it'll just make it harder for him later. Run back home now."

I couldn't move. I just stood there in shock at hearing these things said to me in such a honey-drenched voice. I had never heard an accent like hers except for Eugene's softer version. It was as if she were singing me a little song.

"What's wrong? Didn't you hear what I said?" She seemed very angry, and I finally snapped out of my trance. I turned away from the green door and heard her close it gently.

Our apartment was empty when I got home. My mother was in someone else's kitchen, seeking the <u>solace</u> she needed. Father would come in from his late shift at midnight. I would hear them talking softly in the kitchen for hours that night. They would not discuss their dreams for the future, or life in Puerto Rico, as they often did; that night they would talk sadly about the young widow and her two children as if they were family. For the next few days, we would observe *tuto* in our apartment; that is, we would practice restraint and silence—no loud music or laughter. Some of the women of El Building would wear black for weeks.

That night, I lay in my bed, trying to feel the right thing for our dead president. But the tears that came up from a deep source inside me were strictly for me. When my mother came to the door. I pretended to be sleeping. Sometime during the night, I saw from my bed the streetlight come on. It had a pink halo around it. I went to my window and pressed my face to the cool glass. Looking up at the light I could see the white snow falling like a lace veil over its face. I did not look down to *see* it turning gray as it touched the ground below.

Understanding the Reading

Complete the next three exercises and see how well you understood the excerpt from "American History."

Exercise 9.4 Multiple-Choice Questions

Answer the following questions about the reading. Circle the letter of your answer.

TIP: Don't try to answer the questions from memory; go back to the text as often as necessary.

1. Judging from context, *lilting* (top of page 188) means
   A. cheerful and joyous.
   B. flowing up and down.
   C. angry and harsh.
   D. accented and unclear.

2. Elena's mother is nagging her about being a señorita now because she
   A. is worried her daughter's lovesickness will get her into trouble.
   B. is unhappy in Paterson and just wants to vent.
   C. is afraid her daughter wasn't working hard enough.
   D. could not understand what caused her daughter's attraction to Eugene.

3. Which statement about Eugene is *not* supported by the selection?
   A. Eugene speaks with a southern accent.
   B. Eugene considers himself superior to the narrator.
   C. Eugene has few friends.
   D. Eugene invited the narrator to his house.

4. The narrator is not particularly upset about President Kennedy's death because she
   A. was not even aware he was shot.
   B. did not vote for him.
   C. doesn't understand the importance of a president's assassination.
   D. is self-absorbed and unfeeling.

5. Eugene's mother can best be described as
   A. a rude supremacist.
   B. an unhappy single mother.
   C. an out-of-place southerner.
   D. a fairly polite social and racial snob.

Exercise 9.5 Short-Answer Questions

Respond to the following questions in one to two complete sentences. Go back to the text, as you did on the multiple choice.

6. Why did Mr. DePalma act as he did when he told the students about President Kennedy? Was he out of line? Explain why or why not.

_____

_____

_____

7. Elena's mother tells her, "You are forgetting who you are . . . You are heading for humiliation and pain." Why didn't she stop her daughter from going?

_____

_____

_____

8. What point might the author be trying to convey by telling us that both of the mothers in this story were crying?

_____

_____

_____

9. If you were writing this story, what conversation would you add between Eugene and Elena the next time they meet?

_____

_____

_____

Exercise 9.6 Extending Your Thinking

Respond to the following question in three to four complete sentences. Use details from the texts in your answer.

10. How does the school romance portrayed in this selection compare with the one from the *Tom Sawyer* excerpt?

_____

_____

_____

_____

_____

_____

Reading Strategy Lesson
Identifying Conflict

Conflict

Conflict is a struggle between opposing forces. With no conflict, there can be no real story. That does not mean that two people have to be in a fight, however; you can have a perfectly good story without having conflict between characters. That's because there are several different types of conflict.

- **a character's struggle against nature**

  When one or more characters must overcome an obstacle placed in their path by a natural force, there is a conflict with nature. A storm causes a shipwreck, and the survivors float in a rubber raft with no land in sight. Sharks circle the raft. The sun is hot and oppressive. The sea provides no drinkable water.

- **a character's struggle against society**

  A character who is in conflict with society may be struggling against poverty, racism, a political system, a class system, a set of values, or some other social convention. If you have read *To Kill a Mockingbird,* you know that the attorney Atticus Finch decides to defend an African-American accused of a crime in a small southern town. Both Finch and his children are oppressed by most of the townspeople. They are in conflict with their racist society.

- **a character's internal struggle**

  Have you ever wanted to do something you shouldn't and had to struggle with yourself to make your decision? Then you have experienced internal conflict. Internal conflicts center around emotions, morals, or ideas. Should the character follow her heart or her head? Which side should she believe?

- **a character's struggle with another character**

  A conflict between two people is not necessarily a violent one. They don't have to duke it out in the street. They may simply engage in a battle of wits, with few words spoken to one another, or they may never even meet. Think of a detective who is chasing a criminal. They have not met or spoken, but they are in conflict. Likewise, characters may conflict simply because they have different ideas, envy one another, or are struggling for power.

Exercise 9.7 Practice the Reading Strategy

Read each situation description below. On the blank line, identify the type of conflict specifically described. Then use your imagination and note what other kind(s) of conflict might also be involved in the situation, even though they aren't presented here.

1. Two men decided to go fishing. They rented a boat and went out into the Gulf of Mexico at 6 A.M. They encountered rough water, and their boat capsized. Now they are trying to hold on to the boat's upside-down hull, hoping to be rescued.

Specific conflict: characters' struggle with _____

Other possible conflicts that could have come before this situation or develop from it:

_____

_____

2. Trevor and Travis are twins, and they are both on the same basketball team. Their dad is watching the game. They both want to be the twin of whom he is more proud.

Specific conflict: characters' struggle with _____

Other possible conflicts that could have come before this situation or develop from it:

_____

_____

3. A Muslim family from Pakistan has just moved to a small community. Both of the parents are doctors. The two children attend public school. The parents are having a hard time getting patients to see them in their private practice. Neither of the children has made any friends at the high school they attend.

Specific conflict: characters' struggle with _____

Other possible conflicts that could have come before this situation or develop from it:

_____

_____

4. Shannon did not study for the math test. In fact, she forgot all about it. Right now she is sitting behind Marcus, who is a very good math student. Shannon can see his paper perfectly, and the teacher does not seem to be watching.

Specific conflict: character's struggle with _____

Other possible conflicts that could have come before this situation or develop from it:

_____

_____

Exercise 9.8 **Apply the Reading Strategy Back to "American History"**

Reread the descriptions of the various types of conflict outlined on page 193. Then, on a separate sheet of paper, write a paragraph describing the conflicts evident in the selection from "American History." State the types of conflict, who is involved, and what each conflict is about. Try to make inferences about conflicts that are not specifically stated in the reading.

Writing Workshop
Using Strong Verbs

What Are Strong Verbs?

Verbs show action. Choosing strong verbs energizes and enlivens your writing. They are your most powerful writing tools. Weak verbs tell the reader only what he or she is expecting to hear.

Weak and boring:	I have to go to the store because we're out of milk.
Strong and interesting:	I have to dash to the store before it closes because I just realized Nadia's guzzled down every drop of milk.

In previous chapters, you practiced turning adjectives into adverbs, and adjectives and verbs into nouns. There are times when you need a certain form of a word, so it's good to know how to play with suffixes and base words to find the one you want.

When you want to make a strong statement, use an active verb. Telling what something *does* is much more effective than just saying what it *is*. Strong verbs help you to be specific about action. Which of the following sentences provides you with a more interesting mental picture? Which one tells you more about what is actually *happening* in the scene?

The clothes are on the clothesline.

The clothes on the line are *whipping and snapping* in the wind.

Strong, active verbs are not just for narratives. Persuasive and expository essays—the kind you are usually asked to write for class and for standardized tests—also benefit from strong verb choices. Which sentence or passage in each of the following pairs tells you more and paints the better picture?

In this selection, Elena is snubbed by Eugene's mother.

In this selection, Eugene's snobbish mother shatters Elena's dreams of romance.

She is nice about it, yet not really that nice, telling Elena to go back home. She doesn't want her son having anything to do with Elena.

Her voice drips with Georgia honey as she dismisses Elena, her outward kindness clearly conflicting with her true feelings. In his mother's eyes, Eugene outclasses Elena, and she prefers his loneliness to a friendship she considers unsuitable.

Using strong, active verbs in your essays and short answers whenever you can will clarify your statements and make them more interesting.

Exercise 9.9 Practice the Writing Lesson: Using Strong Verbs

Rewrite each sentence below, changing the verbs to stronger, more active verbs. Revise the sentences in any other ways you wish to make them more appealing and interesting.

1. Molly ate dinner.

   _____

2. I looked at the clock.

   _____

3. Louis went down the road.

   _____

4. The dog barked.

   _____

5. Nathan hit the ball.

   _____

6. The cat was friendly.

   _____

7. The flowers bloomed.

   _____

8. The tree fell.

   _____

9. The car went by.

   _____

10. The horse was in the pasture.

    _____

Exercise 9.10 Apply the Writing Lesson to Revise a Paragraph

On a separate sheet of paper, rewrite the following paragraph using strong verbs to make it more interesting.

> The best thing about winter is the ice skating rink at the shopping mall. Our parents take us. Sometimes we take the bus there. We stay all day. The ice rink is in the middle with the shops all around. There are two levels. Shoppers sit and watch skaters from the second level. Some of the skaters are really good. Even if you cannot skate very well it is still fun. There are restaurants at the mall, shops, and of course you can just hang out and talk. One of my friends takes figure-skating lessons. She wants to be in the Olympics. She goes to the mall with us, but she never leaves the ice except to rest a little.

Grammar Mini-Lesson
Compound-Complex Sentences

What Is a Compound-Complex Sentence?

A **compound-complex** sentence consists of at least two independent clauses and at least one dependent clause. Let's break down a compound-complex sentence from "American History."

> I felt dishonest, but
> INDEP. CLAUSE   CONJ.
>
> I liked my secret sharing of his evenings,
>   INDEP. CLAUSE
>
> especially now that I knew what he was reading,
>   DEP. CLAUSE
>
> since we chose our books together at the school library.
>   DEP. CLAUSE

1. If you just had independent clauses joined together—*without* any dependent clauses—you would have what is called a **compound sentence:**

> I felt dishonest, but I liked my secret sharing of his evenings.
> INDEP. CLAUSE   CONJ.   INDEP. CLAUSE

A compound sentence consists of two or more independent clauses. Notice that you usually use a coordinating conjunction (*and, or,* or *but*) when joining these clauses.

2. Once you add a dependent clause into the mix, you are making the sentence more complex, thus forming a **compound-complex sentence**. Look again at our original example:

> I felt dishonest, but I liked my secret sharing of his evenings, especially now that I knew what he was reading, since we chose our books together at the school library.

The compound-complex sentence allows the narrator to explain her situation fully. It gets in a lot of information but remains clear and easy to follow.

Exercise 9.11 Practice Forming Compound-Complex Sentences

Each item contains a compound sentence and a simple sentence. Combine them into a compound-complex sentence.

Hint: Change the simple sentence to a dependent clause beginning with one of the following: although, as, because, now that, since, that, though, when, which, who.

Example: The future is beginning to look brighter, and we can all breathe more freely. The worst seems to be over.

<u>The future is beginning to look brighter, and we can all breathe</u>

<u>more freely now that the worst seems to be over.</u>

1. The gong sounded. The seconds quickly left the ring, and the two opponents advanced to meet each other.

   _____

   _____

   _____

2. Mrs. Applebaum is out, but I can connect you with her secretary. She may be able to answer your question.

   _____

   _____

   _____

3. We were extremely careful, or we might have slipped on the pavement. It was very icy.

   _____

   _____

   _____

4. Visibility was almost zero. The pilot had to attempt a landing, for he was running low on fuel.

   _____

   _____

   _____

5. The days are growing shorter, and you can feel the chill in the air. Winter is approaching.

_____

_____

_____

Exercise 9.12 Forming Compound-Complex Sentences with Three Sentences

Each item contains three simple sentences. Combine all three sentences to make one compound-complex sentence.

1. The argument was settled. The athletes returned to their positions. Play resumed.

_____

_____

_____

2. We were on time. We might have missed the bus. The driver would not wait.

_____

_____

_____

3. I had bought a ticket for the concert. I came down with a cold. I was not able to go.

_____

_____

_____

4. The rent is overdue. There are several other bills, too. They all must be paid somehow.

_____

_____

_____

5. Amanda could not stay. Everyone else remained. We had to get the paper done that day.

_____

_____

_____

Polish Your Spelling

IE or EI?

In some words, the sound of long *e* as in *evening* is spelled *ie* (*achieve*, *believe*). In certain other words, the same sound is spelled *ei* (*ceiling*, *receive*).

You have probably heard the little rhyme that can help you remember whether you should write *ie* or *ei*. The rhyme remains a good way to recall the rule:

Write *i* before *e*	(*brief, chief, fierce, piece, yield*)
Except after *c*	(*conceit, deceit, perceive*)
Or when sounded like *ay*	(*sleigh, vein, freight*)
As in *neighbor* and *weigh*.	

As is often true with the English language, there are some exceptions to the rule. The seven most common exceptions are these:

either	neither	foreign	height
leisure	seize	weird	

Exercise 9.13 Practice Spelling IE and EI Words

Insert either *ie* or *ei* and rewrite each word on the blank line.

1. p___ ___ce _____
2. v___ ___n _____
3. conc___ ___vable _____
4. f___ ___rce _____
5. bes___ ___ged _____
6. fr___ ___ght _____
7. w___ ___gh _____
8. for___ ___gner _____
9. disbel___ ___f _____
10. y___ ___ld _____

Unit Three Review

Vocabulary Review

A. Match each word with its definition.

DEFINITION		WORD
_____	1. a feeling of ill will	a. supercilious
_____	2. long series of passing events	b. eerie
_____	3. fallen into disrepair	c. refuge
_____	4. give in to another's wishes	d. infatuated
_____	5. foolishly attracted to someone	e. panorama
_____	6. emotionally moving	f. animosity
_____	7. protection from danger	g. dilapidated
_____	8. feeling of pleasure and happiness	h. poignant
_____	9. peculiar and mysterious	i. defer
_____	10. haughtily disdainful	j. elation

B. Match each word with its synonym.

SYNONYM		WORD
_____	11. lessen	a. incisive
_____	12. embarrassment	b. petulant
_____	13. attentively	c. disquieting
_____	14. successive	d. humiliation
_____	15. comfort	e. diminish
_____	16. biting	f. evoke
_____	17. peevish	g. subsequent
_____	18. elicit	h. solace
_____	19. partying	i. intently
_____	20. disturbing	j. revelry

C. Match each word with its antonym.

ANTONYM	WORD
_____ 21. lovable	a. enthralled
_____ 22. polite	b. exultation
_____ 23. sadness	c. latent
_____ 24. delighted	d. vigilant
_____ 25. optimistic	e. furtive
_____ 26. immodesty	f. sardonic
_____ 27. neglectful	g. impudent
_____ 28. straightforward	h. abominable
_____ 29. bored	i. distraught
_____ 30. evident	j. self-effacement

Grammar Review

The underlined portions of the paragraphs may or may not contain errors. If there is an error, circle the letter of the correction in the answer choices. If there is no error, choose D.

Idenity theft and idenity fraud are terms
            (1)
that are used when referring to all types
            (1)
of crime involving a person wrongfuly
  (1)   (2)
obtaning and using another person's
        (2)
personal data in some way that involves
  (2)
fraud or trickery. Typicaly for economic
         (3)
gain. You need protect yourself from
 (3)

1. A. Identity theft and identity fraud are terms that are used when you're referring to all types of crime
   B. The terms "identity theft" and "identity fraud" are used to refer to all types of crime
   C. Identity theft and identity fraud are terms that refers to all types of crime
   D. no change

2. A. obtaining and using another's personal data
   B. wrongfully obtaining and then also using the data of another person
   C. wrongfully obtaining and using another person's data
   D. no change

3. A. fraud or trickery for typical economic gain.
   B. fraud or trickery, typically for economic gain.
   C. Fraud or trickery. Typically for economic gain.
   D. no change

identity theft. <u>Your fingerprints, which are</u>
                          (4)
<u>unique to you, and cannot be given to</u>
                          (4)
<u>someone else.</u> This is not true of your
            (4)
personal data. "Personal data" means
your Social Security number, your
bank account or credit card number,
<u>your telephone calling card number, and</u>
                          (5)
<u>other valuable identifying data can be used.</u>
                          (5)
If these are obtained by an identity thief
you could be in big trouble. In the U.S.
and Canada, <u>people have reported</u>
                          (6)
<u>withdrawals made from their bank accounts</u>
                          (6)
<u>without their permission.</u> Even worse is
            (6)
when a person's identity <u>is taken completely</u>
                                      (7)
<u>over.</u> <u>Debts and crimes are committed as</u>
 (7)   (8)
<u>the victim.</u> In most cases a victim not
      (8)

4. A. Your fingerprints, which are
       unique to you, can't be some-
       one else's.
    B. Your fingerprints, which are
       unique to you, cannot be given
       to someone else.
    C. Your fingerprints, which is
       unique to you, cannot be given
       to someone else.
    D. no change

5. A. your telephone calling card
       number, and other valuable
       identifying data that can be
       used to commit fraud.
    B. your telephone calling card
       number, and other valuable
       identifying data. That can be
       used.
    C. your telephone calling card
       number, and other valuable
       identifying data, to commit
       frauds.
    D. no change

6. A. there have been reports of
       moneys being taken out of
       their bank accounts without-
       their permission.
    B. people have reported, with-
       drawals made from their
       bank accounts without their
       permission.
    C. there have been reported mon-
       eys being taken out of their
       bank accounts without their
       permisson.
    D. no change

7. A. is taken in complete.
    B. is taken over completely.
    C. is wholly taken.
    D. no change

8. A. Debts are run up and crimes
       are committed in the name of
       the victim.
    B. All the debts and crimes that
       happen are due to the victim.
    C. Debts and crime is committed
       in the name of the victim.
    D. no change

only loses the money the thief steals. But
                    (9)
victims also has to pay people to investigate
    (9)
the crime and help to restore his reputation and credit rating. How does someone
                                (10)
get your personal data is stolen in different
                    (10)
ways. He could be listening when you give
(10)
your credit card number on the phone. He
goes through your trash to look for checks
and bank statements that have identifying
information. A real find is a preapproved
                      (11)
credit card application. The thief fills it
                    (11)
out and sends it in, changing the address
                    (11)
to his postoffice box. Then all he has to do
                    (11)
is wait for the card to arrive. Identity
            (11)
criminals also "phish" for information on
the Internet. Or get you to order some-
                (12)
thing using your credit card, but they
                (12)
never send you anything they just wanted
                    (12)
the number.
    (12)

9. A. only loses the money the thief
        steals but also
    B. only loses the money the thief
        steals. But also
    C. only loses the money, the thief
        steals, but also
    D. no change

10. A. How does someone get your
        personal data? It can be stolen
        in different ways.
    B. Someone can make the theft of
        your data in different ways.
    C. In different ways, your per-
        sonal data can be stolen.
    D. no change

11. A. A real find is a preapproved
        credit card application, no
        problem, they just change the
        address to thier post office box
        and wait for the card to arrive.
    B. Finding a credit card applica-
        tion, the thief changes the
        address on it and then waits
        for the card to arrive.
    C. A real find is a preapproved
        credit card application. They
        just change the address to
        they're post office box and
        wait for the card to arrive.
    D. no change

12. A. Internet, or get you to order
        something using your credit
        card which is the only thing
        they wanted.
    B. Internet, or get you to order
        something using your credit
        card. Your order never arrives,
        but they have what they want:
        your card number.
    C. Internet. Or, get you to order
        something using your credit
        card. They never send you any-
        thing they just wanted the
        number.
    D. no change

People who steal your identity can <u>max out your credit cards. Get loans</u> <u>(13)</u> <u>in your name, and generally pose as you</u> <u>(13)</u> <u>and ruin your life.</u> <u>Fortunately,</u> <u>Congress</u> <u>(13)</u> <u>(14)</u> <u>made identity theft a federal offense in</u> <u>(14)</u> <u>1998.</u> That doesn't mean you can (14) stop worrying or that the government <u>will catch every theif red-handed.</u> You still (15) should tear up or shred anything with your information on it before you throw it out. Don't respond to spam e-mails. Always be aware that someone may be looking over your shoulder—literally or in cyberspace.

13. A max out your credit cards, get loans in your name, and generally pose as you.
    B. charge your credit cards to their limit, get loans in your name, and generally ruin your life by posing as you.
    C. charge your credit cards to its limit, get loans in your name, and generally ruin your life by posing as you.
    D. no change

14. A. Congress fortunately decided identity fraud was an offense in 1998.
    B. Congress found identity fraud offensive in 1998.
    C. Fortunately, Congress made identity fraud in 1998 an offense.
    D. no change

15. A. will catch every theif who comits fraud.
    B. will catch every thief who commits fraud.
    C. will catch any thief who commit fraud.
    D. no change

Spelling Review

A. Insert *ei* or *ie* to spell each word correctly.

1. n___ ___ghbor

2. rec___ ___ver

3. ch___ ___f

B. Circle the word in each row that is misspelled.

4. exhaust   debtor   ajacent   typewriter

5. aquainted   knuckle   pneumonia   yolk

6. unknown   climber   ajoin   plumber

7. almond   wrist   anser   knee

C. Add *-or* or *-er* to each word.

8. elevate   _____

9. labor   _____

10. senate   _____

Choose one of the following topics. Plan your essay. Write your first draft. Then revise and edit your draft, and write your final essay. Be sure to identify your audience, purpose, and task before you begin planning.

> *My Ántonia, Tom Sawyer,* and *Ethan Frome* are all set at least 100 years ago. Compare and contrast the settings in terms of their appeal to the reader. Which setting is the least threatening and most inviting? Which setting seems the most unpleasant? Support your opinion statements with examples from the selections.
>
> OR
>
> In "American History," Elena experiences her own personal tragedy. How does it compare with the tragedy of President Kennedy's assassination in terms of immediate impact and long-term effects?

Unit Three Extension Activities

 SPEAK/LISTEN

Celebrating Writers' Lives and Work

Choose one of the authors included in this unit (Mark Twain, Willa Cather, Edith Wharton, or Judith Ortiz Cofer). Research the author's life and accomplishments. Find at least three new facts about the author and a paragraph or a poem written by him or her that you feel is especially important. Present the biographical information to the class. Then read the paragraph or poem and discuss it as a group.

 EXPLORE

Universal Themes in Literature

The theme of this unit is "Love and Friendship." With a partner, use a quotations book or Web site and gather at least eight quotations about love and friendship that relate to several (or all) of the selections you have read in this unit. Take notes below each quotation, explaining the connections you found. Present your findings to another pair.

 WRITE

Sensory Descriptions

In Chapter Eleven, you learned about sensory images. Spend some time in a spot rich in appeal to the senses, for example a noisy cafeteria or a soccer game. Try to stand outside the activity around you and make a list of all the sensory images you notice. When you have listed about ten images, revise your descriptions to make them seem as real to a reader as they were to you.

CONNECT

Promoting Great Books

Divide into groups. Each group should be assigned one of the readings. Remember that each reading comes from a novel (*Tom Sawyer*, *My Ántonia*, and *Ethan Frome*) or from a collection of writings ("American History" is from *The Latin Deli*). Imagine that your group works at a publishing company and has to design a book jacket for the book you have been assigned. One person should do research to find out more about your book. Another should collect books of different types so the group can see what kinds of things are included on book jackets. A third person should locate several art choices for the group to vote on. Another person should write words that will appear on the jacket—usually a brief summary, reviews, and author information. At your final meeting, put everything together. Present or display the book jackets.

Defining Moments

Chapter Ten

Prereading Guide
Words to know and ideas to consider before you jump into the reading.

A. Essential Vocabulary

Word	Meaning	Typical Use
deliberate (*adj*) de-LIB-ur-ut	in a leisurely but determined manner; unhurried	After a few weeks of dedicated, *deliberate* knitting, Stephanie had almost finished the blanket for her sister's baby.
dilemma (*n*) dih-LEM-uh	a situation that requires a difficult choice; predicament	David could not decide between two colleges, so he turned to his guidance counselor for help with his *dilemma.*
edifice (*n*) ED-uh-fiss	a building, especially an impressive one; structure	My dad's office is located on the thirtieth floor of the new *edifice* on the public square.
expendable (*adj*) ek-SPEN-duh-bul	able to be used up; easily replaceable; unnecessary	I debated whether to put her present in a fancy keepsake tin or an *expendable* box.
facet (*n*) FASS-ut	1. one of many flat cuts on a gemstone 2. an aspect of a situation; side	The diamond, with perhaps as many as 100 *facets*, sparkled blindingly. This problem has a number of *facets*, and we need to consider each one.
hapless (*adj*) HAP-luss	not favored by luck; unfortunate	The *hapless* family in *The Grapes of Wrath* moved from one place to another in search of work.
protrude (*v*) pro-TROOD	to project outward; extend	It was difficult to drive the bedroom furniture home from the store because my new desk was *protruding* out of our trunk.
relinquish (*v*) re-LINK-wish	to let go of or give up, usually unwillingly; yield	After considerable pleading and tugging, I got Joe to *relinquish* my shoe.
sinuous (*adj*) SIN-yoo-us	curvy and winding; wavy	The Appalachian Trail is a *sinuous* path that runs from Georgia to Maine.

Word	Meaning	Typical Use
terrestrial (*adj*) tur-EST-ree-ul	relating to the earth or land; worldly	In the larger sense, even fish are *terrestrial* beings because they are part of the earth.

B. Vocabulary Practice

Exercise 10.1 Sentence Completion

Using your new vocabulary knowledge, choose the best way to complete the following sentences. Circle the letter of your answer.

1. We _____ in the mountains because the roads are sinuous.
   A. drive slowly
   B. can ignore speed limits

2. The 85-year-old man was able to _____ because of his deliberate pace.
   A. play the violin
   B. finish the marathon

3. The speaker presented only one _____ of the problem; I wish he had given us the full picture.
   A. edifice
   B. facet

4. Porcupines are _____ because of their many protruding quills.
   A. best avoided
   B. cuddly pets

5. Many of us hate to see them destroy the old edifice, _____.
   A. a huge oak tree
   B. a city landmark

6. You can borrow my pencils, since they're _____, but I would never give you my lucky eraser.
   A. expendable
   B. priceless

7. With _____ people to transport and one small car, we found ourselves in a dilemma.
   A. three
   B. ten

8. Every year, hundreds of hapless people _____.
   A. are victims of disasters
   B. win the lottery

9. Most turtles enjoy both _____, but some are strictly terrestrial.
   A. rivers and streams
   B. water and land

10. Throughout American history, natives were repeatedly _____ to relinquish land.
   A. asked or forced
   B. eager and happy

Exercise 10.2 Using Fewer Words

Replace the italicized words with a single word from the following list.

protrudes	edifice	expendable	dilemma	terrestrial
relinquish	sinuous	deliberately	facets	hapless

1. The phenomenon of *earth-related* magnetism was used even in primitive compasses. 1._____

2. I got my sister to *unwillingly give up* her plans to wear my new outfit by convincing her I should be the one to wear it first. 2._____

3. Forty flavors of ice cream! Talk about a(an) *situation that requires a difficult choice*! 3._____

4. The best place to fish is where the fallen pine *projects outward*. 4._____

5. There are many *sides to this issue* that we don't understand. 5._____

6. Environmentalists argue that old growth forests are not *easily replaceable* resources that we should sacrifice lightly. 6._____

7. I saw the blueprints and drawings for the Forresters' new home. It's going to be quite a(an) *impressive building*. 7._____

8. Cycling *in a leisurely but determined manner*, Rakesh logged 50 miles a week. 8._____

9. Most people who are *not favored by luck* keep hoping for better times. 9._____

10. The Mid-Atlantic Ridge is a(an) *curvy and winding* spine of land that lies beneath the ocean. 10._____

Exercise 10.3 Synonyms and Antonyms

Fill in the blanks in column A with the required synonyms or antonyms, selecting them from column B. (Remember: A *synonym* is a word similar in meaning to another word. An *antonym* is a word *opposite* in meaning to another word.)

	A	B
_____	1. synonym for *structure*	facet
_____	2. synonym for *predicament*	protrude
_____	3. antonym for *hurried*	expendable
_____	4. synonym for *wavy*	dilemma
_____	5. antonym for *fortunate*	deliberate
_____	6. synonym for *worldly*	sinuous
_____	7. antonym for *keep*	edifice
_____	8. synonym for *side*	terrestrial
_____	9. synonym for *extend*	hapless
_____	10. antonym for *necessary*	relinquish

C. Journal Freewrite

Before you begin the reading on the next page, take out a journal or sheet of paper and spend some time responding to the following prompt.

TIP: Don't worry about grammar and spelling; just write what comes to mind. The purpose of freewriting is to explore ideas, not to produce a polished work.

> Many parks and other natural areas post a sign that says, "Take only pictures. Leave only footprints." What do you think this sign means? How important do you think it is to do what the sign says—very, somewhat, or not at all important? Explain.

from Setting Free the Crabs

by Barbara Kingsolver

About the Author
Barbara Kingsolver
(1955–) grew up in
Carlisle, Kentucky, in a
home full of books. She
was not allowed to
watch television as a
child and instead was
encouraged to read,
write, and listen to
music. She graduated at
the top of her college
class in zoology and
worked as a research
assistant, technical
writer, and freelance
journalist. Kingsolver's
writings reflect her
strong support for
human rights and her
apprehension about
environmental destruc-
tion. She has written
novels, essay collec-
tions, poetry, short sto-
ries, and magazine and
newspaper articles. In
this slice-of-life essay
excerpt, she and her
family stroll along a
beach on Sanibel Island,
Florida.

At the undulating line where the waves licked the sand on
Sanibel Island, our three pairs of human footprints wove a
long, <u>sinuous</u> path behind us. Littoral zone:[1] no-man's-land,
a place of intertidal danger for some forms of life and of
blissful escape for others. The <u>deliberate</u>, monotonous call
and response of the waves—assail,[2] retreat—could have held
me here forever in a sunlight that felt languid as warm honey
on my skin. So we moved in a trance, my mother, my daughter, and I, the few sandblasted clamshells and knotty whelks
we had gathered clacking together in the bag that hung care-
lessly from my fingertips. Our practiced beachcombers' eyes
remained on high alert, though, and eventually my daughter's eye caught the first true find of our day: a little horse
conch,[3] flame orange, <u>faceted</u>, perfect as a jewel. *Treasure.*

My daughter wanted to take it home, I know. She turned
it over, already awed like any lottery winner by the stroke of
sudden wealth and the rapid reordering of the mind that tells
itself, *Yes! You did deserve this.*

And then her face fell. "Uh-oh," she said. "Already
taken."

"Oh, shoot," my mother said. "Is it alive?" There are
laws, on Sanibel, about taking live creatures from the ocean.

"Well, not the conch—that's gone. But a hermit crab's in
the shell."

Two small white claws <u>protruded</u> from the opening. The
sluggish gastropod[4] that had been architect and builder of
this magnificent orange <u>edifice</u> had already died—probably
yesterday, judging from the condition of the shell—but as
any house hunter can tell you, no home this gorgeous stands
empty for long. A squatter crab had moved in.

"Oh, they don't care if you take *those*," my mother reas-
sured her. "There are thousands of hermit crabs on this
beach."

---

[1]the shore of a body of water
[2]attack
[3]spiral-shelled marine mollusk
[4]a soft invertebrate covered by a shell, for example, clam, mussel,
oyster, snail

She was right, of course, though I could not help thinking, There are thousands of us on this beach, too—at what point do we become expendable? But I said nothing, because I had nothing sure to say, and anyway I was more interested in hearing how my daughter would respond. I decided to watch my leggy, passionate ten-year-old walk into the jaws of this dilemma by herself.

She looked up, uncertain. "But it's a living creature, Grand-mama. We can't kill it just because we want a shell for our collection."

My mother, like every grandmother, wants her grandchildren to have the sun, the moon, and the stars, all tucked into a box with a bright red bow. If my daughter really wanted this shell, Grand-mama was going to give her an out. "Well," she said, summoning remarkable creativity, "can't we find it another shell?"

My daughter pondered this. She knows, as I do, that a hermit crab won't give up its shell just because you want it. It will hold on. It will relinquish a claw or a head, or whatever else you manage to pull off, rather than come out. Were we going to take this thing home and set out an array of alternatives in front of it, as if it were a hapless shopper who'd won a dazzling spree? Some hermit crabs, the bigger ones with reddish claws, are game for a certain amount of terrestrial adventure, but this one wasn't that kind. Away from the littoral zone, this tiny life would give up its ghost within a few hours. I know this, I'm ashamed to say, from experience. So I waited, as did my husband, who had jogged up to join us, wondering what our little life-and-death huddle was all about.

My daughter looked at the creature in her hand for a long time and then said firmly, "No. We can't kill it."

"Anyway, it has the best shell on this whole beach," Steven said, quick to nail a few planks of support to her decision lest it should wobble. "It deserves to keep it."

So we handed it over to him, and he tossed it far out into the surf, to brood out there however a crustacean[5] mind may brood upon a catastrophe narrowly escaped in the cradle of a human child's hand.

---

[5]shellfish such as crab, lobster, and shrimp

Understanding the Reading

Complete the next three exercises and see how well you understood "Setting Free the Crabs."

Exercise 10.4 Multiple-Choice Questions

Answer the following questions about the reading. Circle the letter of your answer.

TIP: Don't try to answer the questions from memory; go back to the text as often as necessary.

1. Which phrase best describes the effect of the waves and sunshine on the author and her family?
   A. agitation and nervousness
   B. relaxation and contentment
   C. confusion and bewilderment
   D. anger and defensiveness

2. When the author's daughter said, "Uh-oh. Already taken," she meant
   A. finders keepers.
   B. that someone else had seen the shell first.
   C. that a live animal was living in the shell.
   D. that a game warden was coming down the beach.

3. The little girl's grandmother probably said, "Oh they don't care if you take *those*," because she
   A. wanted to clarify the rules for her granddaughter.
   B. disagreed with her daughter about following rules.
   C. did not think the rules applied to hermit crabs.
   D. wanted her granddaughter to be happy.

4. Steven said, "Anyway, it has the best shell on the whole beach," because he
   A. wanted his daughter to feel good about her decision.
   B. knew his information was factual.
   C. wanted his daughter to change her mind.
   D. wanted to make the grandmother feel foolish.

5. "Knotty whelks" (paragraph 1) most likely refers to
   A. pieces of rope.
   B. a type of shell.
   C. pieces of glass worn smooth by the sea.
   D. rocks covered with barnacles.

Exercise 10.5 Short-Answer Questions

Respond to the following questions in one to two complete sentences. Go back to the text, as you did on the multiple choice.

6. The author says that the littoral zone is "a place of intertidal danger for some forms of life and of blissful escape for others." To what forms of life is it dangerous? To which is it blissful?

_____

_____

_____

7. Why do you think the author gave her daughter no advice about whether she should keep the shell?

_____

_____

_____

8. How does the author's question—"At what point do we become expendable?"—connect with the issues raised in this essay?

_____

_____

_____

9. Do you think the author's daughter made the right decision? Explain why or why not.

_____

_____

_____

Exercise 10.6 Extending Your Thinking

Respond to the following question in three to four complete sentences. Use details from the text in your answer.

10. The theme of this unit is "Defining Moments." A defining moment is an important point in your life when a decision is made, a thought or idea is suddenly very clear, or a significant event occurs. What is the defining moment for the girl in this story?

_____

_____

_____

_____

_____

Reading Strategy Lesson
Understanding Figurative Language

What Is Figurative Language?

Figurative language contains figures of speech, devices that use language in an imaginative way. Figures of speech make unexpected comparisons or change the everyday meaning of words. Figurative language is the opposite of literal language, the *actual* meaning of words. When you say, "Andrew is a real brain," you don't mean that Andrew is *literally* a brain, and the people who hear you don't picture a mass of brain tissue at Andrew's desk. They know you mean that Andrew is intelligent.

Authors use figurative language to paint vivid mental and sensory pictures that keep their readers interested. Figures of speech are useful for stating your ideas in a new way and for clarifying them. In this lesson, we'll concentrate on the two most commonly used ones—similes and metaphors.

What Is a Simile?

A simile compares two apparently unlike things, feelings, or actions using a connecting word: *like, as, as if, than.*
In "Setting Free the Crabs," Barbara Kingsolver writes,

> The deliberate, monotonous call and response of the waves— assail, retreat—could have held me here forever in a sunlight that felt languid as warm honey on my skin.

A "sunlight that felt languid *as* warm honey on my skin" is a simile that compares the slow, listless feeling of the sunlight to that of warm honey. This figure of speech appeals to your sense of touch and helps the scene come alive in your mind.

Similes are not reserved for great literature; we use them in our daily speech. Here are four similes you may have already heard:

> I wandered lonely as a cloud.

> My love is like a red, red rose.

> She looked as if she'd been struck by lightning.

> Swifter than a speeding bullet—Superman!

How Is a Metaphor Different from a Simile?

A metaphor also makes a comparison but does not use the connecting words. A metaphor says or implies that one thing, feeling, or action *is* another. For example, you may have heard people say that "the road of life has its twists and turns." That is a metaphor comparing our journey through life, with its challenges and obstacles, to a journey down a winding road.

Look at another metaphor and see if you can figure out the comparison:

A constellation of gum wrappers littered the ground.

Here, the arrangement of the wrappers is being compared to a constellation. This is a vivid way of showing us exactly how the ground looked.

Exercise 10.7 Practice the Reading Strategy: Identifying Figurative Language

Read each quotation from the selection. If it contains a simile, write **S** on the blank line. If it contains a metaphor, write **M**.

_____ 1. "She turned it over, already awed like any lottery winner by the stroke of sudden wealth . . ."

_____ 2. ". . . a little horse conch, flame orange, faceted, perfect as a jewel."

_____ 3. "'Anyway, it has the best shell on this whole beach,' Steven said, quick to nail a few planks of support to her decision lest it should wobble."

_____ 4. "The sluggish gastropod that had been architect and builder of this magnificent orange edifice had already died . . ."

_____ 5. "I decided to watch my leggy, passionate ten-year-old walk into the jaws of this dilemma by herself."

Exercise 10.8 Apply the Reading Strategy

Search other selections in this text, your language arts textbook, newspapers, magazines, or other sources. Find at least three similes and two metaphors. List them below and identify each with **S** or **M**.

1. _____

2. _____

3. _____

4. _____

5. _____

Writing Workshop
Creating Similes and Metaphors

In Chapter Six, you learned about clichés and why it is important to avoid them. You also practiced replacing worn-out phrases with new, interesting ones.

The same similes and metaphors are often used over and over, falling into the category of cliché. Try creating new comparisons instead—using an unexpected simile or metaphor in your writing will give your ideas vitality and power.

Call on your imagination to complete the exercises that follow. Shoot for the unexpected, and have fun!

Exercise 10.9 Practice the Writing Lesson

These similes and metaphors are so overused they no longer work. Write an imaginative replacement for each one on the blank line.

1. She's the apple of her daddy's eye.

   _____

2. The newborn infant seemed as light as a feather.

   _____

3. He's as cool as a cucumber.

   _____

4. It's a jungle out there.

   _____

5. Lisa looked as pretty as a picture.

   _____

6. Your hands are as warm as toast.

   _____

7. The traffic was murder.

   _____

8. Your feet are as cold as ice.

   _____

9. The mall was a zoo.

   _____

10. He's as strong as an ox.

    _____

The Power of Figurative Language

The incident described in this chapter's selection takes place in about five minutes. It begins with a description of the scene and how the characters are feeling. Then comes the discovery of the shell and the conflict over whether it should be kept. Finally comes the resolution, the decision to throw it back into the ocean.

Despite its brevity, the passage contains so many similes and metaphors that we feel we've taken a minivacation to Sanibel Island. The following exercise challenges you to take your readers on a similar imaginary trip.

Exercise 10.10 Apply the Lesson to Your Own Writing

Think of a place with which you are very familiar. It does not have to be a faraway or exotic place. Somewhere in your neighborhood is fine. Begin your story by describing that place. Then add a conflict: a choice that you had to make. Resolve the conflict by writing about your decision. In your description, use at least two similes and one metaphor. Remember to appeal to your readers' senses so they get a "you are there" feeling.

Grammar Mini-Lesson
Using Possessives Correctly

The Possessive of Nouns

The **possessive** is the form of a noun that indicates ownership or possession.

The italicized nouns in the phrases below are **possessives**:

Rachel's hair	hair belonging to Rachel
students' money	money belonging to the students
women's rights	rights possessed by women
girls' names	the names of the girls

Notice that by using the possessives, we are able to express ideas in fewer words and avoid choppiness.

Why do some possessives end in 's (*Rachel's, women's*) while others end is s' (*students', girls'*)? Understanding the answer to this question is one of the keys to using possessives correctly.

1. If the possessor is a singular noun, add 's.

the student's hand

the girl's hat

the bird's nest

Charles's books (Names ending in *s* still need 's to make them possessive because they are singular nouns.)

2. If the possessive is a plural noun that ends in s, add only an apostrophe.

For instance, if there are several students who raise their hands, several girls with hats, and more than one bird in the nest, you would write

> the students' hands
>
> the girls' hats
>
> the birds' nest

3. If the possessor is a plural noun that does not end in s, add 's.

Women is already the plural of *woman,* so *women's* is the possessive. Other examples:

> salesmen's earnings
>
> children's playground

Exercise 10.11 Practice Using Possessives for Conciseness

Reduce each phrase to fewer words by using a possessive.

1. bicycle owned by the girl   _____

2. uniforms of the police officers   _____

3. toys belonging to the children   _____

4. wishes of my parents   _____

5. mother of the baby   _____

6. duties of congressmen   _____

7. shirts for men   _____

8. mouth of the horse   _____

9. problems facing the city   _____

10. the letter Nicholas wrote   _____

Exercise 10.12 Additional Practice Using Possessives

Write the correct possessive form of the noun in parentheses.

1. My _____ name is Taylor. (sister)

2. A _____ job is not an easy one. (firefighter)

3. In early fall, the stores have a good selection of girls' and _____ coats. (women)

4. Did you notice the sad expression on the _____ face? (camel)

5. The game will be played in the _____ gymnasium. (boys)

6. Why are these _____ shoes so much more expensive than the men's? (ladies)

7. I remembered the title but forgot the _____ name. (author)

8. _____ house is on the next corner. (Jacob)

9. The valet parked the _____ cars. (gentlemen)

10. In their campaign speeches, most candidates promise not to waste the _____ money. (taxpayers)

Polish Your Spelling
Verbs Ending in -CEED, -CEDE, and -SEDE

1. Only three verbs end in *-ceed*:
   exceed (be more than)   proceed (go ahead)   succeed (do well)

2. Other verbs with the same final sound end in *-cede*:
   recede (draw back)   cede (relinquish)   accede (agree)
   secede (break away)   concede (give up)   intercede (inter-
   precede (come before)   vene)

3. There is only one verb that ends in *-sede*:
   supersede (replace, take the place of)

Exercise 10.13 Practice the Spelling Patterns

Write in the correct -ceed, -cede, or -sede word to complete each sentence.

1. The crab decided to (draw back) _____ into its shell.

2. These instructions (replace) _____ the old ones.

3. I am ready to (intervene) _____ for you.

4. A parade will (come before) _____ the game.

5. Are you ready to (give up) _____?

6. Do you think we will (do well) _____?

7. (Go ahead) _____ to the nearest exit.

8. Your spending should not (be more than) _____ your earnings.

9. The Confederacy decided to (break away) _____ from the Union.

10. They will (agree) _____ to our proposal.

Chapter Eleven

Prereading Guide

Words to know and ideas to consider before you jump into the reading.

A. Essential Vocabulary

Word	Meaning	Typical Use
appreciable (*adj*) ah-PREESH-uh-bul	able to be perceived; measurable	It seemed just as cold at noon as it had in the morning; there was no *appreciable* difference in temperature.
besiege (*v*) be-SEEJ	to surround or attack on all sides, with weapons and troops or with questions and pleas; harass	The moment the courthouse doors opened, reporters *besieged* the young rock star who had been accused of a crime.
fastidious (*adj*) fas-TID-ee-us	particular about details of dress, food, manners, etc.; picky	Cats are *fastidious* animals that spend hours a day grooming themselves.
gaudy (*adj*) GAW-dee	overly colorful or ornamental; flashy	Some people enjoy the attention they get when they wear *gaudy* jewelry and clothing.
judicious (*adj*) joo-DISH-us	using sensible judgment; wise	My mother says she is simply being *judicious* when she asks me where I'm going and when I'll be back.
laborious (*adj*) luh-BOR-ee-us	requiring a great deal of work or effort; strenuous	Building interstate highways across the nation was a *laborious* task.
preposterous (*adj*) pre-POSS-tur-us	totally senseless or unbelievable; ridiculous	It is *preposterous* to imagine you will be able to write your term paper all in one evening.
profusion (*n*) pro-FEW-zhun	a large or excessive amount; abundance	A *profusion* of wildflowers blooms along the roadsides in the spring.
retrospection (*n*) ret-tro-SPEK-shun	the act of looking back over past events; review	She spent hours in *retrospection*, trying to determine what went wrong with their friendship.

Word	Meaning	Typical Use
veritable (*adj*) VARE-ih-tuh-bul	1. verifiable and authentic; genuine	A *veritable* blizzard made it impossible to see anything but white.
	2. Note: *veritable* is often used for emphasis or exaggeration when something is really *not* factual.	There's a *veritable* war every day in our urban streets.

B. Vocabulary Practice

Exercise 11.1 Sentence Completion

Using your new vocabulary knowledge, choose the best way to complete the following sentences. Circle the letter of your answer.

1. A _____ would be a judicious choice, since rain is predicted.
   A. raincoat
   B. sweater

2. There is no appreciable difference between _____.
   A. the bus and the subway
   B. freezing rain and sleet

3. The _____ provides a profusion of information.
   A. basketball court
   B. library

4. _____ combine to form a veritable rainbow.
   A. Green and blue
   B. Sunshine and moisture in the air

5. Retrospection is a valuable tool if you want to _____.
   A. build a storage chest
   B. learn from your mistakes

6. Besieged by the enemy for weeks, the soldiers were _____.
   A. running short of supplies
   B. hopeful of winning the battle

7. Getting _____ turned out to be more laborious than we'd imagined.
   A. to school on time
   B. the old wallpaper off the wall

8. Alyssa was much too fastidious to enjoy _____.
   A. wilderness camping
   B. an evening at a fine restaurant

9. Your excuses are preposterous, and you _____ have an extension on your paper.
   A. may not
   B. may

10. She bought gaudy jewelry since she _____.
    A. likes to attract attention
    B. prefers a more simple style of dress

Exercise 11.2 Using Fewer Words

Replace the italicized words with a single word from the following list.

appreciable besieged fastidious gaudily judiciously

laborious preposterous profusion retrospection veritable

1. With his long white beard, he looks like a(an) *verifiable and authentic* Santa Claus. 1._____

2. My science project is going to be *requiring a great deal of work.* 2._____

3. Benjamin felt *attacked on all sides* when his friends started asking him to explain why the team had lost the game. 3._____

4. *Looking back over past events* is especially interesting if you keep a journal. 4._____

5. He is so *particular about details* that I'd prefer he buy his own clothes. 5._____

6. The *excessive amount* of money and supplies collected for the new homeless shelter is heartening. 6._____

7. Surely she must have realized that she had dressed much too *colorfully and ornamentally* for a solemn occasion like this! 7._____

8. Although this sweater is marked a size 10 and that one is labeled a 12, no real difference is *able to be seen.* 8._____

9. Everyone agreed that we should proceed slowly and make the final decision *using sensible judgment.* 9._____

10. Many people thought the astronomer Copernicus's theories were *totally senseless and unbelievable.* 10._____

Exercise 11.3 Synonyms and Antonyms

Fill in the blanks in column A with the required synonyms or antonyms, selecting them from column B. (Remember: A *synonym* is a word similar in meaning to another word. An *antonym* is a word opposite in meaning to another word.)

	A	B
_____	1. antonym for *unwise*	gaudy
_____	2. synonym for *abundance*	besiege
_____	3. antonym for *immeasurable*	preposterous
_____	4. synonym for *flashy*	judicious
_____	5. antonym for *easy*	retrospection
_____	6. synonym for *picky*	appreciable
_____	7. synonym for *harass*	veritable
_____	8. synonym for *ridiculous*	laborious
_____	9. synonym for *review*	fastidious
_____	10. synonym for *genuine*	profusion

C. Journal Freewrite

Before you begin the reading on the next page, take out a journal or sheet of paper and spend some time responding to the following prompt.

TIP: Don't worry about grammar and spelling; just write what comes to mind. The purpose of freewriting is to explore ideas, not to produce a polished work.

> Imagine that you have just been given a few hundred dollars. What *should* you do with it? What *could* you do with it? What *would* you do with it? Explain your reasons.

Reading 14

A Pair of Silk Stockings

by Kate Chopin

About the Author

Kate Chopin (1850–1904) was born in Missouri when it was the gateway to the western frontier. Her father, a founder of the Pacific Railroad, died when she was five. Two years later, she lost her brother George to typhoid fever. She attended the Academy of the Sacred Heart, where she was an honor student known for her brilliant storytelling. At the age of 19, she married a cotton broker, Oscar Chopin, and had six children over the next 12 years. Her husband died when she was just 31, and she lost her mother the following year. Her disillusionment with life—and especially with women's lack of control over their own lives during her time—is evident in much of her writing.

Little Mrs. Sommers one day found herself the unexpected possessor of fifteen dollars. It seemed to her a very large amount of money, and the way in which it stuffed and bulged her worn old *porte-monnaie* gave her a feeling of importance such as she had not enjoyed for years.

The question of investment was one that occupied her greatly. For a day or two she walked about apparently in a dreamy state, but really absorbed in speculation and calculation. She did not wish to act hastily, to do anything she might afterward regret. But it was during the still hours of the night when she lay awake revolving plans in her mind that she seemed to see her way clearly toward a proper and <u>judicious</u> use of the money.

A dollar or two should be added to the price usually paid for Janie's shoes, which would insure their lasting an <u>appreciable</u> time longer than they usually did. She would buy so and so many yards of percale[1] for new shirt waists for the boys and Janie and Mag. She had intended to make the old ones do by skilful patching. Mag should have another gown. She had seen some beautiful patterns, <u>veritable</u> bargains in the shop windows. And still there would be left enough for new stockings—two pairs apiece—and what darning that would save for a while! She would get caps for the boys and sailor-hats for the girls. The vision of her little brood looking fresh and dainty and new for once in their lives excited her and made her restless and wakeful with anticipation.

The neighbors sometimes talked of certain "better days" that little Mrs. Sommers had known before she had ever thought of being Mrs. Sommers. She herself indulged in no such morbid <u>retrospection</u>. She had no time—no second of time to devote to the past. The needs of the present absorbed her every faculty.[2] A vision of the future like some dim, gaunt monster sometimes appalled her, but luckily to-morrow never comes.

---

[1] fine woven cotton cloth
[2] ability, power

Mrs. Sommers was one who knew the value of bargains; who could stand for hours making her way inch by inch toward the desired object that was selling below cost. She could elbow her way if need be; she had learned to clutch a piece of goods and hold it and stick to it with persistence and determination till her turn came to be served, no matter when it came.

But that day she was a little faint and tired. She had swallowed a light luncheon—no! when she came to think of it, between getting the children fed and the place righted, and preparing herself for the shopping bout, she had actually forgotten to eat any luncheon at all!

She sat herself upon a revolving stool before a counter that was comparatively deserted, trying to gather strength and courage to charge through an eager multitude that was besieging breast-works of shirting and figured lawn.[3] An all-gone limp feeling had come over her and she rested her hand aimlessly upon the counter. She wore no gloves. By degrees she grew aware that her hand had encountered something very soothing, very pleasant to touch. She looked down to see that her hand lay upon a pile of silk stockings. A placard near by announced that they had been reduced in price from two dollars and fifty cents to one dollar and ninety-eight cents; and a young girl who stood behind the counter asked her if she wished to examine their line of silk hosiery. She smiled, just as if she had been asked to inspect a tiara of diamonds with the ultimate view of purchasing it. But she went on feeling the soft, sheeny luxurious things—with both hands now, holding them up to see them glisten, and to feel them glide serpent-like through her fingers.

Two hectic blotches came suddenly into her pale cheeks. She looked up at the girl.

"Do you think there are any eights-and-a-half among these?"

There were any number of eights-and-a-half. In fact, there were more of that size than any other. Here was a light-blue pair; there were some lavender, some all black and various shades of tan and gray Mrs. Sommers selected a black pair and looked at them very long and closely. She pretended to be examining their texture, which the clerk assured her was excellent.

"A dollar and ninety-eight cents," she mused aloud. "Well, I'll take this pair." She handed the girl a five-dollar bill and waited for her change and for her parcel. What a very small parcel it was! It seemed lost in the depths of her shabby old shopping-bag.

Mrs. Sommers after that did not move in the direction of the bargain counter. She took the elevator, which carried her to an upper floor into the region of the ladies' waiting-rooms. Here, in a retired corner, she exchanged her cotton stockings for the new silk ones which she had just bought. She was not going through any acute mental process or reasoning with herself, nor was she striving to explain to her satisfaction the motive of her action. She was not thinking at all. She seemed for the time to be taking a rest from that laborious and fatiguing function and to have abandoned herself to

---

[3] a transparent linen or cotton fabric

some mechanical impulse that directed her actions and freed her of responsibility.

How good was the touch of the raw silk to her flesh! She felt like lying back in the cushioned chair and reveling for a while in the luxury of it. She did for a little while. Then she replaced her shoes, rolled the cotton stockings together and thrust them into her bag. After doing this she crossed straight over to the shoe department and took her seat to be fitted.

She was <u>fastidious</u>. The clerk could not make her out; he could not reconcile her shoes with her stockings, and she was not too easily pleased. She held back her skirts and turned her feet one way and her head another way as she glanced down at the polished, pointed-tipped boots. Her foot and ankle looked very pretty. She could not realize that they belonged to her and were a part of herself. She wanted an excellent and stylish fit, she told the young fellow who served her, and she did not mind the difference of a dollar or two more in the price so long as she got what she desired.

It was a long time since Mrs. Sommers had been fitted with gloves. On rare occasions when she had bought a pair they were always "bargains," so cheap that it would have been <u>preposterous</u> and unreasonable to have expected them to be fitted to the hand.

Now she rested her elbow on the cushion of the glove counter, and a pretty, pleasant young creature, delicate and deft[4] of touch, drew a long-wristed "kid"[5] over Mrs. Sommers's hand. She smoothed it down over the wrist and buttoned it neatly, and both lost themselves for a second or two in admiring contemplation of the little symmetrical gloved hand. But there were other places where money might be spent.

There were books and magazines piled up in the window of a stall a few paces down the street. Mrs. Sommers bought two high-priced magazines such as she had been accustomed to read in the days when she had been accustomed to other pleasant things. She carried them without wrapping. As well as she could she lifted her skirts at the crossings. Her stockings and boots and well fitting gloves had worked marvels in her bearing—had given her a feeling of assurance, a sense of belonging to the well-dressed multitude.

She was very hungry. Another time she would have stilled the cravings for food until reaching her own home, where she would have brewed herself a cup of tea and taken a snack of anything that was available. But the impulse that was guiding her would not suffer her to entertain any such thought.

There was a restaurant at the corner. She had never entered its doors; from the outside she had sometimes caught glimpses of spotless damask and shining crystal,[6] and soft-stepping waiters serving people of fashion.

When she entered her appearance created no surprise, no consternation, as she had half feared it might. She seated herself at a small

---

[4]skillful
[5]dress glove made of goat leather
[6]linen tablecloths and glassware

table alone, and an attentive waiter at once approached to take her order. She did not want a <u>profusion</u>; she craved a nice and tasty bite—a half dozen blue-points,[7] a plump chop with cress, a something sweet—a crème-frappée,[8] for instance; a glass of Rhine wine, and after all a small cup of black coffee.

While waiting to be served she removed her gloves very leisurely and laid them beside her. Then she picked up a magazine and glanced through it, cutting the pages with a blunt edge of her knife.[9] It was all very agreeable. The damask was even more spotless than it had seemed through the window, and the crystal more sparkling. There were quiet ladies and gentlemen, who did not notice her, lunching at the small tables like her own. A soft, pleasing strain of music could be heard, and a gentle breeze was blowing through the window. She tasted a bite, and she read a word or two, and she sipped the amber wine and wiggled her toes in the silk stockings. The price of it made no difference. She counted the money out to the waiter and left an extra coin on his tray, whereupon he bowed before her as before a princess of royal blood.

There was still money in her purse, and her next temptation presented itself in the shape of a matinée poster.

It was a little later when she entered the theatre, the play had begun and the house seemed to her to be packed. But there were vacant seats here and there, and into one of them she was ushered, between brilliantly dressed women who had gone there to kill time and eat candy and display their <u>gaudy</u> attire. There were many others who were there solely for the play and acting. It is safe to say there was no one present who bore quite the attitude which Mrs. Sommers did to her surroundings. She gathered in the whole—stage and players and people in one wide impression, and absorbed it and enjoyed it. She laughed at the comedy and wept—she and the gaudy woman next to her wept over the tragedy. And they talked a little together over it. And the gaudy woman wiped her eyes and sniffled on a tiny square of filmy, perfumed lace and passed little Mrs. Sommers her box of candy.

The play was over, the music ceased, the crowd filed out. It was like a dream ended. People scattered in all directions. Mrs. Sommers went to the corner and waited for the cable car.

A man with keen eyes, who sat opposite to her, seemed to like the study of her small, pale face. It puzzled him to decipher what he saw there. In truth, he saw nothing—unless he were wizard enough to detect a poignant wish, a powerful longing that the cable car would never stop anywhere, but go on and on with her forever.

---

[7] oysters
[8] ice cream
[9] Book and magazine pages used to be printed on folded paper, and you had to cut the folds at the outer edges.

Understanding the Reading

Complete the next three exercises and see how well you understood "A Pair of Silk Stockings."

Exercise 11.4 Multiple-Choice Questions

Answer the following questions about the reading. Circle the letter of your answer.

TIP: Don't try to answer the questions from memory; go back to the text as often as necessary.

1. Judging from context, a *porte-monnaie* (paragraph 1) is most likely a
   A. suitcase.
   B. purse.
   C. backpack.
   D. duffel bag.

2. In the second paragraph, Mrs. Sommers thinks mostly about what?
   A. all the things she will buy for herself
   B. a trip she is preparing to take
   C. how much easier her life once was
   D. all the things she will buy for her children

3. The paragraph beginning, "Mrs. Sommers after that did not move in the direction of the bargain counter," (bottom of page 230) indicates that Mrs. Sommers was
   A. trying to decide if she should take the stockings back.
   B. planning how she would spend the remaining money on herself.
   C. taking a break from having to plan her spending so carefully.
   D. trying to find a motive for her actions.

4. The narrator probably included the detail about Mrs. Sommers leaving the waiter a tip to show that Mrs. Sommers was
   A. enjoying appearing to be wealthy.
   B. a very generous woman.
   C. once a princess of royal blood.
   D. in possession of so much money she could easily give some away.

5. Mrs. Sommers's attitude toward the play is different from that of the other playgoers because
   A. she is not dressed as gaudily as the other women.
   B. it is a rare experience for her, while they are merely killing time.
   C. she laughs even though the play is a tragedy.
   D. it was the first time in months she had eaten candy.

Exercise 11.5 Short-Answer Questions

Respond to the following questions in one to two complete sentences. Go back to the text, as you did on the multiple choice.

6. In the last paragraph, Chopin writes, "It was like a dream ended." Why is this choice of words particularly appropriate at this point in the story?

   _____

   _____

   _____

7. Give an example of a simile or metaphor in this reading and explain what it shows.

   _____

   _____

   _____

8. What evidence can you find in the story that Mrs. Sommers had not always had to worry so much about money? Be specific.

   _____

   _____

   _____

9. Do you think it was all right for Mrs. Sommers to spend all the money on herself? Why or why not?

   _____

   _____

   _____

Exercise 11.6 Extending Your Thinking

Respond to the following question in three to four complete sentences. Use details from the text in your answer.

10. What is Mrs. Sommers's defining moment? What does she realize that she dared not admit to herself until that moment?

    _____

    _____

    _____

    _____

    _____

    _____

Reading Strategy Lesson
Words with Multiple Meanings

One of the more confusing things about the English language is that many of our words have more than one meaning. In the course of reading, you may frequently come across a familiar word that is confusing because it does not seem to make sense in the sentence.

Look at the following example from "A Pair of Silk Stockings":

> The needs of the present absorbed her every *faculty*.

If the only meaning you know for *faculty* is "the teachers in a school or college," then this sentence will be a mystery to you. If you know that *faculty* also means "mental ability," the meaning of the sentence is quite clear. Mrs. Sommers had been absorbed in thinking about how to spend the money—using all of her mental abilities, or *faculties*.

Other examples whose meanings are footnoted in the selection are *lawn* and *kid*. What do you think of first when you hear or see these two words? Most of us think of an expanse of grass and a small child. Looking back at the footnotes, how are the words used in this selection?

When you run across a familiar word used in an unfamiliar way, you can use context to determine its meaning or you can look it up. Either way, the next time you see it used in this second (or third, or fourth) way, you'll recognize which meaning the author intends and your comprehension will improve.

Exercise 11.7 Practice the Reading Strategy

The familiar words below are used in the selection. In column A, write the meaning the author intended for the word in this story. In column B, write another meaning for the word. The first one has been done for you.

Word	A	B
1. bout (p. 230)	trip	boxing match
2. retired (p. 230)		
3. charge (p. 230)		
4. speculation (p. 229)		
5. reconcile (p. 231)		
6. study (p. 232)		

Exercise 11.8 Apply the Reading Strategy

In each sentence, a familiar word is used in an unfamiliar way. On the blank line, write a brief definition or synonym of the italicized word as it is used in the sentence.

1. Mr. Johnson said he would take my ideas into *account*.

   _____

2. Copper is a good *conductor* of electricity.

   _____

3. This brick chimney *draws* well.

   _____

4. She has a very *dry* sense of humor.

   _____

5. He was the best tight *end* the team had ever had.

   _____

6. The *gravity* of this situation cannot be overemphasized.

   _____

7. I'll *mat* the painting and get it framed.

   _____

8. The Chilkoot *Pass* was the hardest part of the Klondike Trail.

   _____

9. The *report* of the cannon was deafening.

   _____

10. The wide *sweep* of prairie extended as far as the settlers could see.

    _____

Writing Workshop
Using Direct Quotations

One way to make your essays more interesting and effective is to use quotations from the story, article, or other selection about which you are writing. Question 8 in "Understanding the Reading" says:

> What evidence can you find in the story that Mrs. Sommers had not always had to worry so much about money? Be specific.

This question asks you to find *evidence*. That means you should look for some passages in the story that you can quote directly and use as your evidence. Your answer to this question might read:

> In "A Pair of Silk Stockings," Chopin says, "The neighbors sometimes talked of certain 'better days' that little Mrs. Sommers had known before she had ever thought of being Mrs. Sommers." This indicates that Mrs. Sommers was better off before she got married, although we are not told exactly what the problem is. We do know that now she is "one who knew the value of bargains." She will stand in line for a long time in order to get one. Later in the story, Chopin tells us, "It was a long time since Mrs. Sommers had been fitted with gloves" and that she "bought two high-priced magazines such as she had been accustomed to read in the days when she had been accustomed to other pleasant things." Clearly, when Mrs. Sommers was younger, she did not have to worry so much about money.

Four things to notice and remember:

1. The title of the story is enclosed in quotation marks. (Titles of short stories and poems are usually surrounded by quotation marks. If you were quoting from a book, however, you would underline or italicize the title.)

2. The quotation marks go only around material that is *directly* quoted from the story.

3. If the quoted material begins with a capital letter in the selection, the capital letter remains in the quotation:

> Chopin says, "The neighbors sometimes talked of certain 'better days' that little Mrs. Sommers had known before she had ever thought of being Mrs. Sommers."

4. Information from the story that is used as evidence in an essay question but is not directly quoted should not be enclosed in quotation marks:

> *She will stand in line for a long time in order to get one* is information from the story, but not a direct quotation, so it is not enclosed in quotation marks.

Exercise 11.9 Practice the Writing Lesson

The following is part of an essay on character motivation in "A Pair of Silk Stockings." Punctuate the title and direct quotations correctly.

> On the day described in A Pair of Silk Stockings, Mrs.
> Sommers does not act as the reader expects her to. We are told
> that she lay awake revolving plans in her mind before she

decided on a proper and judicious use of the money. She had planned to spend it all on clothes for her children and was excited by the vision of her little brood looking fresh and dainty and new for once in their lives. At this point in the story, Mrs. Sommers seems to be motivated by motherly concern and pride.

She sets out on a shopping bout, a word that implies fighting rather than a pleasurable trip, and tries to gather strength and courage to charge through an eager multitude that was besieging breastworks of shirting and figured lawn. It is then, sitting at the counter, that she touches the silk stockings, and an all-gone limp feeling comes over her. After the daring act of buying herself the stockings, the motivation for the shopping trip changes. For once, she is going to enjoy herself.

Exercise 11.10 Apply the Writing Lesson

On a separate sheet of paper, answer the short-essay question that follows. Include at least two direct quotations and one piece of information from the story that is not a direct quotation but still offers evidence for your answer.

What evidence can you find that Mrs. Sommers's lunch at the restaurant is a very special occasion for her?

Grammar Mini-Lesson
Common Usage Problems

You've learned that many words have more than one meaning and that you can improve your reading comprehension by recognizing the meaning an author intends. Likewise, there are words whose meanings are often confused. You can improve your writing by being careful to use these words correctly.

The table on the next page will help you learn the differences in meaning and spelling of commonly misused words.

Commonly Misused Words	
accept, except	To *accept* is to agree to something or to receive something. *Except* means something is left out. *Except* can also be used in place of *but.*
advice, advise	You *advise* someone. What you give him or her is *advice.*
a lot	This is two words. Do not spell it as one (*alot*).
allusion, illusion	An *allusion* a reference to something. An *illusion* is a figment of your imagination.
among, between	*Among* refers to a group of three or more ("*among* the students in our class"). *Between* refers to two people or two groups ("*between* you and me").
beside, besides	*Beside* means "at the side of." *Besides* means "in addition to."
fewer, less	*Fewer* describes things that can be counted. (There are *fewer* than five shirts in my closet.) *Less* is used when referring to a quantity or degree of something. (I like him *less* and *less.*)
formerly, formally	*Formerly* means "before" or "previously." *Formally* means in a formal way. (*Formerly* people could not dress *formally* for weddings if they had only one set of clothes.)
further, farther	Use *farther* when comparing distances and *further* for anything else. (Brady can kick the ball *farther* than he ever has before. Now if only he would worry more about *furthering* his education.)
hopefully	When you write "Hopefully, the author will write another book soon," you're saying the author is full of hope. Instead, say "I hope the author writes another book soon."
imply, infer	You *infer* something from what you read or hear. The writer or speaker is *implying* what you are *inferring.*
irregardless	Don't use this. Just use *regardless,* or you will be writing the opposite of what you really mean.
proceed, precede	*Proceed* means "to go forward." *Precede* means "to go ahead of." (The faculty *preceded* the students as they all *proceeded* into the auditorium for graduation.)
whether, weather	*Whether* is the word to use in phrases like "whether or not," while *weather* refers to things like rain, sunshine, and temperature.

Exercise 11.11 Practice Using the Correct Word or Phrase

For each sentence, write the correct choice on the line.

1. I'd like to (except, accept) _____ his gift, (except, accept) _____ I feel it is too expensive.

2. I'm not sure (whether, weather) _____ the (weather, whether) _____ will cooperate with our plans to eat outside.

3. (Hopefully, I hope) _____ my GPA will improve.

4. I'm not sure what you are trying to (imply, infer) _____. Am I (implying, inferring) _____ correctly?

5. (Regardless, Irregardless) _____, I'm going to the dance.

6. (Proceed, Precede) _____ with caution—someone (proceeded, preceded) _____ us.

7. You can choose (among, between) _____ fish, chicken, and pasta, and (among, between) _____ pie and ice cream.

8. Magicians are masters of (allusion, illusion) _____.

9. (Formerly, Formally) _____ she was living in a small farming town where people rarely dress (formerly, formally) _____ for dinner.

10. You have (fewer, less) _____ math problems than I do, so your homework will take (fewer, less) _____ time.

Exercise 11.12 Apply the Lesson to Revise a Paragraph

Read the following paragraph. Circle the misused words and write in the correct forms.

Weather you realize it or not, I implied from your speech that you are not very enthusiastic about the testing program. You have not really excepted it as the way to measure how much our students are learning. I don't have any allusions about how well our school will do. Hopefully, our students will do well and we can precede with our other learning tasks as we did formally. Irregardless, the testing program is here to stay.

Polish Your Spelling

-ABLE or -IBLE?

1. You can be sure that an adjective ends in *-able* rather than *-ible* if you can trace it to a noun ending in *-ation*:

Noun	Adjective
adoration	adorable
adaptation	adaptable
alteration	alterable
commendation	commendable
imagination	imaginable
irritation	irritable
presentation	presentable

(*Exception: sensation → sensible*)

2. Many adjectives have no *-ation* nouns to which they can be traced, yet they end in *-able*. Here are some to review.

Commonly Used -ABLE Adjectives

accountable	advisable	available	believable
changeable	charitable	comfortable	comparable
conceivable	consumable	debatable	dependable
desirable	despicable	disposable	excusable
favorable	hospitable	incurable	inevitable
manageable	memorable	miserable	objectionable
perishable	predictable	profitable	reasonable

3. When you add *-ible* to a noun, look for the "*ib*" in the noun or in a related word that you know how to spell. Also, study this list of commonly used *-ible* adjectives.

Commonly Used -IBLE Adjectives

accessible	audible	collapsible	contemptible
digestible	divisible	edible	eligible
feasible	flexible	forcible	horrible
incredible	indefensible	indelible	inexhaustible
intelligible	invincible	invisible	irresistible
legible	negligible	permissible	plausible
possible	responsible	sensible	tangible

Exercise 11.13 Practice the Spelling Patterns: -ABLE or -IBLE?

Add -*able* or -*ible* to form the correctly spelled adjective.

	-ABLE OR -IBLE	ADJECTIVE
Example:	invis_____	invisible
1.	exhaust_____	_____
2.	unreason_____	_____
3.	unmanage_____	_____
4.	irresist_____	_____
5.	dispos_____	_____
6.	plaus_____	_____
7.	account_____	_____
8.	inhospit_____	_____
9.	forc_____	_____
10.	inflex_____	_____

Chapter Twelve

Prereading Guide
Words to know and ideas to consider before you jump into the reading.

A. Essential Vocabulary

Word	Meaning	Typical Use
admonition (*n*) ad-mun-ISH-un	a mild scolding or reprimand; warning	We were sorry we had ignored Mom's *admonition* to wear our scarves and boots.
aspect (*n*) AS-pekt	a characteristic, part, or feature of something; element	Huge bodies of water are only one *aspect* of the Great Lakes area.
engender (*v*) en-JEN-dur	to create or cause to be created; produce	He *engendered* considerable suspicion when his crimes came to light.
infirm (*adj*) in-FIRM	weak or feeble, particularly from old age; ill	Nursing homes are filled with people who are *infirm*.
luxuriant (*adj*) lug-ZHUR-ee-unt	growing abundantly; lush	The first thing you notice about Savannah is her *luxuriant* black hair.
nomadic (*adj*) no-MAD-ik	moving frequently from one home to another; migratory	Many early native tribes in America were *nomadic*, moving to various places where food was plentiful for a time.
preeminent (*adj*) pre-EM-ih-nunt	exceeding others in importance; leading	Dr. Foster is *preeminent* in the field of computer systems analysts.
tenuous (*adj*) TEN-yoo-us	without much support or strength; shaky or insubstantial	The two neighbors had a *tenuous* relationship, arguing constantly over noise and pets.
unrelenting (*adj*) un-re-LENT-ing	continuous and determined; unyielding	During rush hour, the traffic on the freeway is *unrelenting*.
writhe (*v*) RYTH	to twist and turn in pain or embarrassment; squirm	I told myself that when I got the tetanus shot, I would not *writhe* and whine.

B. Vocabulary Practice

Exercise 12.1 Sentence Completion

Using your new vocabulary knowledge, choose the best way to complete the following sentences. Circle the letter of your answer.

1. My grandmother needs _____ because she is infirm.
   A. a lot of help
   B. no help

2. _____ are aspects of large cities.
   A. General stores
   B. Skyscrapers and mass-transit systems

3. In the seventh inning, we had a tenuous _____ the opposing team.
   A. stretch with
   B. lead over

4. When my father introduced me as his _____, I writhed in embarrassment.
   A. baby girl
   B. youngest daughter

5. _____ grow luxuriantly in Hawaii.
   A. Beaches
   B. Flowers

6. Fans of rap say it engenders _____.
   A. pride and self-improvement
   B. violence and apathy

7. I gave my little brother an admonition for _____.
   A. doing well on his math quiz
   B. not staying out of my room

8. By February in Maine, it seems as if _____ are unrelenting.
   A. blueberries
   B. snowstorms

9. The preeminent reason for settlers to move west was _____.
   A. free or cheap land
   B. having enough space to keep horses

10. Many birds fly _____ in spring and fall in a nomadic pattern.
    A. from tree to tree
    B. north or south

Exercise 12.2 Using Fewer Words

Replace the italicized words with a single word from the following list.

admonition aspect   engendered infirm   luxuriant

nomadic   preeminent   tenuous   unrelentingly writhing

1. She wasn't really angry, but she made sure   1._____
   we listened to her *mild scolding*.

2. *Twisting and turning in pain*, I held my   2._____
   breath while the doctor examined my
   sprained ankle.

3. One *characteristic, part, or feature* of the   3._____
   beaches on summer weekends is that they
   are crowded with all sorts of people.

4. When there is money at stake, alliances on   4._____
   reality shows are *without much support or
   strength*.

5. It was splendid driving through Yellowstone   5._____
   and seeing the *abundantly growing* trees,
   flowers, and grasses.

6. Images of September 11 on the news *caused*   6._____
   to be created a desire in people all over the
   world to help New Yorkers recover.

7. *Continuously and with determination*, my   7._____
   little sister plays a very annoying video game.

8. Rio de Janeiro is Brazil's *exceedingly*   8._____
   important urban center.

9. The Masai who live in southern Kenya are   9._____
   herders who are *frequently moving from
   one place to another*.

10. If you are *weak and feeble*, everyday tasks   10._____
    become huge accomplishments.

Exercise 12.3 Synonyms and Antonyms

Fill in the blanks in column A with the required synonyms or antonyms, selecting them from column B. (Remember: A *synonym* is a word similar in meaning to another word. An *antonym* is a word opposite in meaning to another word.)

A		B
_____	1. synonym for *squirm*	engender
_____	2. synonym for *element*	nomadic
_____	3. antonym for *yielding*	aspect
_____	4. synonym for *insubstantial*	infirm
_____	5. antonym for *sparse*	writhe
_____	6. synonym for *produce*	preeminent
_____	7. synonym for *migratory*	admonition
_____	8. antonym for *healthy*	unrelenting
_____	9. synonym for *leading*	tenuous
_____	10. synonym for *warning*	luxuriant

C. Journal Freewrite

Before you begin the reading on the next page, take out a journal or sheet of paper and spend some time responding to the following prompt.

TIP: Don't worry about grammar and spelling; just write what comes to mind. The purpose of freewriting is to explore ideas, not to produce a polished work.

People of all cultures have myths, legends, and folktales that are passed down from one generation to the next. What purpose is served by keeping these stories alive? Include your own anecdotes from family or friends if you wish.

from The Way to Rainy Mountain

by N. Scott Momaday

About the Author
N. Scott Momaday
(1934–) was born
"Navarro Scott
Mammedaty" in
Oklahoma in the heart
of Kiowa country. His
parents, both teachers,
worked in different
cities in the Southwest,
exposing him to Navajo,
San Carlos Apache, and
Hispanic cultures. In his
own words, he "fell in
love" with both English
and Spanish words. This
led him to a PhD in
English from Stanford.
He is regarded as one of
the most important
Native American writers
and was the first to be
widely read. He taught
at Berkeley, Stanford,
and the University of
Arizona. His poetry and
fiction make use of his
multicultural back-
ground. This selection is
part of his introduction
to his Pulitzer Prize-win-
ning novel, *The Way to
Rainy Mountain.*

A single knoll rises out of the plain in Oklahoma, north and west of the Wichita Range. For my people, the Kiowas, it is an old landmark, and they gave it the name Rainy Mountain. The hardest weather in the world is there. Winter brings blizzards, hot tornadic winds arise in the spring, and in summer the prairie is an anvil's edge. The grass turns brittle and brown, and it cracks beneath your feet. There are green belts along the rivers and creeks, linear groves of hickory and pecan, willow and witch hazel. At a distance in July or August the steaming foliage seems almost to <u>writhe</u> in fire. Great green and yellow grasshoppers are everywhere in the tall grass, popping up like corn to sting the flesh, and tortoises crawl about on the red earth, going nowhere in the plenty of time. Loneliness is an <u>aspect</u> of the land. All things in the plain are isolated; there is no confusion of objects in the eye, but *one* hill or *one* tree or *one* man. To look upon that landscape in the early morning, with the sun at your back, is to lose the sense of proportion. Your imagination comes to life, and this, you think, is where Creation was begun.

I returned to Rainy Mountain in July. My grandmother had died in the spring, and I wanted to be at her grave. She had lived to be very old and at last <u>infirm</u>. Her only living daughter was with her when she died, and I was told that in death her face was that of a child.

I like to think of her as a child. When she was born, the Kiowas were living the last great moment of their history. For more than a hundred years they had controlled the open range from the Smoky Hill River to the Red, from the headwaters of the Canadian to the fork of the Arkansas and Cimarron. In alliance with the Comanches, they had ruled the whole of the southern Plains. War was their sacred business, and they were among the finest horsemen the world has ever known. But warfare for the Kiowas was <u>preeminently</u> a matter of disposition[1] rather than of survival, and they never understood the grim, <u>unrelenting</u> advance of the U.S.

---

[1]natural character and temperament

Cavalry. When at last, divided and ill-provisioned, they were driven onto the Staked Plains in the cold rains of autumn, they fell into panic. In Palo Duro Canyon they abandoned their crucial stores to pillage[2] and had nothing then but their lives. In order to save themselves, they surrendered to the soldiers at Fort Sill[3] and were imprisoned in the old stone corral that now stands as a military museum. My grandmother was spared the humiliation of those high gray walls by eight or ten years, but she must have known from birth the affliction of defeat, the dark brooding of old warriors.

Her name was Aho, and she belonged to the last culture to evolve in North America. Her forebears came down from the high country in western Montana nearly three centuries ago. They were a mountain people, a mysterious tribe of hunters whose language has never been positively classified in any major group. In the late seventeenth century they began a long migration to the south and east. It was a journey toward the dawn, and it led to a golden age. Along the way the Kiowas were befriended by the Crows, who gave them the culture and religion of the Plains. They acquired horses, and their ancient <u>nomadic</u> spirit was suddenly free of the ground. They acquired Tai-me, the sacred Sun Dance doll, from that moment the object and symbol of their worship, and so shared in the divinity of the sun. Not least, they acquired the sense of destiny, therefore courage and pride. When they entered upon the southern Plains they had been transformed. No longer were they slaves to the simple necessity of survival; they were a lordly and dangerous society of fighters and thieves, hunters and priests of the sun. According to their origin myth, they entered the world through a hollow log. From one point of view, their migration was the fruit of an old prophecy, for indeed they emerged from a sunless world.

Although my grandmother lived out her long life in the shadow of Rainy Mountain, the immense landscape of the continental interior lay like memory in her blood. She could tell of the Crows, whom she had never seen, and of the Black Hills, where she had never been. I wanted to see in reality what she had seen more perfectly in the mind's eye, and traveled fifteen hundred miles to begin my pilgrimage.

Yellowstone, it seemed to me, was the top of the world, a region of deep lakes and dark timber, canyons and waterfalls. But, beautiful as it is, one might have the sense of confinement there. The skyline in all directions is close at hand, the high wall of the woods and deep cleavages of shade. There is a perfect freedom in the mountains, but it belongs to the eagle and the elk, the badger and the bear. The Kiowas reckoned their stature by the distance they could see, and they were bent and blind in the wilderness.

Descending eastward, the highland meadows are a stairway to the plain. In July the inland slope of the Rockies is <u>luxuriant</u> with flax and buckwheat, stonecrop and larkspur. The earth unfolds and the limit of the land recedes. Clusters of trees, and animals grazing

---

[2]looting and theft
[3]the U.S. Army fort in Oklahoma

far in the distance, cause the vision to reach away and wonder to build upon the mind. The sun follows a longer course in the day, and the sky is immense beyond all comparison. The great billowing clouds that sail upon it are shadows that move upon the grain like water, dividing light. Farther down, in the land of the Crows and Blackfeet, the plain is yellow. Sweet clover takes hold of the hills and bends upon itself to cover and seal the soil. There the Kiowas paused on their way; they had come to the place where they must change their lives. The sun is at home on the plains. Precisely there does it have the certain character of a god. When the Kiowas came to the land of the Crows, they could see the dark lees of the hills at dawn across the Bighorn River, the profusion of light on the grain shelves, the oldest deity ranging after the solstices.[4] Not yet would they veer southward to the caldron of the land that lay below; they must wean their blood from the northern winter and hold the mountains a while longer in their view. They bore Tai-me in procession to the east.

A dark mist lay over the Black Hills, and the land was like iron. At the top of a ridge I caught sight of Devil's Tower upthrust against the gray sky as if in the birth of time the core of the earth had broken through its crust and the motion of the world was begun. There are things in nature that <u>engender</u> an awful quiet in the heart of man; Devil's Tower is one of them. Two centuries ago, because they could not do otherwise, the Kiowas made a legend at the base of the rock. My grandmother said:

> Eight children were there at play, seven sisters and their brother. Suddenly the boy was struck dumb; he trembled and began to run upon his hands and feet. His fingers became claws, and his body was covered with fur. Directly there was a bear where the boy had been. The sisters were terrified; they ran, and the bear after them. They came to the stump of a great tree, and the tree spoke to them. It bade them climb upon it, and as they did so it began to rise into the air. The bear came to kill them, but they were just beyond its reach. It reared against the tree and scored the bark all around with its claws. The seven sisters were borne into the sky, and they became the stars of the Big Dipper.

From that moment, and so long as the legend lives, the Kiowas have kinsmen in the night sky. Whatever they were in the mountains, they could be no more. However <u>tenuous</u> their well-being, however much they had suffered and would suffer again, they had found a way out of the wilderness.

---

[4]the two times of the year when the sun is farthest north of the equator (around June 22) or farthest south (about December 22). In North America, they represent the longest and shortest days of the year.

Understanding the Reading

Complete the next three exercises and see how well you understood the excerpt from *The Way to Rainy Mountain.*

Exercise 12.4 Multiple-Choice Questions

Answer the following questions about the reading. Circle the letter of your answer.

TIP: Don't try to answer the questions from memory; go back to the text as often as necessary.

1. The selection is told in what point of view?
   A. third person omniscient
   B. first person
   C. third person limited
   D. second person

2. The author made the journey from Yellowstone to Rainy Mountain because
   A. he wanted to visit his grandmother's grave.
   B. he wanted to trace his ancestors' pilgrimage.
   C. Rainy Mountain was the place his grandmother had always lived.
   D. all of these.

3. What ended the Kiowas' "golden age"?
   A. They had no choice but to surrender to the U.S. Cavalry.
   B. They were bent and blind in the wilderness.
   C. They left the mountains for the plains.
   D. The Crows defeated them.

4. The Kiowa people gave the knoll in Oklahoma the name "Rainy Mountain" because
   A. they believed it was where Creation began.
   B. it always seemed to be raining on the misty mountaintop.
   C. the people felt gloomy when they were forced to move there.
   D. the weather there is extremely hard.

Exercise 12.5 Short-Answer Questions

Respond to the following questions in one to two complete sentences. Go back to the text, as you did on the multiple choice.

5. Give an example of Momaday's figurative language and explain how it helps you picture the scene.

_____

_____

_____

6. What are the Smoky Hill, the Red, the Canadian, the Arkansas, and the Cimarron? Why were they important to the Kiowa and the Comanche?

_____

_____

_____

7. What significance might this selection have for today's Kiowa children and teens?

_____

_____

_____

Exercise 12.6 Extending Your Thinking

Respond to the following question in three to four complete sentences. Use details from the text in your answer.

8. Explain how Momaday's retracing of his ancestors' journey helped him to define who he was.

_____

_____

_____

_____

_____

_____

_____

Journal Freewrite

Before you begin the second reading in this chapter, take out a journal or sheet of paper and spend some time responding to the following prompt.

TIP: Don't worry about grammar and spelling; just write what comes to mind. The purpose of freewriting is to explore ideas, not to produce a polished work.

Suppose you are moving from the country to the city, or vice versa. What will you miss most about your present life? What will make the change easier for you?

Sparrow's Sleep

by M. L. Smoker

About the Author

M. L. Smoker (1975–) is a member of both the Assiniboine and Sioux tribes, and currently works for the Indian Education Division of the Office of Public Instruction in Montana. Her first book of poems, *Another Attempt at Rescue*, won national acclaim, and she was invited to read her poetry at the Smithsonian Institution's National Museum of the American Indian. Smoker received the Richard Hugo Scholarship at the University of Montana and the Arianna and Hannah Yellow Thunder Scholarship at UCLA. In an interview with *The Great Falls Tribune*, she said, "Poems hold a special kind of power. They give people a lot of room to explore their emotions and their heart." Her poetry draws on the landscape, her relationships with her family and friends, and her native heritage.

As a child she would trouble herself each bedtime over the hours. Her father, who built her a bed of five mattresses stacked one on top of the other, would say *you don't have to worry about those things*. But she could never fully believe him and she could never stop herself from counting, well into the night, anxious over the school nurse's <u>admonition</u>: *at least eight hours, healthy children need at least eight hours*. And she wanted to be like all of the other kids. She wanted a horse and her old house back and all of the family they had left behind in that small reservation town. It was soon after they left that she refused to sleep on any bed that had a frame lifting it from the ground—something about all that empty space being too much like the hours spent hovering over the road in their Dodge as they drove farther and farther away. An hour, then two, then sometimes three would pass and eventually her father would come to sit quietly in a chair in the corner of the room. Only then could she lose track of the restless addition and subtraction, of the distance between one place, one life and another.

Understanding the Reading

Complete the next three exercises and see how well you understood "Sparrow's Sleep."

Exercise 12.7 Multiple-Choice Questions

Answer the following questions about the reading. Circle the letter of your answer.

TIP: Don't try to answer the questions from memory; go back to the text as often as necessary.

1. "As a child, she would trouble herself each bedtime over the hours" is a reference to
   A. Sparrow's feeling that her bedtime was too early.
   B. the hours spent riding from the reservation to Sparrow's new home.
   C. the school nurse's warning that children need eight hours of sleep.
   D. the hours Sparrow's father sat with her.

2. Sparrow's father told her *"you don't have to worry about those things"* most likely because he
   A. knew it was past her bedtime and wanted her to go to sleep.
   B. wanted her to stop worrying about the family left behind.
   C. thought the school nurse was wrong.
   D. didn't want her to be like all of the other kids.

3. Sparrow refused to sleep in a bed with space beneath it because
   A. she was afraid monsters were hiding under the bed.
   B. it reminded her too much of the trip away from the reservation.
   C. she was used to sleeping on the floor.
   D. she wanted to defy her parents.

4. Which of the following best states the message of this poem?
   A. Children should never be moved from one home to another.
   B. Children should get plenty of sleep.
   C. Moving from one kind of life to another can be traumatic for a child.
   D. If a little girl wants a horse, she should have one.

Exercise 12.8 Short-Answer Questions

Respond to the following questions in one to two complete sentences. Go back to the text, as you did on the multiple choice.

5. What would be another appropriate title for this poem? Why?

_____

_____

_____

6. How does Sparrow's sense of place influence her feelings?

_____

_____

_____

7. How is Sparrow's dilemma similar to that of immigrants who come to the United States?

_____

_____

_____

Exercise 12.9 Extending Your Thinking

Respond to the following question in three to four complete sentences. Use details from the text in your answer.

8. Sparrow experienced a difficult kind of defining moment, or change. When do you think it occurred? Explain.

_____

_____

_____

_____

_____

_____

Reading Strategy Lesson
How to Read a Poem

Have you ever read a poem and thought, "I have no idea what this is about"? Almost every reader of poetry has thought that, especially upon first reading a poem. Poets choose their words carefully for meaning, sound, and even look. A reader who works just as carefully can begin to answer the question, "What might this poem mean?" Here are some techniques for reading poetry.

1. Read the title. What does it suggest about the poem you are about to read? In the selection you have just read, "Sparrow's Sleep," the title suggests that the poem is about sleeping. A sparrow is a small bird, and perhaps a light sleeper. Reading on, you understand that Sparrow is a girl. Does the image of a small bird shape your impression of the girl?

2. Read aloud if possible. The first time you read a poem, it helps to read it aloud or listen to someone else reading it. Since most poems are short enough for you to read them a number of times, you do not have to think about *every* aspect of a poem the first time you read it. Read slowly and thoughtfully to get a feel for the poem. How would you describe the mood or tone of "Sparrow's Sleep"?

3. Look at the poem's structure. How is it built? Are there parts or sections? "Sparrow's Sleep" has only one section or stanza, which is written in free verse, that is, with no pattern of rhyme. The first line is indented and the poem reads like a very short story. How does this structure add to the poem's message?

4. Read according to the poem's punctuation. Pause or stop at the end of a line only if there is punctuation there that says you should. If there is a comma, pause briefly. A semicolon or colon indicates a longer pause. A period, question mark, or exclamation point tells you to come to a complete stop. No punctuation at the end of a line means that you go on reading to the next line without pause. "Sparrow's Sleep" is written as a paragraph, so reading according to the punctuation may be easier than with other poems you will encounter.

> As a child she would trouble herself each bedtime (continue) / over the hours. (full stop) Her father, (short pause) who built her a bed of five (continue) / mattresses stacked one on top of the other, (short pause) would say (continue) / *you don't have to worry about those things*. (full stop)

5. Look back at the poem to see what stands out. Different things will stand out to different readers; notice what elements of the poem capture your attention. What words, phrases, images, or ideas catch your eye when reading the poem? Exploring the meaning of these captivating details can illuminate the poet's intended meaning.

One striking image in "Sparrow's Sleep" is the bed made of "five mattresses stacked one on top of the other." This image may remind some readers of the fairy tale "The Princess and the Pea," in which only the real princess is sensitive enough to feel the pea placed under many mattresses. Like the princess, Sparrow is very sensitive. The move from her home has deeply affected her.

You probably noticed the repetition of the word "hours" in "Sparrow's Sleep." Look again at all the places where the word appears. What are the different hours mentioned in the poem? Why are hours so important to Sparrow?

What is another detail of the poem that captured your attention?

What does that detail reveal?

6. Paraphrase the poem. Restate what the poem presents in your own words. While writing, think about your impression of the title, your response to the first reading, your observations about the poem's structure, and the understanding you gained by exploring the poem's details.

Exercise 12.10 Practice the Reading Strategy

Reread "Sparrow's Sleep," on your own or with a partner, per your teacher's guidelines. Go through the six strategies outlined above. Write your paraphrase of the poem on a separate sheet of paper.

Exercise 12.11 Apply the Reading Strategy to a New Poem

Work with a small group. Two people in the group should take turns reading the poem "The New Colossus" aloud, following the rules for reading according to punctuation. Be sure to read the note about the poet. Then discuss the title and speaker, examine the structure, and think about the elements of the poem that stand out to you. Look up words or references you don't understand. Take notes as you discuss what the poem means. Finally, write a one-paragraph paraphrase of the poem on your own.

Emma Lazarus was a Jewish-American poet who envisioned the Statue of Liberty as a symbol of hope for the thousands of immigrants who came to America each year in search of better lives. This poem is inscribed on the pedestal of the statue.

The New Colossus
by Emma Lazarus

Not like the brazen giant of Greek fame,
With conquering limbs astride from land to land,
Here at our sea-washed, sunset gates shall stand
A mighty woman with a torch, whose flame
Is the imprisoned lightning, and her name

Mother of Exiles. From her beacon-hand

Glows world-wide welcome; her mild eyes command
The air-bridged harbor that twin cities frame.
"Keep, ancient lands, your storied pomp!" cries she
With silent lips. "Give me your tired, your poor,
Your huddled masses yearning to breathe free,
The wretched refuse of your teeming shore.
Send these, the homeless, tempest-tossed to me,
I lift my lamp beside the golden door!"

Writing Workshop

Found Poems

Many students of N. Scott Momaday's writing have called him a "prose poet." This means that although his writing is technically prose, it is so lyrical and expressive that it reads like poetry.

Here is a short passage from *The Way to Rainy Mountain*, presented as a poem:

>At a distance in July or August
>the steaming foliage seems almost to writhe in fire.
>Great green and yellow grasshoppers
>are everywhere in the tall grass,
>popping up like corn
>to sting the flesh,
>and tortoises crawl about on the red earth,
>going nowhere
>in plenty of time.

Exercise 12.12 Practice the Writing Lesson

Choose another passage from *The Way to Rainy Mountain*. On a separate sheet of paper, lay out the words as a poem. Check your poem by reading it out loud. How does it sound? Play with the lines and words until you feel that the phrasing is just right. Then write your final poem and share it with the class.

Finding Your Own Poems

Found poems don't have to come from spectacular literature. You can find them almost anywhere. Take this one, fashioned from a real estate ad:

>**Dream Home**
>Granddaddy oaks line the winding drive
>that leads to this country estate.
>Four bedrooms, three baths,
>a barn and a pond
>on five wooded acres,
>a fabulous place
>to entertain friends or just enjoy
>all the space.

Exercise 12.13 Apply the Writing Lesson

Look for a piece of writing that you can make into a poem. Play with the lines and words until you like the way it sounds when you read it aloud. Write your final draft and share the result with your classmates.

Grammar Mini-Lesson

Misplaced Modifiers

What Is a Modifier?

To *modify* means to limit or change something. You might modify your vacation plans because you run out of money. If you've rearranged the furniture in your bedroom or added some new posters to the wall, you've modified the room.

In language, adjectives and adverbs are **modifiers**. They describe, explain, or tell how much or in what way. Adjective and adverb phrases are also modifiers. In the following examples, the modifying word or phrase is underlined. The arrow points to the word or group of words it modifies.

Leslie Marmon Silko, a Native American writer, is best known for her novel, *Ceremony*.

Tired after a long walk, Lindsay took a nap.

My cats are both black.

Where is the computer to be repaired?

Exercise 12.14 Practice Identifying Modifiers

Following the previous examples, draw a line under the modifier and an arrow to the word or word group that it modifies.

1. The school play was a sensational success.

2. I like him even though he is bossy at times.

3. John Sutter, a California settler, found gold at his mill.

4. The children with muddy boots should take them off at the door.

5. This economic recovery plan is sensible and necessary.

6. The city is suffering from a housing shortage.

7. Dominic was managing the store by himself.

8. A priceless painting was stolen from the museum.

9. Strikers circling the plant assured that no one got past them.

10. Tofu is becoming more popular.

Misplaced Modifiers

A **misplaced modifier** makes a sentence illogical or confusing because of where it is placed in the sentence.

Example:
> A can of soda sat on the desk that Jessica had been drinking.

It sounds as if Jessica had been drinking the desk! How can we fix the sentence?

> Jessica had been drinking soda from the can that sat on the desk.

To decide if a modifier is misplaced, draw an arrow to the nearest word it could modify. Does it make sense? If it does not, the modifier is probably misplaced.

Consider this sentence with a misplaced modifier:

> Walking down the road, the hot asphalt burned our bare feet.

It sounds as if the hot asphalt was walking down the road. To make it clear that this was not the case, we can reword the sentence:

> The hot asphalt burned our bare feet as we walked down the road.

To make your sentences say what you mean, place your modifying words and phrases as close as possible to what they modify. Here's another example:

> The boy was driving the car with a baggy T-shirt.

Have you ever seen a car wearing a baggy T-shirt? Put the boy and his T-shirt closer together:

> The boy in the baggy T-shirt was driving the car.

Exercise 12.15 Correcting Misplaced Modifiers

The following sentences contain misplaced modifiers. Rewrite each sentence to clarify the meaning.

1. Many people are sentenced by judges who may be innocent.

   _____

   _____

2. The rush-hour commuters headed for the trains with frowns.

   _____

   _____

3. The Congress voted not to drill for oil in the Arctic Refuge recently.

   _____

   _____

4. Requiring too many repairs, I sold my old car.

   _____

   _____

5. Looking at the girl's palm, her future was told by the psychic.

   _____

   _____

6. Racing down the field, we watched the receiver catch the ball in the end zone.

   _____

   _____

7. Unlike black bears, people who camp in Alaska must realize grizzlies can be aggressive.

   _____

   _____

8. Running out of gas, the storm forced many to stay put who should have evacuated.

   _____

   _____

9. Farmers were hurt by severe drought throughout the Midwest.

   _____

   _____

10. Jorge solves our technical problems, who is good with computers.

    _____

    _____

Polish Your Spelling
100 Spelling Demons

Nearly everyone has difficulty spelling certain words in the English language. That is why there is only one winner in the National Spelling Bee! The 100 words on the list below are among the most commonly misspelled words.

accidentally	accommodate	achieve	acknowledge
acquire	aerial	aggravate	appropriate
argument	assassin	athlete	bachelor
because	beginning	benefited	bureau
business	category	chaos	chief
colleagues	commemorate	commission	commitment
committee	comparative	compatible	competent
conscious	correspondence	courteous	criticism
desperate	deterrent	disappoint	disastrous
dissatisfied	efficient	eight	embarrass
environment	equipped	especially	essential
exception	exercise	extraordinary	fascinate
February	foreign	forty	friends
gauge	government	guardian	harass
height	history	hypocrisy	illiterate
illuminate	immediately	immigrant	incidentally
independent	Internet	irrelevant	irreparable
irresistible	judgment	knowledge	livelihood
maintenance	medicine	miniature	necessary
negotiable	neighbor	noticeable	occasional
occurrence	omission	parallel	privilege
rhythm	scholastic	scissors	seize
separate	strategy	tendency	truly
twelfth	unconscious	usually	valuable
view	Wednesday	weird	withhold

Exercise 12.16 Create a Personal Spelling List

After reading the list of spelling demons, go back and circle the 20 words with which you think you have the most trouble. Have a partner read the words to you while you write them on a separate sheet of paper. Then change places and test your partner. When you have both finished, check your paper with the list to see how well you did. Rewrite any words you missed and make them part of your personal spelling list.

Unit Four Review

Vocabulary Review

A. Match each word with its definition.

	DEFINITION		WORD
_____	1. impressive building	a.	protruding
_____	2. mild scolding or warning	b.	veritable
_____	3. little support or strength	c.	facet
_____	4. flat surface on a gemstone	d.	preeminent
_____	5. moving from place to place	e.	sinuous
_____	6. attacked on all sides	f.	tenuous
_____	7. curvy and winding	g.	admonition
_____	8. exceedingly important	h.	nomadic
_____	9. verifiable and authentic	i.	edifice
_____	10. projecting outward	j.	besieged

B. Match each word with its synonym.

	SYNONYM		WORD
_____	11. predicament	a.	retrospection
_____	12. abundance	b.	fastidious
_____	13. element	c.	terrestrial
_____	14. picky	d.	gaudy
_____	15. produce	e.	writhe
_____	16. squirm	f.	aspect
_____	17. review	g.	dilemma
_____	18. ridiculous	h.	engender
_____	19. flashy	i.	preposterous
_____	20. worldly	j.	profusion

C. Match each word with its antonym.

ANTONYM	WORD
_____ 21. unwise	a. appreciable
_____ 22. necessary	b. relinquish
_____ 23. yielding	c. infirm
_____ 24. fortunate	d. laborious
_____ 25. healthy	e. luxuriant
_____ 26. immeasurable	f. deliberate
_____ 27. keep	g. unrelenting
_____ 28. sparse	h. expendable
_____ 29. hurried	i. judicious
_____ 30. easy	j. hapless

Grammar Review

Each of the following sentences *may* contain an error in the word or phrase that is underlined. Circle the letter of the error or, if there is no error, mark D.

1. When the first <u>European settler's</u> arrived in <u>North America,</u>
                        A   B
several hundred different <u>native tribes</u> were spread out across
                            C
the continent. <u>No error</u>
             D

2. <u>Irregardless</u> of where they lived, native people had
      A
<u>adapted to the climate</u> and used the natural resources
         B
<u>that were available to them</u> for food and shelter. <u>No error</u>
         C   D

3. Tribes <u>that lived</u> in the <u>Northeast</u> used wood <u>from the vast</u>
           A   B   C
<u>forests</u> for their houses, canoes, and tools. <u>No error</u>
   C   D

4. In the dry desert land of the Southwest, <u>native peoples'</u>
                                              A
dwellings were made of adobe, <u>a type of sun-dried brick</u> that
                                    B
was used to build <u>apartmentlike dwellings</u>. <u>No error</u>
                        C   D

5. In the Arctic, <u>there was little vegetation</u>, but the people there
   A
   <u>excepted</u> the subzero <u>weather</u> and learned to survive by hunting
   B   C
   sea mammals and fishing. <u>No error</u>
                                  D

6. The languages, <u>social customs</u>, clothing styles, and <u>spiritual</u>
                        A   B
   <u>beliefs</u> differed <u>alot</u> among the various tribes. <u>No error</u>
    B   C   D

7. The first <u>European explorers'</u> arrived in the 1500s and the
                    A
   native people <u>had to face</u> challenges <u>they could not have</u>
                       B   C
   <u>imagined</u>. <u>No error</u>
       C   D

8. <u>Many</u> of the tribes <u>set up trade arrangements</u> with the early
    A   B
   explorers, <u>friendly toward them.</u> <u>No error</u>
                        C   D

9. As more and more settlers <u>arrived, however,</u> native people were
                                    A
   <u>pushed off the land</u> where they had always lived, <u>destroying</u>
          B   C
   <u>ways of life</u>. <u>No error</u>
        C   D

10. Another tragedy <u>of which many people</u> are not aware is that
                          A
    some tribes, <u>along with their languages and cultures</u>, were
                              B
    completely exterminated by European diseases <u>to which they</u>
                                                      C
    <u>had no immunity</u>. <u>No error</u>
          C   D

Spelling Review

Circle the letter of the correctly spelled word on each line.

1. A. consede   B. conceed   C. concede

2. A. exaustible   B. exhaustible   C. exhaustable

3. A. aknowlege   B. acknowledge   C. acknowlege

4. A. disposable   B. disposible   C. desposible

5. A. excede   B. exceed   C. exsede

6. A. hieght   B. heighth   C. height

7. A. suceed   B. succede   C. succeed

8. A. Wensday   B. Wednesday   C. Wenesday

9. A. recede   B. receed   C. resede

10. A. truely   B. truly   C. truley

Writing Review

Choose one of the following topics. Plan your essay. Write your first draft. Then revise and edit your draft, and write your final essay. Be sure to identify your audience, purpose, and task before you begin planning.

Compare and contrast Momaday's journey to the reservation at Rainy Mountain with Sparrow's journey away from her reservation. Explain how both journeys led to a clearer sense of identity for the two travelers.

OR

The theme of this unit is "Defining Moments." Choose a defining moment in your life. Explain something that happened that changed how you looked at an idea, a person, or yourself. Then compare your defining moment with that of one of the characters or authors in the selections in this unit.

Unit Four Extension Activities

 SPEAK/LISTEN

Retelling Histories

N. Scott Momaday's grandmother passed along the tribal history through her stories. Nearly everyone who has lived for a long time has stories to tell. If possible, interview an elderly relative about your family's history—places your ancestors lived and how they made a living, for example. Alternatively, interview an elderly neighbor or someone from a senior housing building. Make sure you have his or her permission to make a DVD, video, or audiotape of your interview. Play the interview for your class and explain what you learned during the interview.

 EXPLORE

What Writing Reveals

Barbara Kingsolver has written short stories, poetry, articles, novels, and essays. Either read several of her other essays or research her on the Internet (where you may find some articles she wrote). Think about how her writing expresses her identity. Who is she? How do her beliefs define her? Then make a character map profiling Kingsolver. Use quotations you found important and explain what each tells you about her. A framework is shown below. Yours should be a full-size page that you can share with your class.

 WRITE

Alternative Endings

Choose a point in "A Pair of Silk Stockings" where the story might have gone a different way. Write the remainder of the story from that point on.

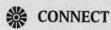 **CONNECT**

Native American History

Work with a group of three or four. As a group, choose a native tribe that lived in your state in 1700. Then assign each group member a different one of these areas to research: (1) extent of the tribe's territory (show on a map); (2) types of shelters (draw, print out, or make copies); (3) main sources of food (with illustrations); and (4) names of lakes, rivers, towns, etc., in your state that come from native languages (with a map). Group members should do their research individually and then come back and share what they've learned with the group, so that everyone has a more complete understanding of the tribe.

Acknowledgments

Grateful acknowledgment is made to the following sources for having granted permission to reprint copyrighted materials. Every effort has been made to obtain permission to use previously published materials. Any errors or omissions are unintentional.

"Crispus Attucks, Martyr for American Independence." Reprinted by permission of Harold Ober Associates Incorporated. Copyright © 1958 by Langston Hughes. From FAMOUS NEGRO HEROES OF AMERICA. Page 7.

Excerpted from "Salt Water Farm" from *One Man's Meat*, text copyright © 1939 by E. B. White. Copyright renewed. Reprinted by permission of Tilbury House, Publishers, Gardiner, Maine. Page 29.

From THE WOMAN WARRIOR by Maxine Hong Kingston, copyright © 1975, 1976 by Maxine Hong Kingston. Used by permission of Alfred A. Knopf, a division of Random House, Inc. Page 71.

Copyright © 2000 From WHERE WE STAND by bell hooks. Reproduced by permission of Routledge/Taylor & Francis Group, LLC. Page 89.

From *Hunger of Memory* by Richard Rodriguez. Reprinted by permission of David R. Godine, Publisher, Inc. Copyright © 1982 by Richard Rodriguez. Page 93.

From THE WEDDING by Dorothy West, copyright © 1995 by Dorothy West. Used by permission of Doubleday, a division of Random House, Inc. Page 115.

From *The Latin Deli: Prose & Poetry* by Judith Ortiz Cofer. Copyright 1993 by Judith Ortiz Cofer. Reprinted by permission of the University of Georgia Press. Page 185.

pp. 60-62 from SMALL WONDER: ESSAYS by Barbara Kingsolver. Copyright © 2002 by Barbara Kingsolver. Reprinted by permission of HarperCollins Publishers Inc. Page 215.

From THE WAY TO RAINY MOUNTAIN by N. Scott Momaday. Used by permission of University of New Mexico Press, © 1969. Page 247.

"Sparrow's Sleep." Reprinted from *Another Attempt at Rescue* © 2005 by M.L. Smoker, by permission of Hanging Loose Press. Page 252.

Photo Credits

Langston Hughes © Robert W. Kelley/Getty Images. Page 7.

Franklin Delano Roosevelt. Courtesy of the Franklin D. Roosevelt Presidential Library. Page 45.

Maxine Hong Kingston © Christopher Felver/CORBIS. Page 71.

Dorothy West © Richard Howard/Getty Images. Page 115.

Mark Twain © Hulton Archive/Getty Images. Page 143.

Vocabulary Index

A
abominable, 139
accountable, 41
admonition, 243
alignment, 111
amalgamate, 25
animosity, 139
antithesis, 41
appall, 25
appease, 41
appreciable, 225
aspect, 243
assail, 41
attainable, 41
avenge, 67

B
besiege, 225

C
classism, 85
conceal, 3
condescend, 85
connotation, 111
conspicuous, 3

D
defer, 139
deleterious, 25
deliberate, 211
despot, 25
dilapidated, 181
dilemma, 211
dimension, 111
diminish, 139
discord, 41
discretion, 111
disquieting, 163
dissuade, 111
distraught, 181

E
eclipse, 67
edifice, 211
eerie, 181
elation, 181
elusive, 85
embattled, 3
engender, 243
enthralled, 181
evoke, 163
exclusive, 111

expendable, 211
exultation, 139

F
facet, 211
fastidious, 225
fiscal, 85
flimsy, 25
flourish, 25
forswear, 25
fume, 67
furtive, 139

G
gainful, 25
gaudy, 225
genocide, 85
gravely, 3
guerrilla, 85

H
hapless, 211
humiliation, 181

I
immaculate, 111
immensity, 67
impudent, 163
incisive, 163
indigent, 85
indignation, 3
infatuated, 181
infirm, 243
intently, 181

J
judicious, 225

L
laborious, 225
latent, 163
luxuriant, 243

N
nomadic, 243

P
palpitation, 111
panorama, 163
peril, 41
petulant, 139
picturesque, 111
plague, 67

poignant, 163
predatory, 85
preeminent, 243
preposterous, 225
profusion, 225
protrude, 211

R
recede, 67
recover, 3
rectify, 67
redeem, 3
refuge, 139
relinquish, 211
reparation, 67
retrospection, 225
revelry, 163
revoke, 25

S
sardonic, 163
self-effacement, 163
sentinel, 3
sinuous, 211
solace, 181
subsequent, 139
sullen, 67
supercilious, 139

T
tainted, 67
taunt, 3
tenuous, 243
terrestrial, 212
tortuous, 111
tyranny, 41

U
unalterably, 41
unimpeded, 25
unrelenting, 243
urban, 85

V
veritable, 226
vetted, 85
vigilant, 181
vindicate, 41
votive, 3

W
writhe, 243

Subject Index